Hellbent & Heartfirst

Books by Kassandra Sims

Falling Upwards
The Midnight Work
Hellbent & Heartfirst

Hellbent & Heartfirst

Kassandra Sims

tor paranormal romance

A TOM DOHERTY ASSOCIATES BOOK
NEW YORK

This is a work of fiction. All of the characters, organizations, and events portrayed in this novel are either products of the author's imagination or are used fictitiously.

HELLBENT & HEARTFIRST

Copyright © 2008 by Kassandra Sims

All rights reserved, including the right to reproduce this book, or portions thereof, in any form.

A Tor Book
Published by Tom Doherty Associates, LLC
175 Fifth Avenue
New York, NY 10010

www.tor.com

Tor® is a registered trademark of Tom Doherty Associates, LLC.

ISBN-13: 978-0-7653-5801-1
ISBN-10: 0-7653-5801-8

First Edition: April 2008

Printed in the United States of America

0 9 8 7 6 5 4 3 2 1

Thank you, Nate,
for being my Jiminy Cricket and allowing
my dreams to happen.

ACKNOWLEDGMENTS

To Jacyn Stewart for use of her name and for reasons better never mentioned anywhere my mom will see: East Nashville is far better than Bastogne, and I love you for yourself, not the "cool" you.

•

To my mom and Aunt Mickey, as always, just for existing.

•

To Allie McKnight for late nights and big thoughts.

•

To Julia Starkey for being my role model and who I want to be when I grow up.

•

Finally, to my editor, Jozelle Dyer, for her patience and dedication to me and my work.

Hellbent
&Heartfirst

CHAPTER ONE

Refugees weren't easy to keep up with at the best of times. The best of times was a concept that rarely appeared in natural disaster areas or war zones. Jacyn Boaz knew from firsthand experience that the difficulty of meeting the needs of refugees and the displaced only increased when many people shared full names, didn't know their social security numbers, had no identification, and were generally traumatized due to the very circumstances that led them to become refugees in the first place. If you added to that free mobility and a lack of communication, then you had the recipe for the sort of unmitigated disaster that was her daily life. After Hurricane Katrina, people came and went all along the Gulf Coast with no permanent home-base or address.

They were fluid, displaced, slipping from aid agency to church to family. People with duplicate names applied for aid and were turned down because there were too many Willie Jacksons for aid groups to know if they were being bilked by conmen. People, all too often, slipped through the cracks of the aid services. This was the second peripheral disaster after Hurricane Katrina.

Jacyn had come home after the hurricane with all of the best intentions of the diaspora, but several months into her stay in Biloxi, Mississippi, she was worn out and worn down, mentally and physically exhausted from looking personal tragedy in the face day after day without being able to offer much more than "We'll try," or "I'm sorry."

In the converted office space given to Oxfam for "reduced" rent, Jacyn looked over the paperwork submitted by one Jacqueline Jackson. Ms. Jackson had been separated from her grandchildren during the evacuation from the Ninth Ward in New Orleans.

"Ms. Jackson, your grandchildren are Pedro Martinez, aged nine, Blessing Martinez, aged seven, and Misty Jackson, aged five?" Jacyn went over the specifics with Ms. Jackson one by one. Sometimes, in their agitation and rush, people misremembered facts or spelled names wrong or wrote in old, wrong addresses.

"Yes, like I wrote there. I think they were goin'

to Utah. No one really said." Ms. Jackson had the pinched look of someone who'd forgotten how to cry. She sat across from Jacyn in an uncomfortable metal folding chair, a twin to Jacyn's own, in a pair of men's shorts, flip-flops, and an Alabama State T-shirt—the uniform for those too harried to pack when rescued from roofs or disallowed from bringing their belongings when evacuated by the military.

Jacyn went over the form line by line with Ms. Jackson like she did with all the other, similar people whom she'd tried to help retrieve lost children. Person by person, case by case, Jacyn felt like her soul was being eaten one personalized nightmare at a time.

Ms. Jacqueline Jackson left, and Jacyn went over paperwork for a six-month-old child, Barry, with his hysterical mother, Juanita. Fifteen cases back-to-back before Jacyn was relieved by another volunteer. She rubbed her eyes and smoothed hands over her two braids—she'd given up on doing anything with her hair besides wearing it in varying braids and buns. She had no one to look good for, no reason to cut or style her hair or wear makeup. As a matter of fact, she'd come to think of looking too put together as something of an insult to all the broken-down, harried folks she attempted to help every day. They related to her better if she wore old, ratty clothes, no makeup, and her hair all a-mess.

When she stepped out into the oppressive humidity

of the Biloxi spring, Jacyn breathed lungful after lungful of semi-solid air. She rolled her head back and forth trying to relieve some of the tension that had been accumulating since her first tear-filled interview with a parent severed from her child almost a six months before. The ritual breathing and stretching only worked when Jacyn believed in it, and lately she'd been believing in it less and less. She was starting to have a hard time remembering Mississippi before the storm. She was starting to have a hard time remembering how to live a structured, work-home-television sort of life free from lows lower than anything Jacyn had ever associated with America—all that sort of thing was supposed to be Over There—and rollicking highs that left her hungover and wiped out.

Her cousin, Amber, pulled up with her radio blaring Toby Keith, tires popping rocks across the cracked cement of the parking lot, and honked her horn in enthusiasm when Jacyn took the five steps to hop in the car. Jacyn's car was being serviced by one of her cousins, and Amber was her temporary roommate and therefore personal taxi service.

"You look like shit." Amber put the car into first and hauled ass, almost burning the tires. Her crayon red hair was fading to dark pink with light brown roots snugged up tight against her scalp. She popped her gum and smiled with deep dimples. "What you need is a drink. Or five."

Unaltered, they looked enough alike to be taken for sisters—light brown hair that went blond in the sun, light brown eyes with upturned noses, and dimples—but Amber kept her hair Crayola-ized, and Jacyn had let Amber put purple streaks in her hair recently. Their hair, combined with the fifteen pounds Jacyn had put on since coming home from stress and the reapplication of home cooking, served to differentiate them, lessening the family resemblance when Jacyn looked in the mirror.

Jacyn smiled at her cousin's exuberance and flipped the radio station to the news. "Why do you leave the radio on that crap?" The car was her aunt's—Amber's mother—and every time Amber returned it, her mama put the radio right back to New Country, something Amber and Jacyn both loathed.

Amber shrugged. "Who cares? I had a lot on my mind." Amber *always* had a lot on her mind. She had just graduated from college the previous spring with a degree in theoretical math and was planning on grad school. She would have started graduate school at Tulane if not for the storm. She was also volunteering in Biloxi, her hometown, but for Habitat for Humanity instead of Oxfam.

Jacyn listened to some plastic, random song bleating out of the speakers compete with the high whine of the air-conditioning. Instead of inland, toward the house, they drove toward the beach.

"Oh, hell no. You're not dragging me to the boats."

Jacyn glared at Amber, trying to intimidate her into submission. She didn't really hold out a lot of hope for that, but there was a first time for everything.

Amber laughed huge and wide, with her head hitting the headrest. "Naw, Buddy's."

Which really was worse. Jacyn groaned and wished she could just go home and get a shower.

Buddy's was a roadhouse cum blues shack that had once been an insurance office before Katrina. The only part of the building that had withstood the storm was the pockmarked cement floor. Some high school friends of Amber's had squatted on the property and rebuilt it piece by piece. One of their relatives had owned the land and previous building and raised an eyebrow but not much else when construction and relief workers started frequenting the place. BYOB to start with, but little by little, Buddy's became an unlicensed speakeasy, known in the right circles as the best place to get decent crawfish or to hear the best local music.

It was also as close to a meat market as you were going to find among the relief worker crowd. Jacyn tended to avoid it after drinking way too much scotch one night and ending up having sex with a Red Cross worker in the bathroom. Amber had no respect for anyone else's grand declarations, though.

They pulled into the broken oyster shell parking lot around seven, and they barely found an empty spot. People up at dawn started drinking early. Jacyn lifted an eyebrow when Amber pulled up the safety break while winking. "Oysters?"

Jacyn couldn't help but smile back. "Yeah." She climbed out of the car laughing. In a lot of ways, it was good to be back home again, back with the people who knew her and might have judged, but judged with love. The sounds of their flip-flops slapping the bottoms of their feet were loud until the hum of the voices and music from inside filtered out into the humidity of the oncoming dusk. Jacyn knocked her hip against Amber's and laughed when she staggered. She ran the back of her hand across her forehead to remove the sweat, which just walking across the parking lot drew out, and wiped her hand on the cotton of her red and white A-line skirt.

"Wonder who's playing tonight?" Amber kicked open the door and swaggered inside.

A chorus of shouts and curses rose when they entered the bar. Jacyn's eyes took a few seconds to dilate in the lava-lamp and novelty-light dimness of the bar. Across the single room, she could see several of Amber's high school friends sitting with people she knew from FEMA and Catholic Social Services. Actually, Jacyn knew pretty much everyone there from work or through relatives. She'd grown up in Gautier, but most of her extended family were in Biloxi and environs.

"Danny's not here, chill." Amber grabbed Jacyn's

arm and tugged her across the room. Jacyn rolled
her eyes and let her cousin manhandle her. Somewhere in the past couple months she'd become her
cousin's *project*, even if Jacyn still wasn't sure what
the aim of the campaign was.

The room was strewn with picnic tables and
benches in haphazard angles. On one end of the
room was a makeshift bar built out of plywood and
Armstrong flooring tiles. The actual color of the tiles
was anyone's guess, since the light by the bar came
mainly from fiber-optic palm trees that threw red
and green light in such a way that nothing you saw
made a whole lot of sense. On the other end of the
room was a six-by-four raised platform that worked
as a stage. The acts could be anything from an emo
cover band to an improvised burlesque show, with
regular side orders of ear-shattering karaoke.

Currently, the radio was being piped into the room:
Pearl Jam or someone who sounded a lot like them to
Jacyn. People shouted over the music, drunk already
or getting there. Jacyn smiled at John Anderson from
FEMA—the guy had a shit job, he was the face of de-
nied claims, which other people besides him actually
rejected. He slid over a shot of something unidentifi-
able in the wacky light. Jacyn shrugged and tossed it
back. She knew she had already been defeated by
Amber and her plans for the evening, so she was going to enjoy it as much as possible.

"Thanks!" Jacyn smiled at John from across the table. He smiled back, and it felt easy; camaraderie in the face of chaos, because he wasn't a threat—gayer than Liberace.

Some friend of Amber's busted up on them with a round of shots. Everyone screamed unintelligibly to Jacyn, tossing back their shots and laughing. She did the same, minus the screaming. She was more of a five-drink screamer. Amber rocked against her shoulder hard, smiling and opening her eyes super wide. Jacyn smiled in response.

"Oysters!" Amber hollered. She stood up and climbed over the bench to fetch a tray of oysters from one side of the bar, where a couple guys sat shucking most of the night. "They don't have oysters where Jacyn's from, you know!" Amber stomped off with Jacyn rolling her eyes at her back.

"I thought you were local." John sipped his beer and looked honestly interested. Looking honestly interested was part of their trade. He was probably bored out of his mind.

"I live in Austin now." Jacyn didn't elaborate on that, didn't go into her sabbatical from the University of Texas's anthropology department or how she wasn't at all sure it was so much a sabbatical anymore and not just the wind up to quitting.

"Texas is a shithole," John said in his broad Midwestern accent. Jacyn felt the laughter spill out before she even realized she was amused. He smiled back at her, some joke of his own in his head. He sure as hell wasn't sharing her joke that she hadn't met a single person in Mississippi who hadn't said something similar. What everyone had against Texas, she had no clue. The antipathy seemed almost universal, though.

Jacyn thought about South by Southwest and her colleagues who grew up in cities and still had to deal with people assuming they were ranchers and rough-necks. She thought about the crisp smell of rain coming on in the distance and the taste of brisket cooked for twelve hours outdoors. Jacyn had her issues with Texas, but they weren't based on the bullshit stereo-types that people got from "Don't Mess with Texas" bumper stickers and people on television with big hair or belt buckles. Her issues revolved around her ex-husband and the sense of listlessness that she just couldn't seem to shake.

"Uh huh," Jacyn replied to John with a smile firmly on her face. Amber thumped back down next to her a second later with two trays of oysters—open-faced, sitting on the half-shell, nestled in cracked iced flanked by little plastic cups of horseradish and ketchup with a tiny plastic fork tossed on the tray with a couple handfuls of saltines. Jacyn's smile turned genuine at the prospect of the food. The rhythm and ritual of doctoring up the oysters felt like home in a way that was inexplicable and ineffable. Oyster on cracker followed by horseradish and ketchup, all shoved into the mouth to be chomped together. Lather, rinse, repeat.

Amber chittered away to someone Jacyn didn't know. Jacyn ate her oysters and sipped at her tequila, settling into the smell of the ocean overlaid with recycled air from the air-conditioning and yeasty spilled beer and cigarettes. She dropped horseradish into her cleavage and didn't feel a single bit self-conscious reaching into her tank top to retrieve it. She didn't even notice when the hippy-rock from the radio faded out into the soft sound of a country-tuned acoustic guitar and a rumbly, gravel-under-butter voice.

Up on the tiny stage sat a guy in a straw cowboy hat with one foot up on the rail of the wooden stool sometimes used as a fruit cutting board. His face was mostly averted, tilted down toward his guitar. He wore a ratty old Willie Nelson T-shirt and holey jeans and boots.

Playin' my guitar, singin' country music
Ain't never thought I'd want to let it go
Standing there, too many things remind me
Of all the little things that made me care
Nearly cried when a spotlight picked out some girl
* standin'*
Who had the exact color of your hair

Being with you a'ways felt like home-comin'
Southern boy, I guess you knew the score

But now the music's all I got without you
And country roads don't take me home no more.

Jacyn hadn't ever had much of a taste for country music, too inundated by it her whole life. It had always carried some kind of stigma that she had mainly managed to shake after many years of self-analysis as an anthropologist. She sometimes deviated from her country-music-hating pattern at Texas dance halls on isolated nights when her friends dragged her out. Jacyn could admit that honky-tonks were made for elongated vowels and songs about cheatin' and heartbreak.

When the guy looked up, Jacyn paused mid-chew and stared. He had a wide, full mouth stretched around his lonesome voice. His long eyelashes were visible even from two tables back from the stage. He slipped into a smile easily, making his already attractive face nearly shocking in its attractiveness—all slightly cleft chin dipping down to his chest and eyelashes brushing his cheek and white flash of teeth. He was a man who knew what he did to women and didn't much care to be fake about that. Jacyn had known a man or two like him, and she'd never had much use for them. Especially one as young as this kid, probably not over twenty-five. All the same, his voice could melt Barbara Bush's panties off. He was also extremely familiar—sharp cheekbones and a crease in the middle of his full bottom lip. She knew him from somewhere, but she knew almost everyone in these parts from *somewhere*.

At the end of the song, several yahoos leaped around, tossing their hats and whooping it up. The singer laughed, and his laughter was even more affecting than his singing voice—coal dark and thick like the air after a thunderstorm.

"Ok, here's one 'bout my mama," the guy said. East Texas probably near the coast in the south. Jacyn could pinpoint accents like nobody's business—mainly because it *was* her business. She studied immigration and settlement patterns and how that affected current culture. Or she had, before Katrina came along at the perfect time for her to get a little change in her life. Now she tried to match displaced children with their families during the day and drank by night.

The cowboy picked up singing a slow ballad accompanied by some complex picking on his guitar. He sang just loud enough to project his voice into the crappy mic and low enough to make his performance seem intimate. Jacyn watched while she finished her oysters, with Amber leaning on her back, watching just as intently.

When the cowboy gave his guitar a hard thrum and said, "I'm Jimmy Wayne, y'all're welcome to buy me a beer," to hoots and hollering, he looked up at Jacyn and Amber with a wink. Amber let out a snort.

"Cute, but cocky. Totally your type." Amber turned back to her conversation, thoughts of Jimmy Wayne probably banished from her mind by the complexities of I-beams fitted to floorboards and whimsies about pressurized wood.

"Too young for me," Jacyn answered the back of Amber's head with a lifted eyebrow.

When Jacyn turned back toward the stage, John and Jimmy Wayne were standing next to the picnic table. Jimmy Wayne had his hat in his hand and was wiping his forehead with the back of his wrist with a long, slow pull. He was watching intently, smiling a little crooked smirk that twisted one side of his mouth into a dimple. The perfect line of his nose—the way his face was absolutely symmetrical from the furrow between his eyebrows, to his nose, the indention above his top lip, and the cleft of his chin—was even more familiar when she didn't have to strain her eyes through cigarette smoke and darkness.

"Hey," he said around his smirk as it stretched out into a full on grin. "John says you're from Texas. Katrina relief?"

He sat down, brazen as you please, propping his guitar case against the end of the table and straddling the bench. Up close he was even better looking— muscled biceps, freckles across the bridge of his nose and high on his sharp cheeks, winged eyebrows, and a flirty tilt to his head that promised shit-kicking or free-range sex acts.

"Nah, I'm from Gautier. I *live* in Austin." Jacyn tipped back her tequila and watched him over the brim of her glass as she drank. He watched right back with an unreadable expression. He ducked his head and tipped his hat back on his head.

"This is gonna sound tore up and six kinds of lame, but have we met before?" He said it with a smile that Jacyn could read immediately as a cover for straight shooting. She was just drunk enough to be flattered and intrigued in equal measure, because this was the sort of guy who didn't need lines, who didn't need to even speak. The cigarettes-and-oil-derrick voice was just icing for the rest of the package.

"I doubt it, but anything's possible." She wasn't drunk enough to say, If we'd've met, baby boy, I'd remember it, sure as shit. Mainly because she figured they probably had met, more than likely when he was in a high school—which hadn't been so very long ago.

"Maybe in Houston a few years ago, at the Marriot off the Galleria? You were wearing a pink cowboy hat and drinking scotch." He leaned in closer as he said it, voice dropping to a whisper. Jacyn's shocked face became hot, and her fingers and toes went dead cold. Oh, yeah, she remembered that night. Most of it. The part up until the two-stepping at the honky-tonk. His face stilled, the smile slipping away into the darkness. He watched her for a couple of ticks. "Don't get like that. It's all good. No harm no foul. Buy me a beer to assuage my ego and we're golden."

Jacyn blinked at him a couple of times, way more embarrassed than a thirty-two-year-old really had a right to be over a one-night stand that she couldn't really remember. It happened to lots of people. However, she felt extremely gypped that *this* was the one-night stand she didn't remember. This boy with his dark blond hair spiked and flattened from sweating under his hat making him all the more attractive for being almost human and long, thick, scarred fingers and eyes full of invitation that promised more than someone his age should be able to pull off.

One beer turned into tequila shots. Amber drove everyone to the Imperial Palace for some cards with Jacyn and Jimmy Wayne laughing and discussing horses. She remembered him then, remembered that he rode rodeo.

Jimmy Wayne Broadus sat in the rebuilt Imperial Palace Hotel and Casino in Biloxi sipping a Johnnie Walker Red Label and watching a clutch of old ladies feeding quarters into whirling and beeping slot machines. Biloxi was still more debris and chaos than remade, but the lure of easy money was always too strong for a lot of people to resist. Even for people who had to cash their FEMA checks to make rent or their Red Cross checks to put a new roof on the house. Displaced people and locals with too much time on their hands were paying the mortgage on the new casinos. Before Hurricane Katrina, casinos in Mississippi had to be built "off shore." Usually that meant they floated right up against the dock one foot off the beach. It was a technical law instituted as a nod to the Old South sensibilities that held no truck in the modern era of petrodollars and Yankee retirees. Gambling was a sin, but one that pulled Mississippi out of the gutter of being the last-ranked U.S. state in every category except poverty.

He'd switched from tequila to scotch, which was about where his mood was, Jacyn notwithstanding. His focus shifted from the old biddies to Jacyn and her cousin—a matched set that he would have pegged as sisters, upturned noses and bowed mouths, deep, round hips and cleavage that could make a man stupider than he was born—playing split high low at the card table he was propped against.

"You did not just play that nine low!" Jacyn threw her head back laughing, the thick, matching braids of her hair flying back and shaking. She was tan from being outside, with the standard scattering of sun freckles on her exposed shoulders. Jimmy Wayne hadn't been all that shocked to run into a random woman from some random rodeo event years ago. His life was full of shit like that. He didn't believe in random much. The whys and wherefores might not be clear yet, might never be, but Jimmy Wayne believed in the bigger picture—just because you see the surface of a lake doesn't mean you can assume that all that's below the reflected sky is fish and plants. Mundane assumptions got people killed and worse.

He was drunk enough to think playing cards was a good idea, but not drunk enough to fall off the stool or prevent himself from losing money he didn't have to lose. Plunking himself down on the other side of Jacyn from Amber, he the tapped the baize to get dealt in. Jacyn turned and looked at him with her unreadable smile. She was smart; he remembered that. A doctor or a lawyer, something professional. He didn't know how she could be, so young, but there you have it—some people didn't waste their lives ranching and rodeoing and doing things people didn't appreciate or believe in.

"Ready to run with the big dogs?" Jacyn's smile lifted her eyelids so that her eyes seemed slightly upturned, exotic in a way he figured wasn't her background, being from Mississippi. She had a good little stack of chips in front of her. He would never have pegged her as a gambler, much less a card sharp.

"I don't talk trash about ladies, so I'm gonna pretend like you didn't say nothin'." He lifted up the edges of his cards and almost groaned at his crap luck. A two of diamonds and a four of spades. Shit luck.

Amber cashed out after two more hands. Jacyn pulled a run that Jimmy Wayne's mood interpreted as superhuman. Too much luck there, hand after hand. He was surprised that the dealer hadn't called the damned security people.

He lost two hundred bucks and all of what was left of his pride. There wasn't much of that. Definitely not two hundred dollars' worth.

Jacyn finally polished off a last swallow of Patrón and slapped the table, nodding to him. "Ready to blow this popsicle stand?" Her face was flushed bright pink from the alcohol and the thrill of victory. Her once-tight braids were coming undone, hair flying every which way, like Willie Nelson on a ten-day bender. She was loose limbed and the left strap of her tank top wouldn't stay up no matter how many times she shoved it back into place.

Even if she didn't remember him right off, he sure as hell remembered her. She'd reminded him of the back injury he'd gotten at seventeen being thrown off a bronc and the knee injury he'd gotten from La Llorona when he was nineteen, for a week afterward. She smiled at him in the way he'd recognized since before he'd really understood what was really being offered, and he smiled back.

Jacyn couldn't find Amber after she cashed out. She didn't really look too hard, honestly. Jimmy Wayne kept up a low drone about how her luck, how he couldn't reckon it, how she was blessed or cursed, one or the other. His voice kept stealing her responses about how she'd pay for her night of cards with some really bad, unlooked-for something, about how her life always played out that way. She was karmatic balance wrapped up in one person—never happy when something good happened because something horrible always followed. Always. So tonight she'd won over three grand at cards, and next week she'd get hit by a car. That's the way her life worked. She opened her mouth to tell him that over and over, but every time she looked over at him her eyes would light on his freckles or the silver hoops in his ears and it slipped away from her.

She was old enough to know exactly where this was going. Even as she flipped her phone open to call Amber, Jimmy Wayne's hand came against the small of her back. They exited the casino right into the wall of suffocating humidity rolling off the Gulf. Sweat immediately popped out all over her skin, coating her in a bubble of slick salt. She didn't really even notice with Jimmy Wayne singing softly under his breath to himself, his hand coming off her back to wrap around her side and pull her flush to his side. They walked through the parking lot, toward where she had no idea, gravel under her flip-flops skittering away, as she dialed Amber's cell and Jimmy Wayne's lips brushed the side of her neck. Jacyn stopped to leave a slurred message for Amber as Jimmy Wayne's hat tipped off; her hand flew out to catch it and he matched the movement. They looked each other in the eye with her hand holding his against the worn straw.

"Good reflexes." He pulled her against him, damp cotton over muscle against her everywhere.

"Uh huh," was all she managed, watching his mouth with her brain function pretty much shut down.

His bracelets made soft clicking noises as they shifted against one another with his movements.

The night was bright with moonlight reflecting off the ocean, white and gray straining against the riot of pink neon from the casino. He leaned down, kissing her with the smoky slide of a whiskey tongue against her mouth, into her mouth, and against the front of her parted teeth. His hat felt heavy in her hand, denser than it really was, the straw seeming to turn to brick or stone. Music blared out of a car passing nearby, and Jimmy Wayne danced them around in a slow circle with one of his legs coming between hers, pulling the cotton of her dress tight with his thick thigh. Around and around, slowly, he crumpled down lower with each spin until her back hit warm metal. His hand reached under her skirt in the back pushing the material up. She dropped his hat on the ground and ran both hands up the deep furrows of his spine.

"Reach in my right pocket for my keys." His lips bumped her ear, words riding his breath, and bringing up all the hair on her body. His thigh rode harder, pressing against her crotch, moving slightly, just enough to make her reach her right hand into his left pocket to feel his erection through the thin cotton. His fingers slid under the leg band of her underwear, palming her ass. "Or keep that up, that's okay, too." He laughed right into her ear, broken glass and the sort of sin that never lives up to expectation.

She managed, barely, to find enough motor control to get her other hand into his right pocket as he rocked against her fingers, lips moving behind her ear in a slip-slip and hum. His keys jangled loudly in the liquid dark when she pulled them out of his pocket. Jimmy Wayne wrapped his hand around hers, his thumb rubbed the veins on the back of her hand, and then he looped a finger through the key-chain. He managed to slide the key into the lock without disengaging, but had to pull away to swing the door open.

Holding the door wide, he bent to retrieve his hat. "Go on and walk away now, if you want. I won't hold it against you," he said, with his face toward the ground. If he was being gentlemanly or just weird, Jacyn had no idea.

"Get in. You gotta be on bottom." She shoved at him at little, laughing and getting a chuckle out of him in return. He climbed into the passenger seat and yanked her along with him so that she sprawled over his lap. His hand on her ass was startling and loud, three quick smacks followed by his bruised laughter.

"Bitch, let me up." Jacyn wiggled until she could get her legs in the truck, one leg coming down on the bench seat of the old pickup, the other being grasped by Jimmy Wayne who held on to her as he slammed the door of the truck. She straddled him and smacked him almost hard on the face. His smile brightened, turning huge and dimpled on both sides of his mouth.

"It's like that, huh?" He gripped both of her thighs and yanked her against his hips as he slid, so he could rock up against her as he leaned around her to slide the key in the ignition and turn the radio on.

"Mood music." She smiled against his mouth as Garth Brooks warbled out of the radio and Jimmy Wayne pushed the straps of her tank top off her shoulders. She fell down into his mouth, kept falling as she got his jeans open without breaking the kiss and he lifted up on one hip to pull his wallet out of his back pocket. She leaned back with her shoulders resting on the dashboard with her ass on his knees as he unfolded her legs and pushed them together to pull her panties off. She teetered, and he laughed, causing her to start laughing again, too. Her eyes snapped shut when he kissed the back of her knee, so she missed the show when he shoved his jeans out of the way and slid the condom on.

"Baby," he whispered against the side of her face as she settled down on him. Her sigh of satisfaction as he met her halfway, rocking up and hitting all the highlights on the way with the first stroke, made her blush, feeling like tiny strokes under her skin.

She pulled his bottom lip into her mouth, and they hit an immediate rhythm of tongue against tongue and hips locking together and pulling apart. Jacyn lost track of everything besides Jimmy Wayne's sharp tobacco and spicy sweat smell and the taste of bourbon and the way her neck couldn't hold up her head when Jimmy Wayne angled her body back with a hand against her lumbar so he could wedge his fingers between them.

Jacyn was something of a specialist in working hungover. She was hardly the only one. Sometimes she wondered how construction workers managed to roof and frame and exert themselves after drinking an entire bottle of Jack the night before. It was one of the mysteries of the universe.

Sitting at her desk in the cranked-up air-conditioning of the Oxfam office, she curled her toes down under themselves to prevent frostbite and stared back at one Misty Rodgers.

"Okay, so what you're saying is that your son was *supposed* to be staying with your aunt and when you got over here from Houston he wasn't there?" Jacyn needed to eat about eight pounds of greasy food and to keep on pretending she hadn't gotten up to the ridiculous antics she had the night before; Misty was not helping her here.

Misty was twenty. Her son, Dylan, was four, and Jacyn's pickled brain was not coping well with her confusing story. It was so garbled that Jacyn's mind kept tossing out snapshots of Jimmy Wayne to entertain her—the curve of his huge bicep, the amber freckles high on his cheeks, his easy laughter and moonlight making his teeth bright against the shadows covering his face.

"Uh-uh. No. Not supposed to. He *was* with my aunt Mary. I know he was because I talked to him on the phone almost every day. But my aunt says he wasn't ever here! How could that happen? Don't y'all keep records or something?" Misty's pale face was spotted a blotchy red from crying and losing her temper. She'd altered between sobbing and screaming ever since she and her aunt had come into the office.

"Sure, we keep records, but if your son's gone missing—after being placed with a family member, that's a law thing, not something we can help with. No matter how much we'd want to." Jacyn sometimes wondered what went through people's heads. She knew that the stress of being displaced, combined with the stress of missing children, could make people just lose their entire minds, but kidnapping wasn't really under the purview of aid organizations. "You need to go to the police and file a missing person's report and they will issue an Amber Alert. I can help you, if you need me to." She couldn't help adding the offer of help. Lord knows this girl looked like she needed it something fierce.

"You aren't fucking listening to me!" Misty shot out of her chair, tears running down her face and her eyes puffing up even more. "Aunt Mary says Dylan wasn't ever here! I talked to him on the phone! How is that possible? How?"

Jacyn had no answer for that, aside from cynical assumptions about Misty's sanity.

"Do you want me to go to the sheriff's office with you?" Jacyn stood up and rounded her desk, pulling on Misty's elbow and patting her on the back in a half hug. She sighed internally and resigned herself to not getting any work done that day while she went through round after round of social services interviews and paperwork with Misty. This wasn't the first time she'd gone through this sort of thing. Stress did weird things to people sometimes. Invented children and created catastrophes were common enough among the mentally ill.

She was glad she'd gotten her car back bright and early that morning, even if at the time she'd been cursing ever being born.

CHAPTER TWO

"So, what'd'ya think?" Clay Boaz, aside from being Jacyn's cousin, was a Harrison County sheriff's deputy. He watched Jacyn with his arms folded over his chest and his legs stretched out in front of him with his backside propped on the edge of his desk. The band of his hat had left a ring indention in his close-cropped light brown hair. He had even more freckles than Jacyn and looked ten years younger than he was because of that.

"Probably a nutjob." Jacyn really couldn't figure out any other explanation that wasn't a whole lot worse.

"Maybe a dangerous nutjob, is what I'm thinking. Could be she wants to get caught, came to you to get some attention. You got no record of the kid at all?" He had a sunburn on his face and arms, and Jacyn wondered if he'd been out fishing recently.

"No, but that doesn't mean anything. I mean, that just means we weren't the aid group who placed him. You know as well as I do that one hand don't know what the other's doing around here." Which was really putting it mildly.

"So it's not out of the realm of possibility that this girl didn't have a son and that she did something to get attention for herself." Clay rubbed a huge hand over his face and across his scalp. His wedding ring caught the fluorescent light from the ceiling. Jacyn remembered him as a sweet, happy man, but this cynical guy had replaced that person when Clay's wife had died from cervical cancer more than a year before. No one talked about that.

"She might just be a benign wacko." Jacyn tended to think most attention seekers were. Clay just stared at her.

"Better safe than sorry." He stood up all the way and reached a hand out to steer Jacyn out into the hall. She felt even more tired and shitty than before, because now Misty Rodgers was going into lockup for forty-eight hours so that the Harrison County Sheriff's Department could be convinced that she hadn't drowned her son in a bathtub or sold him to organ harvesters.

"Seriously, Clay, she's probably just a freak. Give her the benefit of the doubt." Jacyn looked up at him and wrapped her hand loosely around his. He looked back down at her. The lines around his eyes hadn't been there two years ago, and the tightness on the edges of his mouth belonged to their grand-daddy not to Clay.

He squeezed her hand. "Sweetheart, the benefit of the doubt is what *you* do. I gotta deal with the hard reality of bad people doing disgusting things. I've learned that a lot of the time, what we don't know can hurt us. Strange things happen in life, you gotta be prepared for that. Now, this girl could just be the run-of-the-mill attention-seekin' wackadoo-dle, but she could also be a lot of other things. We'll get to the bottom of it. Two days isn't all that long measured out in a whole life."

And that was really a crying shame, because Clay had been one of the sweetest people Jacyn had ever known, once upon a time. She felt like every time she'd reached the limit of her capacity to break for someone else she got a limit-increase by the karma bank. Most of the time, she tried not to think in karma and kismet heavy metaphors, be-cause she had a very curious relationship with luck. Sometimes, she seemed to go on a roll, like anything she wanted would just plop right in her lap for the asking, other times it seemed like her luck brought her the worst sort of country-song-lyrics heartbreak.

* * *

Jacyn was staying in what had once been a rental property that her grandparents owned. Now, Jacyn and Amber lived there rent-free, but they paid all the same. Random favors for a whole army of relatives and having to "yes, ma'am" and "no, sir" like they were kids again. Jacyn had moved to Austin for a reason. She remembered why every time her grandmother called up and "asked" Jacyn to tote her around in her grandmother's Grand Marquis from the grocery store to one friend's house after the other. Sometimes Jacyn didn't answer the phone when it rang. The old, Southern Bell–issued, ivory plastic clunker of a phone that Jacyn associated with old folks (who thought technology was something for deviants and Yankees) would ring and ring, and Jacyn would sit in the kitchen staring at it.

The moss green linoleum was original to the house. As were the avocado appliances and white-and-gold fleck countertops and starburst wallpaper with matching drapes on the window above the sink. Jacyn sat at the pockmarked dinette listening to the phone ring, thinking about Misty Rodgers and where Amber was. Jacyn really didn't think Misty was dangerous. Jacyn tended to be a decent judge of character. But everyone could be wrong from time to time.

"Hey! Look who I found!" Jacyn twisted in her chair to see Amber bounding into the kitchen wearing an "F the President" T-shirt and cutoffs with Jimmy Wayne trailing her. She seemed mighty pleased with herself, flashing her huge smile and raising her eyebrows.

Jimmy Wayne smiled with deep lines next to his eyes and dimples on the corners of his mouth. His University of Texas T-shirt was stretched tight around his biceps and his jeans had grease stains and tears in the worn light blue denim. He was wearing a wrist cuff and the billion bracelets she remembered moving against her skin—human-warmed leather and cold silver and turquoise.

"Hey," Jacyn said, equally annoyed and pleased. Amber was a damned meddler. She was also smug as hell as she stomped around the kitchen flinging open the fridge and pulling out three Miller Lites.

"Whatcha wanna do for supper?" She handed Jimmy Wayne a beer. "Maybe grill out?"

Amber slapped a beer on the table in front of Jacyn and didn't wait for a response. "I'll run over to the store and grab some steaks and, what? Make me some macaroni and cheese?" She smiled down at Jacyn and tugged on her pigtail.

Jacyn couldn't help laughing back at Amber. The girl just didn't know what the words *no* or *none of your business* meant. Which pretty much made her a Southerner.

"You know I'll make you whatever you want."
Jacyn popped open her beer and looked over at
Jimmy Wayne, who was being a little too silent for
Jacyn's taste. "You like macaroni and cheese?"

"I'd fight you over that, but I don't hit girls."
Jimmy Wayne sipped his beer. "Does that mean I'm
invited for supper?"

"Now you're insulting *me*. If there's food and
you're here, you're invited." If this had been her regular life, back in Austin, and her one-night stand had
waltzed into her kitchen with someone, it would have
been uncomfortable and surreal. In Biloxi, now, it
was par for the course.

Amber snatched Jacyn's keys off the table and
skipped out of the house just like she skipped in to
it—with an air of self-satisfaction. Jacyn sighed and
took a long pull on her beer. She stood up and
snapped her fingers toward the dinette. "Go on and
sit down. You waitin' on an engraved invitation?"

Jimmy Wayne lifted one side of his mouth and
pulled on his beer. "Maybe any kind of invitation
would be great." But he crossed the kitchen to pull
a chair out with his foot and sat down. "You don't
want me here, I'm gone." His voice lifted the hair
on the back of her neck, all low rattle and rusty
Texas sand.

She felt weird, but not in a way that she would
have figured on before being in this position. She
didn't care that he was there. Looking over at him,

at his short dark blond hair and too-long eyelashes and perfectly swelling mouth, all she really felt about him was intrigue and want. Nothing strange about him sitting right there in her kitchen drinking crappy beer and staring back at her with his chin tilted up in invitation or challenge.

Jacyn yanked the fridge open and winked at him. "I can't imagine you get sent away very often." And that was the gospel truth made even more concrete when he laughed in a deep rumble that was uninhibited and comforting in a strange way.

"Yeah, well, the Lord was good to me on some accounts. I won't lie about that."

Jacyn pulled cheese and milk and chicken broth out of the refrigerator and looked over her shoulder at Jimmy Wayne. "Modesty is really hot in a man." She rolled her eyes.

"Hey, it ain't braggin' if it's true." He laughed again, all loose limbs and head thrown back. Jacyn shook her head and laughed along. "Can I help?"

She had a few suggestions about how, exactly, he could help her, but she had no plans to put on a show for Amber. He stood up and walked over to stand really close behind her as Jacyn put water on to boil for the macaroni.

"My mama taught me how to cook." He bumped against her back, and over the humid smell of salt in water heating she could smell the combined scent of his bath products, deodorant, and the spicy tang

of sweat. He wasn't being subtle here. To be completely honest, she had no *idea* what his deal was.
She had to be at least six years older than him, average in every way, and nothing all that special.
Maybe less than not special, being so worn down
from the last six months—her personality bleeding
out with the effort to make some kind of a difference.

Maybe she was easy for him, just there within
reach. Jacyn hated herself a little for being the sort
of person who thought someone was too good for
her. She had no idea when she had become this
woman. Actually, she'd had no idea she was this
woman until Jimmy Wayne slid two fingers under
her T-shirt at her waist and under the frayed waist-
band of her jeans.

He pressed her against the edge of the counter
with his weight and kissed the side of her neck
while the two fingers became his whole hand slipping across her stomach and up to touch the wire of
her bra. One of his legs shoved between hers and
the hand not rubbing against the underside of her
breast pressed against the fly of her jeans. She let
her head fall back on his shoulder, and his mouth
slid open and wet across her cheek.

Even as she twisted toward giving in completely,
she wondered what the hell she was doing. She almost laughed that the real issue she had with screwing Jimmy Wayne right there in the kitchen in broad

daylight with all the drapes open and the doors unlocked wasn't that she hardly knew the guy and he
might even be stalking her, but that she didn't want
to have to live down having Amber walk on it.

A drop of water from the pan popped onto her
arm. Instantly, she was shocked back to reality. She
grabbed Jimmy Wayne's arm, gripped him against
his bracelets, and turned her head away from his
mouth.

"Why don't you get the grill going?" It took a
piece of her soul to say that with the muscles of his
chest pressing into her shoulders and the nap of his
stubble moving ticklish against her neck.

Arms slackened and he was somewhere away
from her instantly. She looked over her shoulder to
watch a lost, hurt look collapse into his easy smile.
"Oh, you don't even know my skills with the grill,
girl."

She felt her face shape itself into perplexity. He
felt rejected by *her*? She didn't think a guy like him
would care one way or another about getting turned
down, since all he had to do was walk ten feet to
find someone else. Maybe he had issues.

"The grill's out back and the lighter fluid and
charcoal are sitting on the porch." She pointed at
the back door. He turned his head that way, the
smile slipping a little again.

"Alright, I'm totally on this." He turned and
walked out the back door with Jacyn watching. She

felt like she should be concerned or confused or interested in Jimmy Wayne's weirdness, but it felt somehow normal, like that was just how he was. Why she thought that, she had no idea.

She pulled out a pan and started grating the cheese for the macaroni. Misty popped back into her mind, and she got another beer out of the fridge.

Jimmy Wayne popped his head into the kitchen, trailing the smell of smoke and the humidity from outside with him. "You got a radio I could listen to?"

Jacyn pointed to the counter next to the fridge. "It's got batteries."

He opened the door wide and left it open as he grabbed the radio. "Grab another beer if you want. Hell, feel free to help yourself to whatever. Everyone else does. It's weird to have to offer." Jacyn smiled at him, genuine with that. Anybody in the house was either family or friends that went back so far they might as well be. Jimmy Wayne smiled brightly at her with the radio under his arm while he opened the fridge and pulled out two beers.

That smile probably broke a whole lot of hearts and would probably break a whole lot more. She wondered if she'd get to be one of those notches. Probably, as things were going.

"You trying to get me to ask you to marry me?" Jimmy Wayne tilted his head to the side, smile firmly in place and chin lifted up high.

"Huh?" Jacyn paused stirring the cheese sauce.

He winked at her. "Don't get pissed off at me here, but you're making homemade macaroni and cheese and got me grilling steaks and you're feeding me beer. That's pretty close to redneck heaven, baby."

Now, normally, when a man who wasn't related to her called her baby, Jacyn had a whole string of retorts.

"You ain't even seen me two-step or ride a horse yet, and I haven't even started in about NASCAR." That was not one of the normal comments that would have rolled off her tongue, and the bark of laughter Jimmy Wayne gave in response to it felt as close to freedom as she'd felt in a while.

Amber barreled in the front door hollering shortly thereafter.

"Guess who I ran into at the Winn-Dixie!" Amber called out from the front of the house, and Jacyn knew immediately that supper had turned into a whole thing. She entered the kitchen trailing Clay and his brother, Mason, and Mason's wife, Mimi, and suddenly the kitchen was packed full of people hugging and backslapping and hauling coolers through the room out back.

Mimi hugged Jacyn so tight she might have cracked a rib and shook her by the shoulders. "Amber tells me you got a new boyfriend. Where's he at?" She screamed it like the damned harpy she was, blond curls bobbing triumphantly around her face. She would be relating every gory detail of this night to anyone and everyone who'd listen for weeks.

"I seriously doubt that's what Amber said." Jacyn rolled her eyes in Amber's direction and got the same expression reflected right back at her. They both started laughing together as Mimi looked between them with her hands on her hips.

"What I said, Michelle Boaz, is that Jacyn was fucking a hotass cowboy. You drew your own conclusions." Amber flipped her the bird.

Mimi went red as Clay entered from the door to the backyard. "I miss all the good shit." He smiled, and Jacyn felt like the world shifted slightly on its axis back toward realignment. "Hey, Jacyn, you oughtta told me that you was seein' JW. We go back."

Mimi huffed out the back around Clay, and Jacyn just gave up the fight on that one. Let them think what they wanted; they were going to no matter what she said or did. "What did I say?" Clay looked genuinely mystified.

"You were too stupid to live, what's new?" Jacyn said over her shoulder with a laugh.

"Every family's gotta have one." Amber piped up.

"I'm gonna go sit in the yard and get drunk." Clay slipped away with a soft click of the door.

"So y'all get it on while I was at the store? I assed

around with the dimwits to give you some time. Goddamn, that boy's fine." Amber popped open a beer and watched as Jacyn shoved the macaroni and cheese into the oven.

Jacyn wished that she had just screwed Jimmy Wayne into the ground in that case. She was always her own worst enemy in any given situation. Mainly though, she wondered how Clay knew Jimmy Wayne.

"You're looking for details here, I didn't fall off the turnip truck yesterday. You're gonna have to get me really plastered to get into the kind of detail you're after, with illustrative sound effects and reenactments." Jacyn almost made it the whole way through that without laughing, but Amber's whoop of pleasure was just too much to withstand.

Jacyn slipped out the back door just as dusk was coming on. The sky toward the Gulf hung low, striped cotton-candy pink and salmon with blue-tinted clouds progressing slowly from horizon to horizon. The bug zapper on the porch buzzed and hummed. Someone had tuned the radio to the Country Oldies station, and Waylon twanged about Texas. There were way more people in the backyard than just the ones who'd traipsed through the house. Other cousins and some of Amber's high school friends. Three or four of Clay's work friends. The neighbors.

Jimmy Wayne stood next to the barbecue with one of Jacyn's aprons tied around his waist with the top smock part folded down. He was barefoot, with a Bud longneck hanging from two fingers, and talking to Clay.

The air smelled like damp heat, mildew from the pile of shingles leaning against the back of the house, and burning charcoal. Jacyn felt a vague sense of contentment wrap around her with the humidity. This was home—folks randomly strolling into the yard and parking themselves, drinking a few beers and eating some decent food, gossip and chatting and the easy camaraderie of not giving a crap what anyone thinks.

Her cousin Macon sat on one of the myriad aluminum folding lawn chairs with the half-busted mesh seats, shucking oysters and opining about next season's college football prospects. Mimi was down on her knees weeding the flowerbed against the fence, probably nursing her extreme dislike of Amber and Jacyn. Amber and her school friends were eating oysters and playing cards, having broken out the Maker's Mark while Jacyn wasn't looking.

While she'd been surveying the scene, Jimmy Wayne had turned his attention to her. He had one corner of his mouth lifted and his beer bottle halfway to it. In the growing dark, he looked less uncomplicated. He exuded something ineffable, something dangerous that wasn't about broken hearts and loneliness in the wake of false connection. His grin bled away, leaving what she read to be an assessing face. She stared right back as he let his hand holding the beer drop down to his side.

"Well, shit, this is the part of the evening where I get to tell you, JW, if you mess with my cousin, I'm gonna be forced to pull a *Walker, Texas Ranger* on your ass," Clay said around a laugh, breaking the moment.

"You just wish you were from Texas, son," Jimmy Wayne shot back, laughing along.

"What century is this?" Jacyn snapped her fingers. "Excuse me, but what's with discussing me like I can't take care of myself? I can use a gun." She was totally going to ignore the assumption of a relationship here. That's just what her people were like, leaping to ridiculous conclusions and always wanting everyone hooked up, married, or on total relationship lockdown.

"Well, hell, that's totally my luck." Jimmy Wayne sighed theatrically. "Couldn't be attracted to the incompetent, fragile petal-type like a smart man."

"Don't make me get the bat, JW." She said Clay's name for him with a little twist that made him look her in the eye in the gloom.

"You're lucky you're so pretty, because people don't usually get to threaten me and keep on breathin'." He said it with his mouth curved back up at the corner.

"The whole shit-kickin' thing don't really work on me," Jacyn replied, shocked at the tone of her voice. She was totally screwed here. One the other hand, she wasn't sure how she was expected to withstand Jimmy Wayne scratching his belly and smearing soot from the grill all over his white shirt, and then laughing his ass off when he realized what he was doing while spilling beer all over himself. He just laughed harder as Jacyn whipped off her overshirt to wipe at his arms and the front of his shirt. He pushed the strap of her tank top up with his finger and let the finger stray across her collarbone.

He had soot on the side of his neck. She wiped it off with her shirt as he ran his hand from her shoulder down to cup her elbow. "How do you know my cousin?"

He cleared his throat. "Would you believe me if I said Clay's a huge rodeo fan?" He made a comically hopeful face with a lifted eyebrow and his mouth parted slightly.

"I guess you *want* to tell me the truth, then." She tugged at one of his belt loops as he tumbled back into his devouring smile.

"Oh, baby, I'm not that easy. You gotta work for it a little. At least pretend you want me for my looks." He leaned down and licked at the side of her face.

She leaned away, and he wrapped his arms

around her waist as she dipped back low. He followed her back until her spine protested and she had to tip off one foot. She wrapped her lifted leg against the back of his knee, forcing him to snatch them both back up, and in his confusion she twisted away with a hoot of triumph.

"Bring your A game, Baby Texas." Jacyn snapped her fingers and pointed at him and twirled away toward Amber and the card game now being played under a circle of tiki lamps. He hadn't succeeded in distracting her from finding out what his deal was, but she let him think so for now.

CHAPTER THREE

They ate shrimp barbecued on skewers and some fish the neighbor fried up lickety-split and the macaroni and cheese and coleslaw someone had brought and hush puppies and snap beans from who knows where. Jacyn was dealt into the card game and beat the hell out of everyone, except one of Amber's friends sporting dreadlocks and about seventy facial piercings.

"You forgot the steaks, right?" Jacyn asked Amber, as she picked shrimp off a bamboo skewer.

Amber blinked a couple times, then fell apart laughing. "Oh, shit. Yeah. That's what I went to the store for, right? I got to the beer aisle and totally forgot."

The sound of cards slapping together in a bridge shuffle cracked out loudly. The bug zapper *zzzzzzz*ed so loud and long, Jacyn suspected a cockroach had made a wrong turn in Albuquerque. She scrunched her toes in the grass and felt the desiccated old wood of the picnic table against the back of her thighs. She rearranged her cards by suit with the highest values to the left and sipped her scotch.

On the other side of the yard, Jimmy Wayne had broken out his guitar, and there was a rowdy sing-along transpiring, with half of her cousins whooping it up between singing Willie and Hank Jr. and Alabama songs.

"It's weird how many educated women end up with roughnecks and rednecks. Some kind of self-hatred or something." Amber tapped the tabletop for two cards. Jacyn didn't even have to wonder what she was jawing on about.

"Wow, that was about as subtle as buckshot to the face." She rolled her eyes and tossed a quarter into the kitty.

"You got a type, there ain't no lying about that. I'm not sure if a rodeo rider is moving up or down from a roughneck who works offshore, but that's neither here nor there. It's hardly just you." Amber was drunk. She didn't usually walk this close to out-right offensive. Nobody brought up her divorce to her face, except in really offhanded and apologetic ways. That just wasn't her family's way. She felt sorta off-put by it, wounded, like Amber was saying it was her fault, that her luck had caused it just like everything else in her life. Draggin' herself from one bad choice to another.

"What the hell is wrong with y'all? This guy's the one-night stand that didn't know when to leave, not my baby daddy." Jacyn needed a lot more to drink to deal with this crap.

"Uh-huh. I'm not buyin' what you're sellin', but even if I was I'm still right." Amber rolled her eyes.

Two of Amber's friends started talking about basketball, and Amber polished off her scotch as Jacyn refilled her glass with about three fingers. "Fold." Jacyn laid her full house facedown on the splintering tabletop and flung her legs over the bench. She was used to winning at cards, and someone else probably would have called and smacked down the winning hand in triumph. Jacyn felt like it was a Pyrrhic victory.

She wandered over to the side of the yard where Jimmy Wayne was playing a country version of a Prince song much to the absolute freakin' delight of his audience and laid down on her back in the grass. The stars were bright with hardly any cloud cover to obscure them. She sipped her drink by lifting her head at a weird angle that hurt her neck.

Jimmy Wayne sang about love gone wrong, and Jacyn wondered if he had the life experience to back up the broken-glass sorrowful timbre of his voice. His voice was strong, teeth-jarring sweet tea, and a long summer evening.

She only realized she'd fallen asleep because she woke up again with a shoulder pressing into hers and the liquid cool feel of silver against her arm. She rolled her head to find Jimmy Wayne smiling with his dimpled grin, his arm under his head highlighting the thickness of his muscles.

"I didn't drink enough to pass out." Why that was the first thing that came to mind, she had no idea. His eyelids fluttered down so that he was looking at her mouth.

"Prob'ly tired is all. You were out late last night," he half-whispered, voice cracking from overuse or fatigue.

"How do you know Clay?" It seemed natural to ask him that again, natural in the way easy confidences and soul-bearing always seemed in the cocooning solidarity of the deep night.

Jimmy Wayne rolled on his side with his elbow propping his head up, pressing into her from shoulder to foot.

"Have you ever found out something that later you really wished you hadn't?" He blew air up like he used to have longer hair, an unconscious tick that he probably didn't even know he had. The same way that Jacyn still pushed up her phantom glasses after having LASIK eye surgery.

"Hasn't everyone?" Because it was a universal truth that ignorance really mainly was bliss.

"This is like that." He sounded more serious than usual.

"You mean, you think my life will be permanently altered finding out you met Clay at a cat house?" She watched his mouth pull up into a smile, feeling a reflective one tug across her face.

"You think I've ever had to pay for it?" He ran his finger against the exposed skin between the bottom of her tank top and the top of her cutoffs. His smile made the bottoms of her feet itch and her stomach roll over.

"I think you're tryin' to distract me pretty damned hard, and that makes me really frickin' curious." Jacyn pinned his hand down against her belly. His warm, calloused palm felt more familiar than it really was, like the palms of so many other men she'd known—her daddy and her uncles, her grandaddys, as well as lovers and friends—men who worked hard for a living, who sweated in the heat for their wages and who did it because they had families they loved.

His eyes lifted back up to hers. "Do you like me?"

And that was a 180 she wasn't expecting. He sounded so earnest, though, so genuinely pained, that she felt something shift inside her, her chest tight and her throat closing up. The night pressed down on them as though the rest of the world had fallen away like glass falling apart around a spider-web crack.

"It's pretty obvious I do," she whispered, not sure why, but feeling compelled to dampen, to huddle down and become still.

"You won't anymore when I tell you what you want to know." His eyelashes brushed the freckles under his eyes. She reached up and touched freckles farther down on his cheek, braille under her finger-tips that meant nothing to her besides that maybe she was out of her depth here. But her entire world was a jumbled confusion of relationships built on extreme circumstances and sorrow.

"There's very little that you could tell me that would surprise me, sweetheart." She'd felt jaded for a lot of years, but Katrina had made that realer somehow. Now she didn't feel jaded, she genuinely *was*.

He turned his face to kiss the inside of her wrist, his soft mouth juxtaposed against the sharp rasp of stubble surrounding it.

"I pretty much own the very little you're thinking of, trust me." His voice had bled to oil derricks and dust, Texan in a way she associated with old folks and country people.

Jimmy Wayne had always had a way with people. Most of it was innate, just a function of his ability to read others, peg them with their flaws and charismas without much judgment. He had always figured that in another life he would have been a great criminal, nearly flawless in his head on who someone really was.

He'd had feeling about Jacyn the first time he met her. He'd trusted her enough to let his guard down, get in close and naked with someone he hadn't known for years. That was something he almost never did. *Almost* never, because it had happened a time or two. But only a time or two. He couldn't really risk himself like that, emotionally or physically. There was always something with a pretty facade waiting in the dark, whether that be a back alley, a smoky bar, or a stretch of piney woods. Jimmy Wayne had always felt sympathy for pretty girls because he knew what it was like to use his looks to his benefit, but also knew what it was like to be trapped into doing it even when he wanted to have a conversation free of sexual innuendo and double-talk.

He laid in the grass under the oppressive spring heat of southern Mississippi feeling mosquitoes landing on his skin and skipping away, feeling the sharp prickle of close-cropped grass scrape against him, feeling his life jig to the left as Jacyn stared him down. Even groggy and half-drunk, she was whip quick and tenacious. He didn't want to upset her world anymore than it already had been. It was fairly obvious she was at loose ends, just skating through her life with no real direction or motivation. He'd seen his share of that since the storm. She was someone he'd like to take out like normal people do, movies and a little two-stepping, maybe picnics and slow walks in the country, but that wasn't his life this time around. This was the make or break here. He could tell her the truth and watch her walk away or he could keep lying and wait for the day she got a restraining order on him because he was a lying, cheating piece of dirt.

"I met Clay a couple years back, when I was in Gulfport chasing down a lamia." He watched her blink slow and drunk. He'd chosen honesty, because he didn't want to draw this out into recrimination and bitter words flung across a kitchen table, anything that could have maybe been killed before conception because he didn't trust her to be a grown-up.

"A what again? Is this a hunting thing?" Her face was pulled down tight with her eyebrows snapping together and her mouth pressing closed. He knew full well that she didn't really think it was a "hunting thing."

"You're bound to know what a lamia is." She was smarter than that. Educated. A teacher.

"I know there's a mythological creature called that. It's a snake-woman or something. It eats babies?" She yawned big, and if there had been better light, he figured he could have counted her fillings.

"The creature's not mythological, and it's not really a snake-woman. It eats babies, though." It not only eats them, it eats them skin first and bit by bit, feeding off of their pain as much as their flesh. Not just babies, either. All children. He didn't want to get into those details if possible. When she clued in that he wasn't joshin' her, he didn't want her nightmares to be too bad.

"So, your big secret that I won't be able to go back on is that you're into role-playing games?" She smiled at him, dimples in both cheeks that probably worked to make people forget anger or annoyance or any other damned thing Jacyn wanted anyone to forget.

"Do I seem like the kind of person to get decked out in robes and a cape to sit around discussing my vampiric bloodline?" He wanted to laugh, because just the idea of that was, well, funny as hell. He'd always wondered about people who were into the goth scene that lived in the South. That sort of thing really boggled Jimmy Wayne, because the last place he'd want to live if his uniform was velvet and wool would be New Orleans or anywhere else on the Gulf. He figured that Seattle or Boston would be better suited to that kind of lifestyle. Who knew what went through some people's minds, though. He didn't judge, just wondered what made people tick.

"You seem like the kind of person who would

spend all his time drinking beer and fishing, but I learned a long time ago that how a person seems doesn't mean jack shit." Jacyn leaned up on her elbows. She rolled her neck back and forth and fixed him with a serious expression, eyebrows drawn down and her bottom lip hardening. "Okay, so you're being serious, right?"

She sighed and closed her eyes as her head sagged back toward the ground exposing her throat. He knew she was clicking through whether he was the dangerous kind of crazy or if he was a harmless wacko. He also thought that exposing your throat like that to anyone who might be carrying a weapon was a sign that she needed to be looked out for.

"See, this whole song and dance would have been more believable if you hadn't included my cousin in your delusion. I know the guy. Ain't no way in hell he'd ever believe in monsters and oogly-booglies. He doesn't even believe in good luck." She sat up all the way, forcing him to do the same.

"Clay didn't know *what* we were after, just that we were goin' after a child killer at the time. He learned soon enough that we weren't after a regular ol' crazy-ass murderer. I think brains prob'ly run in your family." He watched her shutting down, deciding to placate him. "I don't expect you to believe a damned word I'm sayin'. You're not an idiot." The anger slipped in just like a firecracker going off. He gets tired of this. Most people like him stick close to one another, like a strict religious sect or an ethnic minority. They marry each other and keep all their secrets in the family. Jimmy Wayne had always thought that was something close to missing the point. If people didn't know what was in the dark, that didn't help them stay alive. The things in the dark believed in human beings all too well. Besides, Clay had kept his head about him on that first hunt and was pretty good at keeping most of his patch of America free of bad things since then. In a way, this was still a family transaction.

"Okay." Jacyn sat up and arranged herself with her hands folded in her lap and her legs crossed Indian style, like she was at Bible camp. Her expression was neutral, completely unreadable. He wondered where she'd learned that sort of blankness and why. Jacyn hardly seemed like the kind of girl who needed to know how to smooth out her personality from her face. Maybe playing cards was where she'd picked it up.

"Lamias are indigenous to the Gulf Coast between Perdido Key, Florida, and Louisiana. Or if they were imported, it was a long ass time ago. Some things out there were here long before white people, some things, though, we brought with us with the syphilis blankets and gun powder." He paused to rub a hand over his face. There was a line here. The more he said, the more likely he was going to sound like a lunatic on a meth bender. But maybe if he explained enough he'd sound believable. This really wasn't his territory, explaining to people who didn't know that all their childhood fears really were true. "I think there's a lamia around here now. You've heard about some missing children, I reckon?" He knew full well she had. He'd talked to Clay about it at length earlier, when he'd first gotten to town and run into Clay by accident. Sometimes life was like that, weird fated kind of garbage like rolling into Clay's town and finding out that another of Clay's cherry-breaking monsters was on the loose. Weird, uncanny, bad luck for someone and good luck for whoever got saved.

Jacyn didn't say anything, and Jimmy Wayne had a long moment to wonder if he'd screwed this up royally. He didn't want to mess this up for his own selfish reasons, but he also knew she'd come into contact with some of the victims' families previously. Her job put her in the position to come into contact with tons of potential victims' families and he could maybe use that knowledge to save someone. He'd put his pride on the back burner to save a child. She might never trust him in the sanity stakes ever again, but if she thought he was harmless enough, maybe she'd help him help someone's baby.

"Okay," she repeated. He knew he was losing her. Even in the dim light of the tiki lamps and Christmas lights on the back porch, he could see her neutrality was masking disappointment and resignation. She'd obviously been way into him. That was never hard to read. He knew what he looked like, and he used it when he had to. Jacyn hadn't been a had-to kind of situation, more of a reciprocated attraction. But the results were the same. He liked her, she liked him, and that had been that. She was smart, though, and funny, and maybe more than a little special and he didn't want to lose his chance at something bigger than floating through each other's lives twice.

"You ain't gotta believe me because I say so." He stood up and wiped the grass off his jeans by instinct more than any desire to be clean. "If you're not scared out of your skin I'm fixin' to kill you and wear your skin as a hat, I can at least prove myself a little bit."

"Oh, yeah?" Jacyn tracked him with her eyes. At first she made no move to get up or follow him. Jimmy Wayne's stomach twisted up. Every time he reached out and got slapped down hurt the same. He had no calluses on whatever secret, invisible organ that some people called the heart—he'd always thought that emotion probably came from the gall bladder or spleen, though, something nasty that was always getting jacked up in car accidents.

Jacyn stood up suddenly, steadying herself with a hand planted firmly on the ground in front of her, and pulled her legs under her. "Fine. Thrill me."

She sort of half-smiled, and he laughed before he even knew he was doing it.

"I knew you couldn't turn me down." He slid a hand against her lower back as she stepped up next to him.

"I can't believe you don't have a better game with all the practice you've probably gotten. It's sorry." She made a mock-angry annoyed face.

"It ain't no game, baby," he said, as he opened the gate in the chain-link fence and held it open for Jacyn. "It's pure truth."

"Uh-huh," she said, with so much sarcasm it could fuel a semi for a month.

He looked up and down the street while smiling easily, just used to being paranoid, even more so when responsible for another person. She made him smile, even when he felt like he might have just ruined what they could have had. "It must get tiresome being so cynical and modern." Her skin was damp under her tank top, the fabric sticking there. Sweat rolled down the backs of his knees and his spine. He wanted to be inside in some arctic-blast air-conditioning after a shower under soft, well-worn sheets—preferably with the radio playing Hank Williams in a low murmur of heartache and with Jacyn heavy and asleep on top of him.

"You're a total crackpot, but you're cute. So if you don't try to kill me, I might not run screaming the other direction. I've known some doozies in my time." Her hair was curly with sweat, plastered against the side of her face, like spit curls that old women worked at for hours.

When they got to his truck—a 1987 F-150 with more dents than straight panels—he pulled down the tailgate and hopped up onto the bed. Jacyn stood next to the taillight watching him. He looked down at her and smiled. "You've got good instincts." She was staying flat-footed on the ground so she could run if he tried anything. He approved of that completely.

"I think me standing here indicates that's hardly the case. Now get on with it."

He laughed as he unlocked the toolbox strapped down to the bed of the truck. Inside were tools, sure, but not wrenches and screwdrivers. More like a shotgun with silver buckshot-filled shells and holy water blessed by every sort of religion he knew a practitioner of and voodoo totems and a petrified chicken slaughtered in a Santeria ceremony.

But most important, he had an imp in a jar he'd been saving to trade in for salt made from the tears of La Llorona. He pulled the mason jar out of the toolbox and looked at the little creature. It looked like a pile of sticks, its natural camouflage. Like the insect in the Amazon or wherever that looked like a tree branch. With this critter, only when animated could you really discern that it was a living, sentient . . . something. This species wasn't dangerous, and

Jimmy Wayne knew several people who kept them as pets. People who also traded in black-market products useful to him.

He got to his feet, feeling the rust and pockmarks on the bed of the truck under his bare feet. Jacyn watched him with her arms crossed over her chest. He held the jar up in front of her face, twisting it so that the street light shone on the little bundle at the bottom. She leaned in, squinting.

"So, you have some sticks in a jar. This is supposed to be proof you're not out of your gourd? Hokay." She hummed at him.

"Untwist the top and breathe into the jar." He shoved it closer to her. She rolled her eyes.

"How about *you* do that?" She lifted an eyebrow and smirked a little. She was toying with him even though she thought he was a psycho. Which made her a little crazy herself, something he didn't dislike in *any* way.

"You need some wonder in your life, lady." He did as she said, though. The metal of the threaded cap screeched in the still night, disturbing the crickets into rubbing their legs together more furiously. When he breathed down onto the imp, the figure leaped to life, scuttling around the bottom of the jar on feet that went *click-clack*, tapping his woodlike fingers against the sides of the glass.

Jacyn's mouth fell open and she snatched the jar toward her face. "What in the hell?"

Jimmy Wayne twisted the lid back down. "When he runs out of oxygen, he'll go back into stasis again."

Jacyn tugged the jar fully out of his hand and lifted it up high. The imp squatted down and stared back at her, twisting his head at comical angles and chittering loud enough to be heard through the glass. His hair looked like moss jutting away from a face marked by mobile eyebrows and an *O* of bark for a mouth. His fingers were tipped with the new green of first spring, bendable, and they pressed on the glass in front of Jacyn's face. "Is this some kind of toy?"

"Some people treat them that way, but not how you mean. It's alive. Just like you and me or a kitten." He paused. "Well, maybe not like you and me, or I hope not too much like you and me, because that's some karma I don't need."

"Where did you get it?" So, she'd moved on from disbelief to curiosity, and that was exactly what he'd been hoping for, but hadn't been relying on. Hope sparked in him that she might be even cooler than he'd thought, just rolling with whatever he tossed out. He wasn't sure if that meant she was even more adrift than he'd thought or if she was just that calm of a character.

"In the woods in Baldwin County, Alabama. There are ass-loads of them running amok there. I think they live off tobacco juice and the dregs of beer left in Bud cans." He smiled at her when she let off a tiny, fox bark of a laugh.

"In which case they should probably infest the cab of your pickup." The imp collapsed all of a sudden into the little heap of sticks again.

"What makes you think I chew chaw?" He tilted his head to the side, watching her.

"You have a Skoal ring in your back right pocket. I'm hardly the FBI here." She tapped her nail against the side of the jar and turned it from side to side.

He smiled, tugging the jar out of her hand. "You got me there."

Jacyn smoothed a hand over her pigtail and watched him with that neutral expression of hers.

"So you kidnap brownies and sell them for a living? Is that common among old rodeo riders?" Her eyes tracked his face but her expression was curiosity more than fear or anger.

"How'd you know that was a brownie?" Jimmy Wayne scratched the back of his neck and tucked the jar back into the cocoon of an old horse blanket he was keeping it in for the time being.

She shrugged one shoulder and crossed her arms over her chest as Jimmy Wayne dropped down to sit on the tailgate of the pickup. "I've read a fairy story or two in my life. I just made it up. How about vampires? Werewolves? Any of that real?"

He couldn't tell if she was asking for real or if

she was baiting him somehow. "Sure. Things aren't as simple as in the storybooks, though. There isn't the sorta categories for things like people want there to be. Maybe there's five kinda vampires, maybe there's only one thing called a vampire and a lot of things that claim to be, I don't know. I just clean up after things that hurt people." That was the best way he could explain that.

Jacyn still didn't look put out, maybe a little skeptical, but she mainly looked like that anyway. "And my cousin knows all this and helps you round up these might-be vampires and snake people who eat babies?"

"Yeah." It wasn't really his place to get into someone else's life story. But he'd already opened that bag anyway.

"Magic is real?" Her expression softened like he'd seen happen plenty of times. Magic was always the thing people wanted to believe in, the thing they wanted to be real, true. Or so they thought they did. Most of Jimmy Wayne's experiences with witches were dodgy at best. Lots of different kinds of magic, lots of different ways to get killed or maimed by it. He wondered what it'd be like to be in awe of something instead of wary of it.

"Sure, lots of kinds of magic in world." He smiled slow and blinked even slower, pulled a hand through his hair and watched her excitement turn to sarcasm.

"Oh, really? Thank god you're so pretty because you sure did hit every branch of the stupid tree when you fell out of it."

He laughed in a sudden loud burst, relieved and feeling bolder than usual with her casual acceptance of his reality—or at least she humored him for being someone unlikely to hurt her, at the very least someone amusing to have around.

"Okay, come by the office tomorrow after five. We can talk. I gotta go to bed now and you're not invited." She smiled real slow and a dimple came up on her cheek. "This time."

Clay was in the kitchen tossing out paper plates and putting macaroni salad in Tupperware when Jacyn slammed the door to the carport open. He smiled at her with the sort of soft-focus pleasure that Jacyn associated with down home. Her cousins hadn't ever been the warring sort, not like so many families she'd seen in her life.

"So." She knew there was probably a protocol to this sort of thing.

"Thought you'd be off with Jimmy Wayne somewhere by now." Laughter threaded his words, making them musical and light. He was a good guy and he liked Jimmy Wayne, which told her more about the Texan than any dating service ever could.

"I sent his sorry ass packin' tonight." She started

undoing her hair, exhausted from the heat and the stress of the day.

Clay looked over his shoulder at her. "Is that so?"

"You ever go huntin' with Jimmy Wayne, Clay? Not pigeon or deer huntin', mind." She would just ask outright, but if Jimmy Wayne were really crazy then that'd embarrass her something fierce. She didn't need another black mark in the man-picking column with anyone.

Clay put down the bright orange container in his hand and turned to face her. "Are you two gettin' serious that fast?"

"What?" That wasn't anything near what she was expecting.

"I expect he showed you some of the stuff in the back of his truck." With his voice pitched low, he dipped his chin down to his chest, watching her closely. She would have thought he'd be super drunk by now, alcohol keeping him company as he walked through the domestic routine, but he appeared totally sober, clear-thinking, and aware.

"Yeah, he did." She paused as he watched her. "It's *true*?" The whole shebang seemed so much realer with this person of all people confirming it for her. She felt slightly light-headed.

" 'Fraid so, sweetheart." He really did sound sad, disappointed, old. He rubbed a hand over his eyes. "This about the disappearances?"

"Yeah." Now the conversation seemed surreal. "Look, I'm gonna hit the hay." She turned and just walked out of the room without waiting for a response.

Her sheets felt gritty and sticky against her skin when she laid down, and she thought about getting back up to shower, but she was just too exhausted to move. She fell asleep and dreamed of winged seahorses.

CHAPTER FOUR

Jimmy Wayne Broadus grew up with a lot of love in his life. Love of the land, love of the wide-arching Texas sky above his head, love of his mama and daddy, love of the Lord. Mississippi was another country to him; the Gulf Coast was full of creatures and a culture he didn't know in the same way he knew Texas. East Texas anyway. Mississippi was closer to what he knew than Laredo, that was damn sure the truth, but it felt strange in his bones all the same. The gas stations sold tamales, which he always thought was odd, but the magic was old, African and native, ancient, and all twisted up together in a way that made him feel uncomfortable. Subtle differences lead to subtle mistakes, and in magic, a mistake was a mistake—subtle might get you a magic coma instead of a magic stasis, but that was a huge freaking difference.

He slept in his truck and dreamed about Jacyn dancing in jerky motions like a film with every few frames removed. She twisted and twirled with tear tracks on her cheeks and a deck of cards in her left hand.

He drifted through the day sharing beers with construction crews to cover information-seeking. He flew under their radar—except the ones from Houston or Harris County who knew him from his rodeo days, which was even better really. It was easy to get details and random facts out of guys so far from home for so long.

Lamia left specific tracks. Not just the bodies of mutilated children, but people with memory lapses or unexplainable artifacts around their homes. Mainly they were the remnants of evidence that a child had once lived in the home, but was inexplicably absent from the minds of the residents. The whole rigmarole was so bizarre that people rarely put all the pieces together. Generally, supernatural beings weren't much like the Hollywood and pop culture concepts of them. Sometimes the legends were dead on—like elves curdling milk and stealing shoes. The more inexplicable and wacko, the more likely a legend was true. The very nature of supernatural beings was a *screw you* to the human concept of the orderly universe, so why they would act

in a way humans found reasonable had always boggled Jimmy Wayne.

At the site of the new Treasure Island, Jimmy
Wayne chatted with some guys on lunch. One of
them was a local with family in the area displaced
from Slidell. They had a missing son who had never
been found after the storm. Oddly enough, his toys
kept randomly turning up in the strangest places in
the house where his parents were living.

He'd heard enough stories just like that to keep
him in town on his way back from Alabama to
Texas. At first he hadn't been sure which kind of
child killer he had on his hands. New Orleans was
always one of those areas most legitimate paranormal investigators or ghost hunters tended to avoid.
Too many spirits, too many supernatural creatures
using the goth community and legends about the
place to cover their actual existence. It was something of an unspoken rule that New Orleans was a
no-go zone for hunters. After Hurricane Katrina, all
the old rules got busted up and rearranged. Old spirits that used to be hemmed in by voudun or Santeria
were let loose across Louisiana, Mississippi, and
Texas. Rumors of bloodletting and exsanguinations
filtered across the Mississippi delta. Refugee towns
like Mobile, Alabama, and Houston hummed with
murmurs of sightings of this and that where nothing
had existed before the storm. Some vampires specialized in children and covering their tracks. He

hadn't been sure about the lamia until he'd talked to Clay.

His night at Buddy's had made his stay more than just a random act of protection for a population completely unaware of his activities. A pretty girl was no laughing matter, but a pretty girl who jumped into his path more than once and could possibly help him find the lamia was something else entirely. Something precious and rare. He'd been on his own, skipping from place to place killing, hunting, with no real home except for the cab of his truck since he'd left the rodeo five years before. He could admit that he nursed a romantic streak that had been like an old wound for most of his life. Women just didn't trust his earnestness, always figuring him for a whoring and boozing type, insincere and a damned fine liar. The same face that made his work easier made his love life doomed. His mama said he'd find someone one day, that he was bound to. By *someone*, she meant a witch from Nacogdoches or some fey girl with leaves in her hair who communed with spirits. Jimmy Wayne wished like hell that was his type. He always went in for sassy girls with attitudes and smarts. The kind who never took him seriously, who thought they saw straight through him, when in truth they were just seeing the stereotype he seemed to represent with his truck and boots and duct-taped cowboy hat.

He slammed the door of his truck shut at sometime

around five P.M. His watch only worked in fits and
starts after he'd gotten too close to an electrical vortex earlier in the year. He'd had it so long he was too
attached to it to get a new one. The air-conditioning
in the Oxfam office wheezed and coughed, an ancient fan groaning and taking the ambient noise
level of the office up from sixty decibels to near
seventy. The receptionist at the old metal desk
looked wrung out. The skin on her forehead was
burned and her nose was peeling. Her light brown
hair was pulled back in a loose ponytail that was
half undone. Jimmy Wayne imagined he could
smell the day-after alcohol fumes from across the
room.

He put on his *smile* when she glanced up at him.
She perked right up, like aspirin in the water of a
vase of wilting flowers. "Howdy." He adjusted his
hat and slouched a little.

"Um, hey." Her returning smile was fluttery, nervous, and barely covered a giggle. She was younger
than he'd thought when he first came in. Barely
twenty. Probably an undergrad intern of some kind.
Easy pickin's.

"Give it up, Baby Texas." Jimmy Wayne's smile
turned genuine at the sound of Jacyn's voice. He
looked over his shoulder to see her pulling a purse
onto her shoulder, wearing a denim skirt and a
white "Habitat for Humanity" T-shirt with a red
tank top under it clearly visible. Her flip-flops

smacked against the soles of her feet as she crossed the room to the front door. "Coming, or are you gonna pick up Jenny?"

"Bye, Jenny." Jimmy Wayne waved at the girl, who looked confused and stunned. He was used to that look.

Back out in the heat, Jacyn watched him from behind her cat eye sunglasses. "You leave a slime trail. You know that, right?"

He laughed so hard his belly hurt at the deadpan tone and twist of her mouth, which looked like she'd been sucking lemons for a week. "Jealous?"

"I already had you. Nothing to be jealous about. You're in the bag. Now, let's get drunk enough so that I'll believe the line of bullshit you're about to spin." She turned so that the sun was haloed around her head, her silhouette a black corona around her like an aura. He watched her walking toward his truck. Just standing there in the gravel-strewn parking lot, he felt like he was confused about this whole breathing thing, unsure where he was or what he was doing there. When she got to the truck, Jacyn turned around and looked back at him. The part of her face that was visible around her sunglasses was set in a wry smile and her hair curled around her face. "Are you simple?"

He smiled in reply. Maybe he was at that. She'd stopped him dead in his tracks with how *alive* she was.

"Get that stick thing out of the back of your truck so I can see it again." Jimmy Wayne circled around the back of the truck and did what she said. He wondered what his life would have been like if he had been the sort of guy who was satisfied with rodeo queens or buckle bunnies. He wondered a little what life was like for people like that as he climbed into the cab of the truck with the mason jar in his hand. It felt natural to do what she said, like he'd been sorta waiting around for someone who didn't fool around with "pretty please" and batted eyelashes.

Jacyn smiled at him as he passed the jar over. Her hair was in two messy braids and she had a scratch on her right cheek. Her laughter, when she unscrewed the lid on the jar and breathed inside, made his belly tighten. When he glanced at her out of the corner of his eye to see her wide-open, curious eyes and mouth parted with her tongue resting on her bottom lip, he got so hard he thought about pulling out his real slick game on her right then and there. She laughed again, sparkling and childlike, and he realized her laughter was just about as good as the feel of her pressed into his chest with her soft curves and sighing breath.

Jacyn didn't think Buddy's or any place else public was right for the sort of conversation she figured she was about to have with Jimmy Wayne.

"Go on up here a little more then turn right by the upturned bathtub on the side of the road." She watched the stick man do jumping jacks or something like them as the truck bounced on the dirt road. It was the rutted access road to her grandparents' fish camp, so it was a good thing Jimmy Wayne had a four by four.

He pulled his hat off and wiped at his forehead with the back of his wrist. "I figure I've passed the psycho murderer test, then."

"I'm holding a living stick guy in a jar on my lap, so, yeah, maybe." Jacyn really wasn't sure what she thought about this crap. This situation was sort of like waking up one day with wings or antennae. The wings or antennae are *there*, so you just have to figure out how to negotiate life with the new appendages. The stick guy was real, that's for sure. He wasn't a robot or some kind of battery-operated toy. She'd discovered that when she'd stuck her hand into the jar and groped around, trying to find out if she had just been too drunk the night before to realize Jimmy Wayne was pulling one over on her. Nope. Besides, she'd also gotten her confirmation from Clay, so that added a whole extra layer of reality to the entire business.

She watched him fiddle with the knob on the radio. His hands were huge, the nails cracked—the ring fingernail on his right hand was split down the middle like he'd injured the bed of the nail somehow. She'd seen tons of similar hands. Her daddy's left thumb-nail was permanently jacked up from a hammering injury when he was a teenager. Working men's hands were scarred hands. Jimmy Wayne had plenty of scars, and not just on his hands. She'd chalked it all up to rodeo injuries.

"How long have you been doing this?" she asked him as he turned down the path that led down to the house. They passed pine trees clustered so close to the dirt road that if she rolled her window down, she could have reached out the window and touched them.

Jimmy Wayne propped a hand on the steering wheel and looked at her from under the brim of his hat. He made a tsking noise and opened his lips to show clenched teeth. "You should prob'ly be care-ful what you ask."

She tilted her head to the side and narrowed her eyes. "If there are things you don't want to tell me, that's fine. How am I supposed to know how to nav-igate the minefield of your life when we hardly know each other at all?" Sex created false intimacy. She knew that damned well.

"Oh, I think we know each other pretty well, just not the details is all." He looked back to the road with the dimpled half-smile of his on his face.

"What the hell does that mean?" The truck bounced so hard she had to grab the oh-shit handle and hold on for dear life. The stick man squawked as he was jostled against the glass pretty hard.

"Welllllll." He drew out the word for several seconds, glanced at her real quick with a huge smile on his face, deep laugh lines furrowing by his eyes, and both cheeks dimpling deep. "You're a smart girl who got smothered by her family and then ran away from home. Just far enough to preclude day trips by your family, but close enough so you could come home when you wanted. You got a good job, an education, but you were homesick. You couldn't just move home, because that would mean failure, so you stuck it out. Maybe you were even married."

Jacyn stared at him with her mouth open. "Are you stalking me?"

He rumbled out a laugh. "So, check yes on the divorced part."

"I was married for five years to a Texaco man." Jacyn figured if he had sussed her whole life out while she was watching the way the sunlight brought out his freckles and turned his stubble slightly red, then she'd just give him the honest truth. She was a little bit flabbergasted that he was so insightful. Maybe she was just that transparent, though.

"You were miserable in your life, so when the storm hit, you used that as an excuse to move home. Now you're smothered by your family and Texas is looking good again." He pulled up to the back of the house, put the truck in park, and turned off the ignition. He propped his hand on the top of the steering wheel and lifted both eyebrows at her. "That about the size of it?"

"So you have me all figured out, but I don't know jack shit about *you*." She flung open the door and deposited the hibernating stick man on the seat before slamming it behind her. She thought about whether he was right and she knew him better than she'd thought about.

He rounded the front of the truck, both hands in his back pocket and his hat set low over his eyes. His mouth was the kind that had probably gotten him into trouble his whole life, just the sight of it alone—full to the point of sinful, pink in a way that would make most women instantaneously jealous— was enough to kill off several IQ points, but what came out of it had definitely gotten his ass kicked on a regular basis. Luckily he was a big enough guy to hold his own in fights.

The open, relaxed set to his face was nearly vulnerable, and she figured he'd been hurt a time or two. Maybe more than a time or two. He could be the sort of man who expected too much and got let down hard. Endless capacity for the pain and suffering of others, which would explain why he'd be here in Biloxi saving other people's children instead of home again to do whatever it is he does.

He followed her into the back of the house and through it to retrieve a bottle of bourbon from the kitchen. They exited through the unlocked side door.

"Do you ranch now?" She turned to follow the little trail around the side of the house that led down to the dock.

"See? I told you that we knew each other better than you were givin' credit for." He bumped against her back, and she turned her head to see him smiling down at her. She might be totally screwed here, because he was entirely too fine to live, and he was working that in a major way. "My brother and mama run the ranch. But I work there when I'm not doing this."

He put a little spin on *this* and trailed a finger under the back of her shirt. She laughed at his sheer cheesiness.

"I'm sure you do a lot of *this* when you're home, too." The trees on the right side of the path fell away down toward the bank of the river, and they descended four steps down onto the wood plank dock.

"That's where you're wrong." His voice was tight, low, obviously annoyed. When she turned back to look at him, his jaw was clenched tight and she could hear his teeth grind together.

"I guess I just pogoed onto a land mine." She lifted an eyebrow and walked down to the end of the dock to sit down and dangle her feet over the edge. It was hot as hell, so she took off her overshirt and rucked up her skirt, kicking off her flip-flops and swinging her feet on the surface of the water. She uncapped the bottle and swigged straight from it.

The opposite bank of the river was denuded in spots. In other places the trees were flattened at the tops. The place right across the river had lost their dock and it hadn't been replaced yet. Her grandparents' boat had been pulled off its moorings and deposited somewhere—who knows where, just one of the thousands of boats randomly flung willy-nilly by the storm.

"I know my good looks would indicate otherwise, but I don't go out cattin' 'round." Jimmy Wayne flopped down next to her and pulled his chew out of his back pocket. He shook it out hard, the tobacco inside thumping against the plastic of the can. "I'm not that sort of person." His voice fell low, cracked on the vowels.

Jacyn watched him pinch a small bit of tobacco and put it into his mouth with his head bent low and his hat obscuring his face. *This* was something she could read pretty easily. She had had a lot of experience with family drama since she'd come back to Mississippi—her own family's and a whole slew of other people's.

"Single mom?" She took another drink of bourbon.

Jimmy Wayne looked up at her with his expressive face pulled back into his watchful open look. "Widow."

Jacyn nodded. She could reckon that he'd taken up this sort of life because of his life drama. He didn't have to tell her that, and his eyes flitted over her face as she pieced all that together.

"Smart *and* pretty." He smiled suddenly, like the sun coming out from behind a cloud. "So shoot. I know you wanna ask me about vampires and werewolves."

His smile really needed to be criminalized immediately, because it made her ability to think stutter and short out.

"Nah, tell me about the baby-eating snake-woman. I'll hit you up about the Anne Rice stuff when I can enjoy it. Also, am I drinkin' alone here?" She held up the bottle and sloshed the contents around.

His eyes dropped half-closed for a second before he spit the tobacco into the water and snatched the bottle away from her. "Like that's ever gonna happen. Gotta go and impugn my manhood. I see how you are now, backstabber."

He took a huge draw on the bottle without coughing or his eyes watering. Jacyn almost sighed. She should have known he wouldn't be swagger-free. She sort of liked it really.

"Ok, here's how it is. Lamia come in every shape and size. They blend. They're creative bitches. How they breed and propagate themselves is still a mystery. To me anyway. If anyone else knows, they ain't sharin'." He passed her the bottle back and she sipped on it.

"Blend how?"

"They look like everyone else. Sometimes they're sexy teenaged cheerleaders, sometimes they're old grannies." Jacyn let the cheerleader comment go, because he was obviously baiting her from the tone of his voice.

"Then how the hell are you supposed to catch the thing?" She would set him up, play the straight man. It felt like a routine, which was strange considering how short a time she'd known him.

"Well, that's the thing. They're predictable. They like to fuck with people. It's part of their game. They don't just eat children, they want to make a big production about it, bring attention to themselves. They shape-shift." He took his hat off and sat it down on the dock next to him all the while keeping his eyes locked on hers.

"So you're telling me Misty Rodgers is the lamia because she's kicking up such a fuss? She's behind the whole thing and getting her jollies by getting attention to boot?" Jacyn could follow the logic, but it wasn't exactly reasonable to her.

Jimmy Wayne's whoop was something out of an old Western, flailing arms and head thrown back. Big as Texas. "Bingo! That's how these creatures operate."

Jacyn couldn't help but laugh.

"Well what the hell are we supposed to do about it, she's in lockup." Jacyn watched the sun reflecting off the wake of a boat that passed them.

"We?" Jimmy grabbed the bottle away.

"You told me all this for a reason. I assume it's to get me to help you somehow."

He swallowed and rested the bottle on his thigh. "Part of the reason, sure." His face defaulted back to the genuine one that she thought might end up breaking her heart. Loneliness was the human condition, but some people were genuinely alone. She felt for him. It must have been nearly unbearable to drive from town to town saving people from things they didn't even believe in with a smile, risking his life maybe, and not have anyone to talk to about it.

"Your family knows? About what you do, I mean."

He bowed his head and picked at the frayed edge of one of the holes in his jeans. "It'd be nigh on impossible for them not to." He sighed. "My mama told me that revenge was a nasty emotion."

Jacyn instantly knew how Jimmy Wayne's mother had been widowed. She reached out and rubbed his back between his shoulder blades. The furrow of his spine was deep, the muscles of his back thick and strong.

"You gotta do what's right for you." She passed him the bottle, and he sat up straighter, grinning.

"That what you really think or the kind of dime-store platitude nervous people hand out at funerals?" He drank as she let her hand drop off his back.

"What do you plan to do about Misty?" She really meant it, but she didn't feel like getting into that kind of emotional conversation with a boy who was going to be gone in a couple days anyway.

He met her eye and for a second she thought he was going to press it, but he just lifted an eyebrow at her. "I was tryin' to convince Clay to let her outta jail. I spun a line of bullshit about grieving mothers and stress." He glanced away toward the water. "He didn't bite."

"No, he wouldn't. Plan B?"

Jimmy Wayne shrugged. "I guess Plan B is to wait for the thing to get its own stupid ass out of jail by hook or by crook and *then* deal with it."

"What do we do in the meantime?" Even as the words left her mouth, she knew how obvious the answer to that was.

Jimmy Wayne cracked up, laughing so hard he splashed bourbon all over her. "Drink and fuck," he managed to get out. "The old standbys, sweetheart."

"Shit, you got that crap all over me." Jacyn wiped at her leg, which was covered in bourbon.

Jimmy Wayne leaned over and down to lick across the top of her thigh. Her hand flew into his hair. He brushed the flat of his tongue from her knee to the hem of her skirt and back again. When he was done, he didn't sit back up, instead he twisted and pushed Jacyn back onto the dock with his weight, turning over to lay on his side.

"Be dark soon." He licked at the corner of her

mouth and she pulled in a breath through parted lips. "Go skinny-dippin'."

His smile pressed against her mouth as his hand wrapped around her inner thigh.

"You can, I can watch," Jacyn whispered when he pulled his mouth away.

"Is that so?" His hand skimmed higher, one finger rubbing the elastic on the leg of her panties.

Frogs croaked loud in the rushes and cattails along the riverbank. A boat sped by sending the dock rocking. Jacyn pushed Jimmy Wayne off and stood up.

"Not drunk enough for public displays, come on." She carried her flip-flops in one hand and the bottle of bourbon in the other. Jimmy Wayne walked quietly enough that she couldn't hear him at all, even though he was close enough to bump into her. The yard running down the water was shaded by several ancient live oaks. In the shade of the trees, azaleas and hostas and a bed of lilies of the valley grew. The leaves and moss under her feet felt right in a way beyond words. The air smelled of dampness and mildew and flowers and dirt—the smell of her youth. She felt out of time, like life wasn't marching on anymore; the heavy feeling of long Sundays and the middle of July during summer vacation settled on her.

The screen door had a huge hole in it that her cousin had kicked there years and years ago. It thumped against the doorframe behind Jimmy Wayne with the familiar thud she'd heard thousands of times before. The house was a split-level, though the back seemed like a basement because it was built into the side of a small hillock. It was cooler down there. All the bedrooms were in that part of the house, each with a window unit air conditioner. The rest of the house had open windows and ceiling fans to deal with the heat.

They walked through the living room, passed the aqua-and-cream brocade couch from 1953, passed the souvenirs from her grandparents' life overseas when her granddaddy was in the army, over the blue shag area rugs, down the steps leading to the dark, shaded part of the house. Her family smiled at her from the walls, five decades of pictures hanging at crooked angles.

She walked into the second bedroom on the left in a bubble of contentment she hadn't felt in so long she had forgotten she ever had. Endless summer days spent on the river and long nights spent playing cards and eating cold leftovers in the kitchen. Her high school years with a boyfriend she had thought was her one and only true love. Right here in that room, on the too-soft, broken-down mattress. She smiled as she flipped the air-conditioning on and up to high and stood in front of it for a couple seconds, the musty smell making her even happier than before.

Jimmy Wayne lay on his back on the candlewick bedspread with his arm under his head and his eyes closed. Jacyn tossed the bottle on the floor and her shoes next to it and climbed onto the bed. It was warm, but not as hot as outside. Just warm enough to bleed all of her energy away when she lay down, sweating, next to Jimmy Wayne. She sank down into the mattress and rolled into him, the mattress bowing so that they lay in a deep depression wedged up together. His arm came from under his head and wrapped around her back, pulling her so that her head was on his shoulder. She fell asleep thinking about yanking his clothes off.

She woke up with her back freezing. Jimmy Wayne had pulled the corner of the bedspread over their legs. The closed door had trapped all the cold air into the room. It was totally dark in the room, which meant it was probably getting dark outside. She really had no desire to move at all. Jimmy Wayne pulled her up against his body with both hands wrapped around her arms so that their faces were level. She opened her mouth for his kiss just as he turned on his side to twist their legs together, her right one coming up over his hip.

They kissed with his hand on her face and neck, lips brushing and barely any tongue. Jacyn kept her eyes closed and touched the freckles high on his cheekbone. It felt like being sixteen again, with Jimmy Wayne not touching her breasts or trying to get his hand under her clothes. He reached behind her and yanked the bedspread over them and settled more firmly against her, sighing into the kiss. She slid her hand under his shirt and up his back, pressing him into her, the resilient feel of his relaxed back muscles under her fingers making her jack her leg over his hip higher.

Jimmy Wayne thrust shallowly against her and twisted his hips just a little, making a humming sound against her mouth. The thrill like they were doing something wrong or that they might get caught was there under the delight of him running his hand up the back of her thigh and under her panties. She bit gently at his bottom lip and pulled it into her mouth when he just went straight for it and started rubbing her off with firm circles of his thumb. Shocks when through her when he started to talk.

"Touch me?" He thrust again to make it clear where exactly he wanted her to do that. He rubbed harder and she gasped and pressed her face into the side of his neck as she popped the buttons on his fly. He started rocking into her hand before she even got a grip, solid and hot against her palm. "Baby," he whispered. "Baby, please."

He flipped them so she was on her back and slid down, pushing her legs apart and her panties to the side. One of her hands touched his cheek and the other pressed at the back of his head as his tongue and lips started to work against her. Her thighs pressed into his shoulders, and by the rhythmic bumping of his right shoulder against her leg she knew he was jacking himself off as he licked and sucked—and that turned her on even more than what he was doing to her.

The looped imagine of him touching himself, hand sliding and fingers working over his own head, his eyes open too wide and then snapping closed, made her legs shake and make her come so hard she forgot how to breathe. Jimmy Wayne held her down with a hand open on her stomach and as she pulled in maybe breath number five, she felt something hot and wet hit her calf.

"You did not."

He bumped his cock against her leg and bit her hip between laughs to indicate how he so totally did. She laughed along with him as he wiped her leg off with the bedspread.

CHAPTER FIVE

Jimmy Wayne wasn't sure what he was supposed to say to the scene in the kitchen when he emerged from the bathroom. Jacyn was standing at the counter cracking ice into a cooler wearing a 1950s-style bathing suit. The straps were thick and set on the outside of her shoulders. The bra area shoved her boobs up like a shelf. The legs had a scrap of material across them like a tiny skirt. It was aqua, like the couch in the living room. She filled it out in a way that made him wish she wouldn't ever wear anything else ever again. Her hair was down. Big curls all the way down her back.

She looked up to catch him staring.

"You wanted to go swimmin', right?" She lifted an eyebrow.

"I did, but now I'm rethinkin' that." He rubbed his bare stomach and looked pointedly at her breasts.

"It's like that, huh?" She turned back to cracking ice, and he got a good look at her ass in the suit. Nice. The problem with going without sex for a long time, and being used to that, is that the urge to do it over and over again when sex reenters the picture is all the more unrelenting. He had some serious shit to deal with here in Mississippi, but all he wanted to do was buy stock in Viagra and Trojan and lay in some beer and chicken.

She had bruises on her thighs in the shape of fingers. He was suddenly embarrassed and angry with himself for hurting her the other night. She hadn't complained, but she'd been plastered, and he was a total jackass for even taking advantage of her to begin with. That wasn't how his mama had taught him to treat women, and Jacyn deserved better than some washed-up rodeo rider whose education pretty much extended to foaling and six different ways to kill a possessed peacock.

He watched the hair curl on the side of her face and was across the kitchen pushing it back behind her ear before he realized he'd even thought about doing that. She looked up at him and smiled.

"I should just put it back up. It makes me nuts." She snapped the lid on the cooler.

"Leave it down." He wrapped a curl around his

finger and kissed it. She looked surprised for a second and he let his hand drop.

"Another man who's a sucker for long hair. Color me not shocked in the least." Grabbing the cooler off the counter she snagged him by a belt loop of the borrowed cutoffs he was wearing and yanked him toward the back door.

She walked backward, pulling him as he reached out and ran two fingers over her collarbone. Her face was flushed dark pink, her mouth swollen from kissing, no makeup, no jewelry, not even earrings. She was about as perfect and real as a woman could get, and he felt that shift inside himself where he tipped right into being the guy who couldn't say no. He wouldn't be able to deny her anything or do anything outside her best interest—even if she didn't agree or want him to. He would alienate her trying to make her happy, trying to keep her with him. He knew it sure as he knew the taste of applewood barbecue or the smell of rain turning clay muddy.

She dropped her hand off his belt loop and turned around to open the screen door. He stood there in the sixty-watt incandescent light, watching her walk down to the water through the screen door until she was lost in the gloom.

"Jimmy Wayne?" she called out to him. She was out in the dark by herself, pleased and content, and he was standing inside, in the light, out of reach. He knew when he opened the door and went out to stand next to her, it would only be the first time in a long string of him doing the same, following wherever she went, until she sent him away.

"Jimmy Wayne!" She screamed it that time, high and strained to carry all the way up from the water. The sound sent adrenaline through him. He banged the screen door so hard he cracked the frame.

She was floating in the river on her back when he waded into the water. He was beyond rationality, heart beating in his mouth and eyes. He splashed and swam out to her, probably thirty feet from shore and pulled her legs down and her against him as he treaded water.

Her eyes popped open. The world had gone all silver and long shadows in the moonlight. "I just wanted you to hurry up," she whispered as her legs started kicking, treading water, too, and her arms came around his shoulders. She already knew instinctively why he reacted like he did. Which was something at least.

"Come on." She pulled away and he let her. His heart didn't slow down much as he watched her swim back toward shore with perfect form, legs scissoring out of the water and glowing white in the moonlight. He followed with much less finesse.

She stood on her tiptoes with her chin barely clearing the water. He pulled her up with his hands under her arms and her legs came around his waist.

"If I start acting dumber than usual, don't get too mad about it." He skimmed his lips over the droplets of water on her cheek.

"Okay," she whispered into his hair.

She had eleventy messages from Amber on her cell phone, after Jacyn and Jimmy Wayne made it back to the house.

Message one: "You better be committing unspeakable acts of sin, because you forgot we were going to Jackson to see Teague Branan tonight."

Message two: "Right. I'm leavin' now. I got someone to take your ticket. You suck beyond the telling of it."

Message three: "I'm worried about you, you skank. Call me or die."

Message four: "You better be fucking dead is all I have to say."

Jacyn deleted each one as she listened. She knew Amber would call back soon. Probably from the show so it would be completely incomprehensible.

Jimmy Wayne popped open a beer and watched her checking her messages. He had stripped off his wet cutoffs and stood in the kitchen butt naked except for the old teal-and-white-flocked towel that was barely tied around his waist. Jacyn thought that he was probably the source of original sin, or at least had sent several women straight to hell just by existing. His broad shoulders bled into those drop-dead arms that made her want to bite him all over. He was muscled but with a thin layer of softness over his muscles, which kept him from having that weird, ripped, hard thing that body builders develop. He was built from working a ranch and (she felt a little strange even thinking this really) from killing monsters.

"Are we stayin' here tonight?" The towel slipped and he reached down to hold it together with his hand.

"How come?" She clicked her phone closed.

He swigged on his beer smiling with his head tilted a little to the side. "My virtuous nature means I don't tool around with . . . supplies of the variety we need. We used my emergency condom the other night."

Jacyn was having a little difficulty comprehending that Jimmy Wayne didn't get serviced on a nightly basis by the Dallas Cowboy Cheerleaders. He must have some deep emotional issues or be religious.

"You trying to keep right with the Lord?" She lifted her eyebrows and pointed at him with her phone.

His face fell into his real expression. "Yeah, sure. You feelin' me out about somethin'?" When she didn't answer after a couple seconds, he lifted the corner of his mouth. "You're not some kind of heathen evangelizer or somethin', because then I'd

have to bust out my Bible and put some old time religion all over ya." She couldn't tell if he was joking
or not. Probably six of one, half dozen of the other.

"I've been saved, but I don't go to church, so you
best keep your Bible thumpin' to yourself." She
turned on her heel and trailed water all over the floor.

"Where you goin'?" Jimmy Wayne called behind
her.

"To see where my boy cousins stash their stuff."
She knew there had to be tons of condoms and
booze stashed all over the place. It was *her* family
after all.

Jacyn stood on the beach near the wooden dock
that used to stretch out into the Gulf for hundreds
of feet, old, worn gray wood, familiar and iconic.
Instead pylons gaped out of the water like broken
teeth, a few planks still clinging on here or there.
Down the convex arc of the white sand, shingles
and beams and pieces of metal littered the strand.
Farther down, upturned boats hulked yards inland,
their hulls sometimes completely intact and sometimes crushed.

Jacyn watched the water lapping around debris
in the shallows. The familiar pattern of the Gulf—
light blue deepening to indigo, streaked with aqua
patches where sandbars collected under the water—
was gone. The water stretched out in unbroken dark
blue, the entire bed of the ocean remade by the

storm. Gulls shrieked and fed off the dead fish strewn all over the beach. She could taste salt in her mouth and couldn't tell if it was spray from water or tears. Not just the buildings were gone, the very topography of the land and water had been remade, homes stolen by a force of nature. Jacyn felt like she had stepped into some alternate Mississippi, that the one she'd known her whole life was beat down and broken up by Katrina to leave a whole new world. People passed her, each looking as helpless and shell-shocked as she felt.

She reached behind her, reached back for something, and her hand touched someone else's.

"Rock bottom looks different when you're looking up out the hole instead of down at the ground," Jimmy Wayne said. She couldn't see him when she turned around, but she felt the calluses and scars of his hand around her own.

She woke up in a tangle with Jimmy Wayne to her phone ringing. She tried to reach around Jimmy Wayne to get it, but he got it first, opening it and pressing it to her ear. His eyes stayed closed the whole time.

"Jacyn? What the hell is *wrong* with you?" Amber barked out. "Where are you? Over at the fish camp?"

"Uh-huh." Jacyn could barely move. Jimmy Wayne pressed his face into her chest, his stubble rasping against her skin, and he lazily pulled her closer with a hand against her back. She touched his short hair. It was thick, prickly, and soft at the same time, depending on how hard she pressed against it.

"You got that fine-ass roughneck out there?" Amber's voice was shredded from screaming at the concert the night before.

"What's up? Are you just calling me for the lowdown, or was there a real, nonpurient point?"

"I guess you haven't seen the news," Amber sighed. Jacyn waited for her to go on. "They found three dead kids in D'Iberville. Mutilated."

"Mutilated how?" Jimmy Wayne sat up abruptly, eyes alert, wide, completely aware.

"I don't know. They didn't release details. I'm sure Clay knows." Her voice cracked into the loud kind of whisper people use when their voices go.

"Who were they?" Jacyn felt like she'd just stepped into a whole new life. Jimmy Wayne telling her *X*, *Y*, and *Z* was one thing, but the evidence made it completely and totally real.

"They haven't identified them." Amber's broken voice sounded more than just exhausted from the concert the night before. The deaths of children affected people strangely at the best of times, which their current lives definitely weren't.

Jimmy Wayne rolled out of bed, his back working, a starburst scar under his right shoulder blade clearly visible in the watery morning light filtered through the oak trees outside. He brushed a hand over his scalp and picked his jeans up off the rocking chair in the corner.

"I'll be home shortly." Even if that wasn't her first or tenth impulse, really. Jimmy Wayne turned to look at her over his shoulder, no smiles this morning, just blue eyes shaded by his eyelashes and something hidden. His jaw tightened as she watched, the muscle jumping.

"Don't bother. I don't want to listen to you have sex all day. It will put me off my food." Amber shifted on the other end of the line, took a drink of something. "I know you're too busy right now with your head up that cowboy's ass. Don't sweat it."

"Are you being passive aggressive, or are you really signing off on me running away to Vegas to get married?" Jimmy Wayne let out a soft bark of laughter at that and leaned down to grab her ankle and yank her off the pillows.

"If you get remarried I get the back meat off the turkey at Thanksgiving, so get crackin'!" Amber laughed in crackling shocks. Jimmy Wayne yanked at her again.

"Are you fixin' to get up, or am I fieldin' this one alone, abandonin' your ass out here to the catfish and God's half acre?" The rasp of his morning voice, soft and pitched to carry even at the low volume, had an intimate feeling to Jacyn that was way more personal than all the other things they'd done together.

"I gotta go," Jacyn said to Amber.

"Yeah, I just bet you do. Slut." Amber hung up.

"I gotta get a shower before we leave." Jacyn tugged her leg out of Jimmy Wayne's grip and swung her legs over the side of the bed. He watched her tugging the bedspread around her, tucking it in at her chest as she got her feet under her. His upturned face with his Flemish Master look—wide, reflective eyes and sybaritic mouth—looked young, his expression watchful and something near worried. "How old are you?"

He blinked slow, face turning toward the carpet. "How come that doesn't sound like a idle inquiry?"

"Just curious is all." Which was sort of the truth.

Looking back up at her, he ran his hand over the top of his head. "Twenty-five."

Eight years younger than her. And she wasn't sure what part of that was more distressing, that almost a decade separated their ages or that it had been eight years since she was twenty-five herself. She still felt about that age.

"I'm a catch, darlin'." He popped his teeth-baring grin, grabbed the bedspread wrapped around her, and jostled her around a bit. "Go on now, get your shower. You can have a whole crisis later, after we do what needs doin'."

He stood up and wrapped around her, rocking her around toward the door and pressing his face into her neck, tickling her with his stubble and making her laugh and struggle to get away. When he finally let go and she turned around to flee, he smacked her on the ass with a giddyap echoing along with the sound of his hand smacking down.

Jacyn figured she was probably done in completely, because she actually laughed at that.

CHAPTER SIX

Jimmy Wayne watched Jacyn out of the corner of his eye as they drove across Back Bay—an inlet of the Gulf of Mexico formed between the peninsula that Biloxi proper sat on and D'Iberville in the north—and down I-90 by Keesler Airforce Base. He let her fiddle with the radio. She changed the station constantly, never listening to an entire song. He couldn't tell if she was restless or if she was just one of those channel-flipping crazies. She'd braided her hair and put on different clothes than she'd had on the day before, a sleeveless cotton dress a size or two too big that looked vintage, like the rest of stuff in the cottage. Yellow with white checks. Her tan looked more pronounced against it. Her knees were scarred, he noticed. Probably childhood injuries, falling off a bike or a skateboard, and he smiled to himself imagining Jacyn as a kid with a skateboard under her arm eating Icees and sassing her parents.

"You think Misty left the kids out and people just now found them? Or you thinkin' something else?" Jacyn flipped the radio from Charlie Daniels Band to Kiss.

What he mainly thought was that he didn't want to have to bother with this case anymore. It was going to take time away from figuring out what he was going to do with himself if Jacyn decided he wasn't anything much but a walking dildo. Dead children affected him on a level that was under active thought. He could feel the anger burn around the spiraling inchoate thoughts about the curve of Jacyn's shoulder and the taste of her, the sound of water lapping against the weathered dock in the dark from the wake of boats, the mildew and Pine-Sol smell of the fishing cottage, the crenulated edges of his uneasiness sharp even when he's doing his best to let that go.

"Leanin' towards thinkin' it's not Misty." He pulled onto Forest Avenue and waited at the light. Sweat beaded under his hat and slipped down his spine. His shirt was plastered to his back, stuck to the cracked vinyl of the seat. Jacyn wiped at the backs of her knees with a Hardee's napkin that was sitting on the dash. The ends of her braids curled up like a cartoon character.

"How come?" Jacyn's voice snapped loud in the front of the car. She had a hair-trigger temper that he thought could lead to some spectacular fireworks between them.

"I've been doin' this all my life. It's a hunch. It just don't feel right." Just like most skills, not all of hunting was about straight facts. There was always that intangible part that wasn't much more than a feeling. Just like relationships.

"Don't feel right? How the hell are we supposed to find the thing if our only candidate is off the list?" She flipped the radio station from Wham! to some kind of salsa music.

He sighed. He'd been trying to field this one without getting his hands too dirty. Some things are best avoided—wet underwear, bare-fisted fighting with grizzlies, and swamp witches. Generally speaking, he'd take the bear baiting over trucking with hoodooists and mambos. Witches and voodoo practitioners were shady in a way that made him feel like there was always something right on the edge of his peripheral vision, but no matter how hard he tried to see it, he never could. He loved the Lord, but he knew there was a whole lot more to Creation than what narrow-minded Bible-thumpers would allow for. All the same, inviting spirits—even ones that people called "saints"—into your life was just asking for trouble. He had no luck with witches, any sort of them. He always seemed to end up with way more than he bargained for when he came into contact with witches.

"I go over to Bayou La Batre and see this swamp witch, voodoo lady." He pulled the truck into Jacyn's driveway leaving it idling.

"Oh hell, no. You think you're ditching me when you're talkin' shit about witches?" She looked totally hell-bent to take this to the streets. More than that, she was excited. She followed his eyes when he tried to look away, grabbed his sleeve, tugging. They both knew he wasn't gonna say no. He threw the car into park.

"Fine, but if she asks you for fingernails or hair, you sure as shit better say no." He snatched the keys out of the ignition and flung his door open, not bothering to roll the window up or lock it. He grabbed the bag on the seat between them.

"Why are we stopping here?" Jacyn caught up to him.

He looked down at her, more than half a foot shorter than him, looking homespun and old timey in her braids and simple, country dress. He could picture her in a paddock with a bridle in her hand or in a field of flowers under the endless Texas sky. Tucking a stray bit of hair that had escaped her braid behind her ear, he said, "I didn't get a shower yet."

He leaned down and kissed her where his finger had been and trailed her hair back, brushing the soft skin behind her ear and catching his breath when she caught hers.

Amber was in fine form when Jimmy Wayne slammed open the door to the kitchen. She had the kitchen table completely obscured with papers with equations all over them. Her hand worked over a half-filled sheet, her crooked writing scribbling out as fast as she could get her muscles to go. She looked up at Jacyn and Jimmy Wayne with an ink-smudged face.

"Y'all don't look too much worse for wear. Must not know how to do it right." Her pen kept working even as she smirked at them. She must be on to something good.

"There weren't no complaints." Jimmy Wayne shifted his bag on his shoulder.

"Moving in already? We'll have to hide all the evidence for when Mawmaw stops by. I don't even want to hear that shit." Her smirk turned into a full-blown shit-eating grin.

"How about you shut the hell up before I smack the sass outta your mouth?" Jacyn was inexplicably annoyed. Amber and she traded barbs and mocked each other, that was their way, and Jimmy Wayne was definitely excellent material for mockery. But she didn't like the jokes one bit this time.

Amber started to laugh and Jimmy Wayne lifted a corner of his mouth.

"Damn, I wish I woulda laid dibs on him now. Wanna share?" Amber snapped her fingers at Jimmy Wayne and made a kissy face at him.

"Highest bidder." Jimmy Wayne laughed back at her, and Jacyn wanted to smack both of them.

"Do you want a shower or what?" She rolled her eyes and left the kitchen, letting Jimmy Wayne trail behind her.

"Baby." He wrapped an arm around her waist and pressed his face into her neck. He smelled like sweat and tobacco and sex. "Don't be like that." He slipped his lips back and forth against her skin. His stubble tickled her and his mouth was open a little so his tongue could lick her skin in little flickers.

Her sigh sounded embarrassingly loud in the white noise of the air-conditioning hum. He pulled her back against him, harder, his hand sliding lower on her belly. She could see where this was going, and as much as her body was totally ready to fuck him into oblivion, she really didn't need Amber to have that kind of ammunition. She peeled his fingers off of her stomach and elbowed him in the side, escaping easily since he didn't resist.

His face was half in shadow when she turned around to point toward the hall closet where the towels lived. "Clean towels there."

"Worth your while to join me." He stepped closer. Telling him no felt like tearing her soul a tiny bit.

"Naw, my cousin."

He smiled and wiped his thumb against her mouth. "Good girls finish last and horny." There was laughter twisted up with the words.

"I think good girls mainly end up under the tires of bad girls. And if you see a good girl around here, you should take a picture for later evidence." She shoved him toward the bathroom, and he stumbled into it, laughing. She yanked the door closed before he could start up again and headed back to the kitchen.

"Wearin' one of Mawmaw's dresses. I'm thinkin' sexcapades transpired," Amber said to her back as Jacyn poured herself a cup of coffee and stuck it in the microwave. "He reminds me a lot of Jared."

Which was, naturally, Jacyn's ex.

"You think?" She didn't see it at all. Jared was taller, dark-headed, loud, and demanding as all hell.

"Same way about him, cocky and full of himself." And that pretty much summed up Jared, but in Jimmy Wayne's case it was just a facade for being lonesome. That much was totally obvious.

"So you're already giving me shit about Jimmy Wayne and he's not even my boyfriend or anything." Jacyn grabbed her coffee out of the microwave and glared at Amber.

Amber didn't look up from her calculations. "If someone slapped you on the back, your face would be stuck like that."

"Better than being stuck with your face as it is." Jacyn sipped her coffee.

"I'm rubber and you're glue." Amber smiled down at her paper.

"Nuh-uh, times infinity." Jacyn shot back.

"I see the maturity level around here has hit negative levels," Jimmy Wayne said as he walked into the kitchen toweling off his hair.

"Damn, land speed record." Jacyn took another drink of her coffee right before Jimmy Wayne snatched it out of her hand and started gulping it down.

"I have hidden talents." And even if she didn't know him, the sleaze factor on that would have been enough to choke a rhino.

"Bust 'em out, then," Amber snorted.

"I accept all major credit cards and cash. No personal checks. Payment upfront." He cocked his hip out and rapped a knuckle on the kitchen table. Amber looked up at him and winked.

"You Mormon or somethin'?" Even Jacyn had to laugh at that.

"Let's hit it." Jacyn grabbed the empty cup from Jimmy Wayne and deposited it in the sink. His eyes, when he looked over at her, were lighter than usual with a rim of blue so dark it was almost black around the edges.

"You're excitable today." He grinned and Jacyn

almost totally reneged on her plan not to embarrass herself in front of her cousin.

"Where y'all goin'?" Amber looked on with interest.

"To the beach," Jacyn answered immediately. The one place Amber would never invite herself along to.

She made a face. "Yeah, good luck with that."

Jacyn walked out the kitchen door. Jimmy Wayne's hand came to rest on the small of her back as they hit the driveway.

"Natural born liar. Shoulda figured on that." He laughed with his face tilted upward.

"Whatever." She looked at it more as family politics. There was no way she could explain the truth anyway. She climbed in the truck, slamming the heavy door behind her.

Biloxi, Mississippi, to Bayou La Batre, Alabama, was about forty miles as the crow flies. However, in reality it was quite a bit more because there was no straight road between the communities right on the coast in Mississippi. Highway 90 and Interstate 10 ran to Mobile, Alabama, which sat at the northern end of Mobile Bay, quite a bit away from the coast. Jacyn and Jimmy Wayne took Highway 90 across the state line into Alabama and then down Highway 188 through Grand Bay.

They drove through Ocean Springs, Gautier, Pascagoula, and into Alabama with Jacyn singing along with the radio and trying to explain what Amber was studying. Something having to do with strings. Jimmy Wayne was more interested in listening to Jacyn talk than her actual point. They passed through the eastern segment of the region devastated by Hurricane Katrina. All of the fishing communities along the coast had been nearly obliterated, smaller stories lost in the media frenzy to cover downtown New Orleans in an endless loop of bloated bodies and flooded buildings. Upended boats and buildings denuded to their foundations lined Highway 188, the people who lived in the area forgotten already in the ruthless search for brand-new suffering.

"When I was a kid, my family always talked about Hurricane Camille like it was the first sign of the apocalypse," Jacyn said, looking out at a little house that had collapsed in on itself like matchsticks. "I always thought they were exaggerating."

"The worst stuff usually sounds like lies in the telling of it," Jimmy Wayne said, as a man who knew the straight facts on such matters. Even his mama and his brother had a hard time swallowing his explanations of demons who fed on the torment of victims whose insides were liquefying one organ at a time, or spirits who took the form of beloved house pets and drank children's souls through their noses. Lots of demons specialized in children to maximize the anguish, since children could often see them plain as day.

"You mean in the middle of the day when the sun washes out the fear of the dark," Jacyn said in a low voice. Jimmy Wayne felt like he'd known her for years, like he'd heard that voice tons of times; it was familiar like the weight of his hat or the coughing of his truck's exhaust.

"Fear of the dark's the only thing that keeps some folks alive." He pulled off of Highway 188 onto a road with no street sign. The pavement was cracked with weeds growing up through the light gray surface. Both sides of the road were lined with loblolly pines and hickories. The road weaved away from even the semblance of civilization toward Little River, the trees thinning out into cypress and tupelo as the swamp crept up on the dry land and seduced it.

The radio crackled to static, and Jacyn fussed with it until they got crackly reception on a country station playing Rascal Flatts.

"I guess I oughta have asked where we were goin' sometime before now." Jacyn looked out the window at the saw grass and lily pads, at the ripples in the water that might be gators and might just be fish under the water.

"You got somethin' against the swamp?"

Jacyn slapped at her arm. "No, I got somethin' against gettin' eaten alive."

"Skin So Soft in the glove box." He leaned over and popped it open for her. It was the sprayable kind instead of the old lotion, which would stick to your skin in thick globs and ruin your clothes.

"God, this shit smells like twelve-year-old hookers." She spritzed herself all the same, then leaned over and squirted the stuff all over him, too. He tried to shy away, but she caught his arm. "Now take your medicine."

She smeared some on her fingers and rubbed it on the back of his neck and ears and on this throat.

"You know, I'm startin' to think you've got a sadistic streak. Either that or you'll use any old excuse to get your hands all over me." He pulled his hat down a little lower and tilted his face up to look at her underneath the brim.

"When you build the shrine to yourself, I suggest you use lead paint, lasts longer." Jacyn wiped her hands off on his jeans and settled back into her seat.

"Put your seat belt back on." He flicked a nail against the latch for emphasis. She rolled her eyes at him and hung her arm out the truck's window, weaving her arm up and down in the air blowing by. He thought about pressing the issue, giving her a lecture about auto safety, but he figured it was pointless since she was purposefully ignoring him to assert independence.

The totems started appearing about then. Tall poles set on the side of the road with little bundles tied to them like tetherballs. Primary-colored fabric tied off with ribbon and topped with feathers. Each pole had a bundle with a different variation—green with white ribbon and yellow feathers, red with black ribbon and blue feathers, yellow with red ribbon and green feathers. Jimmy Wayne had never asked too many questions about those damned things. He really didn't want to know what was in them or what the point of them really was. Most voodoo wackos agreed with him about calling down spirits, but their religion was really too complicated to pay too much attention to. He knew some basics that he'd picked up here and there—a bad witchdoctor was called a boko, and that those suckers could cause more trouble than a fifteen-year-old girl with a grudge; that an ougan was a regular, non-evil witchdoctor; and that the whole possession business was all too freakin' real.

Jacyn watched the Crayola juju balloons knock around the polls on the breeze with open curiosity. "How can this exist and no one says anything about it?"

"People see what they want to. You know that as well as I do." He was starting to wonder if most of the things she said out loud were more for other people than herself.

"Yeah, you're right about that." Jacyn flipped the radio off when even the crappy country station they were getting went on the fritz. Jimmy Wayne knew that not a whole helluva lot of people came this way without meaning to, and even if they did, they probably would chalk what they found up to "Southern eccentricity," a concept that threw a blanket over the fact that almost all of the supernatural activity in America outside of California and the big cities took place below the Mason-Dixon Line and west of the Rio Grande. It made it convenient for Jimmy Wayne, at any rate.

"So, voodoo?" Jacyn shot him a look with her eyebrows together and her mouth open slightly. Totally into this crap. He sort of remembered when he used to feel that way. Been a long time, though.

"Yup. Voodoo, but don't call it that, man. I don't need the drama, or to wake up alive in a coffin or some shit." The cement of the road ended, turning into a gravel path set in a sort of levee raised up through the swamp. He flipped the four-by-four on and slowed down even more. The road ended in a stretch of closely clustered trees about a hundred yards down the track. "We're gonna have to walk the last part of the way," he told Jacyn as they bumped across the gravel.

"It wouldn't be a creepy story about backwoods voodoo if that weren't the case. There better be bones clicking together in the trees or you're totally fired." She knocked his hat back on his head, smiling as he parked the truck. He smiled right back.

"I didn't know I'd been hired." He turned and

grabbed her arm as she popped open the door. She pivoted her head around to look him in the face, eyes dropped low in amusement. "Seriously, don't take any wooden nickels." Her smile brightened and she laughed a little.

"I know how to deal with religious lunatics, babe. I'm from Gautier." His eyes dropped to her mouth, and he wasn't really thinking too much about her personal safety or magic or dead children anymore. She pulled out of his grip before he could start anything.

He climbed out after her feeling the heavy oppressive feeling of strong magic. Some magic smelled like ozone. Some tasted like pepper on your tongue. Voodoo felt like gravity had been ratcheted up a notch or two. He took off his hat as he stepped around the front of his truck and wiped his forehead with the back of his wrist.

The trees were hung with yet more of the tacky, bright-feathered gris-gris bags. Without thinking about it, he stepped nearer to Jacyn and put his hand on her back. She ignored him, which was fine. He didn't necessarily want to get into a whole episode about women's lib and girl power and all that bullhockey.

For a short time before chaos erupted, their breathing and the sounds of Jacyn's flip-flops were loud in the gloom of the sycamore and hawthorn. A ruckus of rhythmic drumming broke out, and Jacyn jumped out of her skin, squealing and leaping into him. They both laughed hysterically—her from adrenaline overload and Jimmy Wayne from the cracking of her blasé attitude. It was easy to be cynical about gunshots until you were staring down a pissed-off redneck with a shotgun.

The drumming picked up again, in a rolling pattern that raised the hair on the back of Jimmy Wayne's arms.

Jacyn opened her mouth to say something, but just as she did, the oungan stepped right into their path like he'd beamed in from the *Enterprise*. He was a big man, taller than Jimmy Wayne, who was six one. His skin was the color of burnt coffee and his hair was almost completely white. He wore a clerical collar with a bright red shirt and black pants. Jimmy Wayne knew that signified what god he worshipped primarily, but not which one that was.

"You took longer than we thought you would." He turned to smile at Jacyn. "You must have been . . . distracted. But that was not unlooked for either."

His accent was all clipped and twisted Creole vowels, not the Pepé le Pew bent backward bullshit from zombie movies. He offered his hand to Jacyn. "Pere Emmanuel."

Jacyn took his hand, polite as hell, smiling the whole time, like she didn't feel like an invisible hand was trying to shove them both down into the dirt. "Jacyn Boaz."

"I know your name, child, but thank you for giving it freely." His teeth were too white for such an old man when he smiled. Jimmy Wayne didn't like how this shit was going one bit. "Some gifts are unlooked for, non?"

"We need some help." Jimmy Wayne thought he was more than telegraphing his annoyance with the set of his shoulders and the scowl, but he really couldn't help it.

The drumming shifted pattern abruptly, becoming more frantic. He'd thought he'd only have to deal with the witch, not the warlock, too. This old man had power, the kind that sort of radiated off him like a corona. They were less safe in this situation than he'd reckoned, and Jimmy Wayne hated getting caught with his pants around his ankles, particularly when he was responsible for someone else.

The oungan dropped Jacyn's hand and turned his smile on Jimmy Wayne. "It's not you who needs the help, though, is it? Who needs our help is the children the baka will slaughter next." He turned, waving his hand for them to follow, and walked back into the trees.

Jacyn poked Jimmy Wayne hard in the side and tightened her face up. That was fine. She could be as pissed off as she wanted. There was no way she could understand the danger that "Pere Emmanuel" could bust out. Jimmy Wayne didn't really know how powerful the guy was, because poking his big nose into some business was bad for his continued status as alive. Her hand wrapped around his arm right above the elbow, and he reached over to pat her fingers.

The warlock's granddaughter wasn't as unworldly as the old man. She was as close to useful as he found the magically inclined. He should have thought this bit through better, though, because if grandpa was interested then there was probably more to this story than he'd figured. He'd been here tons of times, so he knew when the trees were about to give over to the open space with three neat wood-framed houses sat in a triangle. They looked like old-fashioned shotgun shacks with wraparound porches. The trees ringing the houses blocked the sun, so it was still gloomy. The drumming was significantly louder when they broke out of the woods.

The oungan waved them along, smiling and seeming friendly and pleased to see them. Jimmy Wayne didn't buy what he was selling. Not because he thought the guy had it in for them, more that he served powers beyond this world; people who viewed the mortal plane that way tended to be inscrutable and unpredictable. He headed straight for the house on the right, toward the drumming, which meant they were dispensing with the welcome wagon shenanigans today then.

Jacyn dropped Jimmy Wayne's arm as they climbed the stairs onto the porch. The house looked normal enough, and she'd been in plenty of similar places. The front room was a living room. Sometimes there was a thin hallway on one side of the house that let a person pass from the front room all the way to the back of the house to the kitchen, but sometimes the rooms opened one into the next so a person had to walk through bedrooms to get to the kitchen. The style usually depended on the age of the house and where it was built.

Pere Emmanuel opened the front door and she followed him with Jimmy Wayne pressing into her back. His body language rang loud and clear that he wasn't thrilled about this, and also that she needed to get a little fear in her life. Jacyn had read a thing or two about voodoo—granted now that she realized monsters were real, maybe her education was seriously lacking—and she knew that most practitioners held no truck with evil spirits. Maybe Jimmy Wayne just distrusted anyone who did magic. It would fit him.

On the other side of the front door, in what normally would have been a living room was a drum circle in full tilt. Men and women sat shoulder to shoulder. Surprisingly enough the whole white clothes thing appeared to be true. The women wore white turbans and loose white blouses and skirts. The men wore white button-down shirts with undershirts beneath and white cotton pants. Pere Emmanuel skirted the circle, and she followed after

him toward the closed door set in the middle of the
wall, mirroring the front door. The room was completely bare except for the people—scarred, well-
scrubbed floorboards and white walls. None of the
drummers paid she or Jimmy Wayne the least heed
as they passed by. When they got to the door, Pere
Emmanuel turned to smile at them.

He opened the door to a riot of color and movement. Women whirled around the room on stomping
feet, all dressed in shocks of bloodred, matching
Pere Emmanuel's shirt. They moved around one another, sometimes meeting with locking fingers or
arms, bodies spinning and heads rolling. Their clapping and stomping, when she concentrated more than
just stared, was in time to the drumming. Along the
right-hand side of the room was a huge altar hung
with red cotton cloth and decked out with knick-
knacks and candles and feathers and plates and cups.
Pere Emmanuel wove between the women, dropping
his shoulders and rolling his hips in his own choreog-
raphy of avoidance. Jacyn waited for either a direction or an invitation, watching the twenty or so
women wail and clap and stomp.

Jimmy Wayne bent and brushed his lips against
her ear. "You can go around, no need to get all
fancy like the priest."

She looked up at him to see one side of his mouth
lifted and his eyes half-closed. He plucked at her
dress and started around the crowd. She watched

the muscles in his back work beneath his sweaty shirt. His jeans hung low on his hips and his shirt rode up to expose his lower back as he moved. When his hand came back to reach for her as one of the women almost danced right into them, she took it by reflex. His fingertips and the balls of his palm under his fingers were callused—the tips probably from playing guitar and the palms from farm work.

Pere Emmanuel picked up a plastic cup off the altar. When he tipped it over, brown liquid poured out onto the floor. His fingers were scarred against the red plastic as he offered the cup to her. She dropped Jimmy Wayne's hand and took the cup. The smell of the rum was strong even a half foot from her face. The liquor hit her tongue with an antiseptic sting and burned all the way to her stomach.

Pere Emmanuel moved his hands in some kind of benediction, his words lost on her as they were in French. He held his hand out, and she passed him back the cup, mesmerized by the fact that this was even happening. The priest repeated the series of ritualized actions with Jimmy Wayne, who surprised her by taking a healthy drink of the rum. The fact that he could practically gulp down straight liquor was typical of him, but she'd sort of expected him to balk more at eating or drinking anything from people he clearly didn't trust.

Jimmy Wayne was full of surprises, though, because after he finished his drink, he upended the cup. "Rest in peace, Daddy," he murmured, and Pere Emmanuel chimed in with a whispered "Amen." He took the cup and set it back on the altar, smiling again. The smiling was maybe a little creepy. If he'd stuck with dour or stoic, he could have passed as a Anglican priest in a strange setting, what with the red shirt. But the wide-eyed smile made her skin itch when added to the weird malaise she'd felt since pulling off the gravel path into the trees. Her limbs felt too heavy, but she thought it was the front end of a heat stroke until she really thought about it. Yeah, probably not a heat stroke, she realized as women fluttered around her chanting in French, with arms flailing about their heads.

The room that should have been a kitchen was lit by candles, the walls painted with signals that made her intrigued, excited, and scared in equal measures. This was *real*. What did that even mean? They were in the middle of a damned voodoo ritual, participants even, in Bumfuck, Egypt, with no hotline to Buffy programmed into their cell phones. Not that they'd get reception out here anyway.

There were about five people in the room. One of them broke off from sketching something on the floor, leaving all the others hard at it, to approach them. The woman was young, with cinnamon skin and dark freckles across her cheeks. Even shorter than Jacyn, she was the washed-clean sort of pretty that's from genes and the personality peeking out of her facial expression. Her eyes were green ringed with brown with sharply curling lashes. She looked at and through Jimmy Wayne when he moved a hand against Jacyn's back.

"I'm Tasha." She offered her hand to Jacyn. Her nails were perfect, white and oval-shaped, but her palm scraped at Jacyn's skin with a slight rasp.

"Jacyn." They shook, and Jacyn withdrew her hand when Tasha smiled with her full lips, exposing teeth as white as Pere Emmanuel's, saying, "Oh, I know."

This chick was creepier than the old dude. Definitely. Her white skirts and shirt were so fresh looking they had to be starched. When she walked away to get back to her sketching, Jacyn noticed her toenails were painted orange.

Pere Emmanuel pointed to a place on the floor, still smiling. "Please, have a seat."

Jimmy Wayne steered her that way, and the ground seemed to pull her down. She landed so hard her tailbone was probably bruised. She pulled her legs together Indian style and tucked her skirt down between her legs to make sure she wasn't flashing everyone in the room. Jimmy Wayne sat next to her, pressing into her thigh to shoulder. His tobacco and sweat smell caused her to relax as incense began to crowd it out. The memory of the smell was enough to reassure her. White-clad figures scuttled around on the floor on their knees, drawing as Pere Emmanuel prayed with his arms raised up. Some of the celebrants drew with red chalk, some rubbed at the chalk with some black powder, others smudged ashes into the pattern. A pattern that made absolutely no sense to Jacyn. Squiggles and nonintersecting lines and swirls.

Pere Emmanuel walked around the crawling people while praying in French, circling them counterclockwise. Jacyn slumped against Jimmy Wayne, feeling his bicep flex under her cheek.

"They're bleeding our energy out to power the magic is all." His arm came around her back to rest on her hip, and he half-pulled her onto his lap with her head resting against his chest. His heartbeat was steady, seeming to sync up with the incessant drumming and foot-pounding and clapping from the other rooms in the house. The incense made the already chewable, humid air almost unbreathable, and Jacyn started pulling in air through her mouth. She thought about the witches, or voodooists or whatever, pulling the energy out of people, envisioned it in her mind as wavering streamers of glowing light sparkling bright with glitter on the edges. In her mind, she could see the light bleeding from Jimmy Wayne's fingertips, ten thin lines of light blue with darker blue sparks outlining them. She saw lilac light arching away from her temples, and spiraling into the signals on the floor. Each of the celebrants contributed—pale yellow and bright orange and fuchsia, each unique.

Jimmy Wayne's heart kept beating with the noise dragging her further and further away from who she'd been a couple days before, the person who measured her life against all the things she hadn't done, things she never would do, the person who tried to make up for that by helping others but never thought that could be enough. Giving away her life energy was probably in the enough category. She remembered, suddenly, with the vivid sort of detail usually reserved for dreams right after waking, meeting Jimmy Wayne in Houston. She could smell the leather of the new purse she'd bought the day before, hear the rattle of glass against glass, feel the hot-to-cold shock of realizing he was actually flirting with her. He'd been wearing a Western-style, red-and-white plaid shirt with pearl snaps and a belt buckle that read "Texas". She'd had a bruise in the shape of that buckle on her hip for a week.

The signal on the floor began to glow, faintly at first, but when all the celebrants began echoing back Pere Emmanuel's words, the squirls and squiggles and lines popped to life brightly enough to leave ghosts of themselves on her corneas. They seemed to be trading a litany back and forth, like a list of names. Jimmy Wayne tightened his hold on her hip. She turned her face up to his to see if there was something wrong as she caught Pere Emmanuel stepping into the ring of the signal, out of her peripheral vision.

The light became unbearably bright, flashing through each of the colors Jacyn had imagined feeding it in the first place, gunshot fast—pucegingervermilionhoneytangerine—enough to cause a seizure. There was a deafening crack like thunder but in her bones and teeth. Her world went blank for a split second. When she blinked her eyes open, all of the celebrants stood around the room in random places looking at her and Jimmy Wayne.

"Do you see it, child?" Pere Emmanuel squatted down in front of her, his eerie smile not cheering her in the least.

She didn't have to ask him what he meant, because clear as his white teeth, there was a ribbon of rainbow light hovering in the air and ending at the door to the next room.

"You'll find the baka at the other end of the rainbow bridge." He stood back up and offered Jacyn a hand. She took it more from reflex than anything else. Jimmy Wayne hauled himself to his feet next to her.

"Next time I want the ritual with the keg of beer and the dancing girls," Jimmy Wayne groused from behind her.

Jacyn felt that something was off, wrong, and it took opening the door to the should-be bedroom to realize that the whole house had fallen completely silent. The room was empty, as was the front room, when they passed through.

"Your luck woulda found that thing, you know," a voice called to them from inside the house. Jacyn turned on the porch to look through the front room into the back to see Tasha watching her steadily.

"What?" Jacyn felt barely steady on her feet, sweat beading and running down the dent of her spine, humidity pressing her down into the earth. The tang of ozone burned in her nose and against her tongue.

"Your luck. You should trust it more."

Jacyn felt something flutter in her chest. She had no idea how this woman could know about Jacyn's relationship with what she called her luck. Her skin broke out in gooseflesh and she was suddenly aware of how otherworldly her life had become.

"Are you comin' or what?" Jimmy Wayne called behind her and Tasha moved out of her line of sight.

She followed Jimmy Wayne, ducking her head down and trying to remember that she wasn't the kind of person to get so easily spooked by anything, even magic and witches.

CHAPTER SEVEN

Jimmy Wayne rolled over onto his hip when he got back into the truck and pulled his Skoal out of his back pocket. "Hand me that can down there." He pointed at one of the empty Bud cans on the floorboard at Jacyn's feet. She lifted an eyebrow but grabbed one and handed it to him. He wedged a pinch of chaw between his gums and cheek, stuck the can between his thighs, and turned the truck around.

"What the hell is a baka?" Jacyn asked as the tires started spitting gravel as they began to head back to what passed for civilization those days in Mississippi. "I'll start there."

When he thought about it, he could see the rainbow glowing ahead of them off into the distance, following the road through the swamp. If he ignored it, it disappeared. Typical voodoo.

"A baka's an evil spirit. A demon. Depends on who uses it. The old Pere meant the lamia, as you surely figured out on your lonesome. Didn't reckon on him being around. Thought we'd just get Tasha and her hoodoo mumbo jumbo." He plucked the can from between his legs and spat into it. "If your next question is how come those freaks knew you, or acted like they did anyhow, don't ask me. All I got's that they're freaks."

"Tasha's awful pretty." Women were sensitive to that sort of thing, probably an evolutionary thing. Jimmy Wayne knew this ritual in and out. He'd never gotten any better about placatin' a female ego when it really counted. Sure, he was hands down the champion when it came to chatting up a girl, but he really had no idea how to keep one around. Reassurances that he didn't have a wandering sort of eye died in the back of his throat. The truth of the matter was that Tasha and her ilk made his skin wanna crawl off his body. He wouldn't be attracted to a witch if . . . well, he couldn't come up with something other than a witch he'd never done, but there you have it in a nutshell.

"She's not you," Jimmy Wayne said after a spell. He expected her to laugh, because he knew it sounded like bullshit, even if he meant it. She didn't, and when he looked over at her, she was looking out the window toward where he could see the rainbow shooting through the molasses-thick Alabama afternoon.

"What do we do when we get to the end of the rainbow?" She flipped the radio back on. Willie Nelson greeted them with his broken, comforting twang.

"Would you laugh if I made a pot of gold joke?" He spit his tobacco into the can and wedged it between the seat and the safety brake.

"Would you laugh if I made one about you being a snake-oil salesman?" She lifted an eyebrow at him and half-smiled. Jimmy Wayne let the tension he'd been holding in out with an expulsion of a laugh. Who would have thought she'd make crappy puns as bad his? Lamia and snakes, rainbows and leprechauns, he wasn't sure which was worse, really.

"I guess I didn't mention my day job. There really is a subtle difference between cobra oil and cottonmouth oil, girl. The stuff's useful as all get out." She punched him in the arm and flipped the radio around the dial, pulling her legs up under her and sitting Indian style in the seat.

"Alright, doofus, lay it on me. How do we kill the lamia? Some kind of arcane ritual on the full moon where we have to let blood and dance around nekkid?" She paused the radio flipping right as he was about to grab her hand.

"I'll need one of those newfangled iPod thingamabobs if you do that all the damned time. Shit."

Some kind of tinkly pop music made him grind his teeth, but he caught her mouthing along with the words, enjoying herself and smiling around the impromptu karaoke. He felt the annoyance burst like a soap bubble. "Anyway, nah. I know you were looking forward to some serious black magic and kinky whatsit, but *I* will just set her on fire."

"Huh. That's all? Lame."

They passed back onto Highway 188.

"Not as lame as losing an eye or getting possessed." He'd like to keep all his appendages, thanks. "Fire kills most things."

"Like vampires?" She asked in a joking tone to cover her bald curiosity. The muscles in his face twitched into a smile.

"I was waitin' on that." He looked over at her open mouth and wide eyes, the bright sunshine picking up her freckles and the gold in her eyes. "Yeah, babe, like vampires." He reached out and tucked a piece of hair that had escaped her braid back behind her ear.

"Awesome!" She snapped her fingers and threw her head back laughing.

The miles slipped away under his tires as they followed the rainbow back to Mississippi, which was hardly any kind of surprise. What was a surprise, though, was that Jacyn could sing along with Waylon and Johnny, and that she had actually been to the Grand Old Opry. More than once! Her best friend from college lived in Nashville, information he filed away for a future roadtrip.

They stopped for food in Gautier, eating oyster po'boys with extra tartar sauce outside some shack that looked like it was built out of scrap cardboard and string. Jacyn slipped into an accent thicker than the batter on the oysters when she ordered, and it was pretty plain that she was letting him see into her real life—the one she'd lived before she'd moved away from home and became the person she was running so hard not to be anymore.

The old lady running the seafood shack wore coral lipstick and smoked a Kent as she rang them up.

"You got a handsome one there, sugar." She winked a blue eye-shadowed eyelid at him, face wrinkled in the way that people only get after a life-time of smoking a pack a day and believing that a dark tan was healthy. He smiled big back at her, tipping his hat.

"Dumber than a sack of hammers, though." Jacyn said in a fake sort of mournful tone.

"That's just the Lord's way of balancin' the scales, honey. Can't give no man that much good luck, against nature." She handed them Cokes and napkins.

They sat at a broken-down old picnic table that was held together with duct tape, the sun blinding and heavy on Jimmy Wayne's exposed skin. Jacyn hummed happily as she ate and wiped crumbs and tartar sauce off his face with her napkin. He forgot totally about the lamia as they ate, forgot about the fact that this wasn't his regular life, just a lazy afternoon outside with a happy, pretty woman getting a little sunburned and tasting the ocean on his tongue. No monsters, no ghosts, no nothing but the moment.

It was seven before they got back to Biloxi. As they passed the line into Harrison County, the rainbow brightened, sparked a bit, like falling stars from the light bridge down to the ground.

"I guess it's on now." Jacyn didn't sound worried, maybe a little tired, her voice breaking up a little.

"I can do this alone." Which he wasn't really sure about. He hadn't expected the little cabal to put the whammy on Jacyn as well as him. Magic was always dangerously unpredictable and that should have caused him to be more alert with Jacyn in tow, but he'd been preoccupied. Understatement of the decade, right there.

The rainbow arced over the Back Bay, over the bridge to D'Iberville. Jimmy Wayne sat up straighter and gripped the steering wheel with both hands. "Listen to me. I know you're . . . well, whatever you are, excited. But when we get where we're goin' you need to listen to me."

"Well, yeah. I don't want to get eaten or anything." She sounded ticked off, like he was babying her, which he completely was. He didn't have time for her independent woman routine, however.

"I'm just sayin'." He pulled off into a ramshackle neighborhood with tumbledown houses, which might have been the product of storm damage or just long-standing poverty.

"Uh-huh." Jacyn hung her arm out the window, tapping her fingers on the side of the door.

The dry mouth and fluttery heartbeat he associated with hunting kicked in as they made a right turn and the rainbow deepened, took on form, became suddenly corporeal, alive with a throbbing that started on the right side and traveled across its width.

"Whoa." Jacyn sat forward, hands on the dashboard, eyes comically wide.

He felt a tugging in his temple, then in his neck, in his carotid, then in his chest near his heart. Jacyn's fingers flew from her face to her neck to her chest.

"Fucking voodoo bullshit. Fantastic." The rainbow shot straight through the front door of a house with a yard full of rioting weeds. The front window was covered by cardboard and duct tape.

"What do we do now?" Jacyn asked as Jimmy Wayne parked the truck on the street. He hopped out and climbed up into the truck bed. His world narrowed to the job. He clicked over the risks a lamia posed—mesmerism by locking gaze, a pheromone released through glands in their faces, venom se-creted by fangs. Under it all was a thrum of fear for Jacyn. He didn't like getting civilians involved in hunts to begin with. He felt about sixty times worse about it this time. From the toolbox he pulled out a plastic container of lighter fluid, a Zippo, and his Glock. The gun he tucked into the back of his jeans, and when he looked up at Jacyn, her face was flushed like she'd just ran a mile. He smiled at her, almost breaking out laughing. He was scared for her for be-ing herself, but he couldn't help but wanna get close to that. What put her at risk is what made her who she was, and he couldn't help but laugh.

"Like that, huh?" The fact that she was turned on by him packing a gun turned him on, and he felt his jeans tighten in the front.

She blushed harder but didn't look away from his face. "It's hot, what can I say?" She stood with her hands on the side of the truck bed, too close to ignore. He went down on one knee and flicked his tongue against her lips. She opened right up, hands immediately on his face, and he forgot that he was trying to tease her. Instantly he fell down, down, down with his eyes closed and the citrus sweet smell of her, the taste of Coca-Cola and salt of her mouth, into everything he could pretend she was offering him. His collar constricted around his neck and he broke away to find Jacyn's fingers twisting his neck tight and cutting off his air.

"This thing first, okay?" She didn't look any more pleased about it than he did. He pulled back and she let his shirt go. The worry was right back.

"Good thing we got something to do, because if you thought that was gonna *stop* me jumping you right here in broad daylight, you need some schooling." He bit his bottom lip and watched her pupils below. They were about three seconds from pitching in the real job to go at it in the back of the truck, and as much as his vital parts were all in favor, the magic was starting to make him sick at his stomach.

"Vertigo." Jacyn gripped the side of the truck again, and her face went pale.

"Hold up. It'll be okay. The fucking magic's getting uppity." He grabbed the lighter fluid and lighter again and climbed back down to the ground.

She passed a hand over her forehead while breathing in through her nose and out through her mouth. She looked fragile, washed out, all too human.

"This is how it's gonna go down." Jimmy Wayne waited for her to reopen her eyes. "You're gonna count to fifty, then you're gonna go knock on the door to flush the lamia out. Then I'm pretty much gonna set the bitch on fire and we run."

Jacyn glared at him. "That's the plan?"

He gritted his teeth, but relaxed when he realized how spanking new she still was to this. Weren't her fault that she had been programmed with the wrong expectations. Hell, he'd been worse—disbelief causing him to be stupid and careless. At least she believed right off.

Dragging his index and middle fingers made into a *V* from her eyes to his back and forth he ducked down to stare her in the eyes. "Listen to me. This isn't some Delta Force commando outing. You're gonna do everything you can to stay safe. That means jumpin' in the bushes and ducking when I yell. You follow my orders and jump when I say jump." He was pretty concerned that she wouldn't listen. She wasn't much for following orders, and he doubted she'd ever been in any real danger in her life. It's not like she went around vacationing in Gaza—probably.

She watched him and crossed her arms over her chest and lifted her chin in the air. "I can take care of myself."

Which is exactly what he didn't want to hear from her. "Lookit here, I can drive your ass right back to your Mawmaw's and park you on the couch with Amber watchin' you like a nanny if you give me any lip about this." He didn't want to hurt her feelings or ruin anything between them by being a total asshole, but he was willing to go down in flames if it kept her safe. Even hating him, at least she'd be alive.

"This isn't the movies, darlin'. It is what it is, dirty and violent and unrewarding. If you don't wanna . . ."

She cut him off. "Can it." She smiled at him to show she wasn't actually angry, but he knew that already anyway. "I know you're worried, I'll be good, promise." Her smile turned sweet, not calculated but excited and vibrant.

Part of him still wanted to take the time to formulate a plan that included her back at her mawmaw's, but the magic was getting way too insistent, making him nauseated and light-headed. He knew they couldn't take the time for the screaming match and the drive back to her place.

"Come on." Her whisper was strained, like the magic was getting to her as much as him.

He got the hint and high-tailed it around the back of the house pulling his gun out of the back of his jeans, using the car in the driveway as cover, then ducking into an azalea bush on the side of the house. His gun flashed in the low, thick sunlight of the oncoming dusk. The soft petals of the flowers and suede nap of the leaves of the shrubs brushed against his skin as he crawled on his knees and jerked his head and gun around the back corner of the house. Nothing but an old, rusted swing set with the swings missing, the slide twisted back in on itself. Upturned, plastic flower pots lay strewn all through the yard.

The back door had one of those old screen doors with the thick aluminum scrollwork over the holey mesh of the screening. He tucked the lighter fluid under his arm and opened the screen door with that hand, gun at the ready. Pausing, he listened for movement. The doorbell rang loudly enough for him to hear it outside. Even with the ridiculous hum of magic sending glass fragments of wrongness through his blood, his heart hit the back of his mouth out of fear for Jacyn. His fingertips throbbed with his pulse as he tested the doorknob to the back door proper. It, naturally, turned under his grip. Most people in Mississippi didn't bother to lock their doors, so why should a monster that could eat an interloper? The door opened with a slight creaking of the plastic seal against the doorjamb.

As he stepped into the kitchen, he heard voices.

"No, just standard follow up," Jacyn said in a bored tone that impressed him.

"Y'all usu'ly work on weekends?" Another female voice answered. He crept through the kitchen with his gun held in front of his face, popping the flip top lid of the lighter fluid bottle open with his thumb. His focus narrowed on the back of the figure standing framed in the doorway as he whipped his head away from the doorway to the kitchen and into the living room.

"Yeah, one of the benefits of aid work along with the crap pay is the luxury of working seven days a week."

"Well, bless your heart," the lamia said opening the door wider. Jimmy Wayne stood up all straight, easing his gun back into his jeans. Jacyn caught sight of him over the woman's shoulder but made no indication of it. All the same, the lamia twitched her head to the right, like she was about to turn around.

"Ms. Jackson," Jacyn said in a harder tone. Jimmy Wayne took that as his opportunity, because the lamia's back went rigid at the sound of Jacyn's voice. He took two rapid steps forward and shot lighter fluid at the lamia's back from her hair to the backs of her legs. She wheeled around, gentle, old lady face melting into scales, mouth opening to show three rows of stiletto fangs. He let off another stream of lighter fluid at her front when Jacyn hollered, "Ms. Jackson!' The lamia instinctively responded to the name she'd been answering to for however long.

"Here I thought you was a nice girl," Ms. Jackson said with an awfully human voice through her monster mouth. Jacyn stared at her with her head cocked to the side. She was backlit by the sun through the camellia bushes in the front yard. Adrenaline focused the actions in the room to parts of seconds that stretched out into days. Jacyn's face was nothing other than curious, eyes open and direct. The back of the lamia's head began to peel away, the skin and hair falling away to leave iridescent scales the size of the palm of his hand.

The rasping of the flint of his lighter against his

jeans got its attention again. But before it could even really start to advance, the chrome and flame flew in a perfect arc to connect with hair and accelerant. The whole scene became surreal as the lamia began to burn on one tiny spot on her forehead, vertically slitted pupils dilating to obscure the amber irises, and a clawed hand flew up to swat at the flames. The lamia's hand was still manicured with false nails painted bright pink. The nails of one hand caught fire and melted as the monster tried to put out the fire. Jacyn watched from right the threshold to the living room with her mouth hanging open and a hand pressed to her belly. Jimmy Wayne watched for a couple seconds to make sure the monster caught good. The flames spread from her face down her neck and she collapsed to her knees rolling into a ball, which facilitated faster burning. He tried to remember that the person the monster had appeared to be had been dead for a long time, that the outer form was just a costume. He tried to think of the dead children and children that would be safe now. All killing was hard, though. He didn't enjoy it like some folks he knew. He figured the sadness and pain he felt for having to take lives was what made him human. When the lamia's entire figure lit in a corona of yellow and blue, he caught Jacyn's eye and flicked a finger toward the truck out front. She turned and walked away without a fight as he watched the monster burn to ash.

Jacyn was in the driver's seat with the engine going so he threw open the passenger side and dove in. She was moving before he got the door shut.

"Burning hair and plastic combined are going on my list of Never Again." Jacyn drove the speed limit and came to full and complete stops at stop signs. She drove like she was used to crime. And that was new.

"You could complain if Jesus showed up handing out hour long orgasms and beer." He slumped back in his seat and clicked his seat belt closed smiling at her. She drove with one hand low on the bottom of the steering wheel and the other in her lap.

"Hell yeah, I would. First off, couldn't Jesus at least bring Maker's Mark? He is the Lord of all Creation after all. Damned cheapskate."

He wasn't sure if it was the giddiness of an adrenaline hangover or her laughing at her own joke that started him on a laughter loop that caused his ribs to ache.

What Jacyn would always remember about that evening was the complex sweet and fruity smell of the wisteria in her yard in full bloom contrasted with the clean sweat and tobacco smell of Jimmy Wayne at her back as she stood in the halo of the back porch light as she opened the back door. The immediate musty smell of the air-conditioning freezing her front while her back was still sweating. The buzz of mosquitos. How it felt like she'd lived those same thirty seconds over and over in a spiral back to her earliest years.

"Jesus Christ, I need a shower," Jimmy Wayne moaned behind her, and she echoed, "Hell yes." Her back stuck to his front from sweat when she took the one step away from him to walk into the kitchen. His hand stayed on her hip, and that felt right and natural in a way that simple words would never be able to capture. Poets and songwriters had tried since words started tumbling out of human beings' mouths, but they kept on making new poems and new songs because no words really did the bone deep, soul high feeling justice.

"Good to be home," Jimmy Wayne sighed into her hair.

Maybe those words were the closest to explaining the feeling, really.

CHAPTER EIGHT

Eight Months Later.

Nashville in the springtime is a series of jagged bursts and deflations. Below-freezing mornings followed by mid-sixty-degree noons followed by rain storms violent enough to rattle teeth. Before she moved there, someone told her that Nashville had three seasons—winter, summer, and tornado. Jacyn had thought that was hyperbole, the sort of good-natured exaggeration that all settled residents of a given area are prone to. She really hadn't figured on the wind. The prewar wood-framed house she lived in shivered and creaked as exuberant gusts snagged the eaves and snuck in under the window frames. Her neighborhood was a cacophony of trains in the distance, cars honking, her neighbors jamming with their friends until four in the morning, and the sudden, shocking gale-force winds.

Mississippi seemed a continent and a lifetime away, even if it'd only been less than half a year ago. Jacyn sat on her porch sipping her coffee and watching her neighbor in his yard. The neighbor would bend and pick up a brown beer bottle, toss it into his plastic garbage bag, and crane his head up to glare toward the house next to his before bending again and repeating the entire enterprise. His yard was separated from the sidewalk by a two-and-a-half-foot high concrete retaining wall, with concrete steps bisecting it and leading to the walkway to his front porch. The arrangement of almost terraced yards was the same for most of the houses on this end of their street, Jacyn's included. She didn't know if the man's neighbors were college students or just musicians, or if he was even right to cast the blame for the beer bottle explosion on his neighbors to begin with. She woke some mornings to find her own yard strewn with empty Jim Beam flasks and KFC boxes and, once, a hair dryer. She'd seen people tossing all sorts of random items out of car windows down in Gallatin—once a window unit air conditioner of all things. East Nashville was just like that—eclectic in the sense that you never knew what was going to be happening at any given moment.

Unlike the orderly, New South of Belmont and the West End—the tidy clean neighborhoods around Vanderbilt and Music Row—East Nashville retained a bit of the grime and rundown attitude of a real working-class part of town and had acquired the sharp-edged sparkle of artist and musician residents. The house that Jacyn shared with her friend Kara was a Craftsman-like deal with a wide front porch across the front, scarred wooden floorboards, and arched door frames. Her roommate was pretty much the reason why Jacyn had left Mississippi after finally giving up on Jimmy Wayne's return. After "a couple weeks" turned into months and his phone calls made her giddy with dread instead of anticipation, Jacyn decided she didn't want to be that person, wasn't gonna be the little lady waiting back at home and pining away. She'd been married once and had learned the hard way that putting her own heart and desires on the back burner for a man just led to worse pain down the road. She wasn't going to do that to herself again. Even if Jimmy Wayne was a slice of homemade lemon pie and a glass of cold milk in the shade. He had his literal demons to fight, and Jacyn had her dignity.

The screen door barked open behind her and Jacyn looked over her shoulder to see Kara standing in the doorway, her striped black and platinum hair newly blown straight and falling perfectly to her shoulders.

"Gonna be late," she said and smiled, the crystal in her nose stud catching the sunshine. Kara was still bundled up in a hoodie with a sweatshirt under it, hating the cold more than just about anything, which was weird to Jacyn since as far as she was concerned Seattle was cold as hell.

Jacyn sighed and got up off the porch swing to follow her roommate into the house. "It's gonna be warm today. This sucks."

Work always sucked, but, really, it wasn't all that bad. Being trapped inside as the nice weather started was always hardest. Jacyn missed the ocean on days like this, when spring was rapidly bending to summer and the outdoors beckoned.

To be fair, Jacyn didn't really hate her job. The simple matter was that her job was just a readjustment. She hadn't taught in a year and a half. She had *never* taught in a Sociology Department before. Tennessee State was one of those smaller state schools that focused mainly on continuing education and practical education. The student body suited her because they weren't all eighteen and overzealous. She didn't think she could cope with exuberant kids high on their first taste of freedom and independence after her last year.

She pulled into the faculty parking lot with Avery—one of the kids on Kara's record label— intoning darkly through the speakers.

It was on a sunny Memphis day, a good church-
　　goin' Sunday.
And I praised the Lord, wished the folks good day,
And then I killed my lady.

A wet, dark night in Germantown, that's where she
　　first betrayed me.
But I stayed my hand till I'd said my prayers
And then I killed my lady.

I never meant to do her harm, but her cruel heart,
　　it made me.
And the sun shone down as I shot her dead,
When I killed my lady

She turned the ignition off and pulled up the safety break on the Civic her cousin Clay had bought her; he just shoved the keys into her hand with raised eyebrows one afternoon after Jimmy Wayne had been gone longer than he apparently liked. It was Clay's version of a plane ticket or a new set of luggage, a sign that she had her freedom and she ought to use it. The song lingered in her mind, whether because of Avery's shaky, quivering voice full of regret, combined with smugness, or because of the contents, she wasn't sure. Murder ballads were traditional enough to feel familiar to most people that the creepiness had worn off. Jacyn heard the horror beneath the words and they disturbed her in an intrinsic way, the same feeling that made her want to make an inappropriate comment or offer a probably unwelcome hand when she saw a woman in the grocery story with a black eye. Avery's song was about a fictitious death, but that didn't make it any less brutal.

The parking lot was full of paper being blown around by the strong spring wind and students running for classes. Jacyn vaguely watched all of the mayhem and exuberance and she felt alone, far from home. She hated herself for thinking about Jimmy Wayne and the crease above his hip when he slept on his side.

Language and Culture wasn't exactly a taxing class for her, but she appreciated that for the most part the students didn't sleep in her class no matter how hungover they were. Since she spent more nights out than not, she thought working through your hangover was one of the most important skills that college could provide. The wind rushed across the street next to the parking lot and across the flat expanse of concrete, sending trees rustling like a freight train in the distance and whipping her hair into a murderous frenzy.

Jacyn spent the rest of the time walking to the lecture room trying to smooth her hair back into the hand-wrought knot she kept it in most of the time these days—a tight twist, with the hair looping around and in on itself to form a self-sustaining bun. She didn't expend much effort these days, not to braid her hair or shave her legs. Not much reason for it, really.

Avery's voice nearly whispering "I never meant to do her harm, but her cruel heart, it made me," went through her mind as she shoved open the door to the classroom and slapped her papers on the table. The class settled down immediately—she was usually later than they were. Jacyn pulled a dry erase marker from the back pocket of her jeans and wrote the word *y'all* in all caps on the white board and underlined it.

"What's the first thing you think of when you hear this word?" She recapped the pen and pushed her glasses up. They sat on her face lopsided because she'd stepped on them getting out of the bathtub months ago and never bothered to get a new pair. Hands shot into the air. "Penny." She called on a girl in her early twenties wearing a Tennessee Titans sweatshirt with her hair pulled back in a severe blond ponytail.

"Ignorant," Penny said with smug satisfaction. This was almost exactly how Jacyn imagined this going.

"David." Jacyn pointed to a chocolate-skinned boy with wire-framed glasses.

"Second person plural," David said with his head ducked down a bit. He was a freshman, a real one, eighteen. He had a way to go on the self-esteem. Jacyn decided to toss him a bone and give him a boost.

"Yup," she said and turned around to write out a chart on the white border. "First person, singular, *I*. Second person singular, *you*. Third person plural, *he/she/it*." She heard chatter behind her but didn't turn. "Yeah, I know you're bored, gimme a second here!" She moved over slightly on the board. "First, plural, *we*. Second, plural, *ye*, *you*, *you all*, *y'all*, *yous guys*, *you guys*. Third, plural, *they*." She turned around and pointed to the various options. "What do y'all think about that?" She smiled as she said it and got laughter rising up from the students like small spooked birds in a field.

Hands went up. "Tanya." She tilted her head at a girl with afro puffs in a track suit.

"Innit that bad grammar, though? I always was taught that *ain't* and *y'all* and words like that weren't real words."

Sometimes teaching was sitting on the dock all day with your line in the water getting burned, all your beer stale or skunky, and skunk spray floating on the wind periodically. Sometimes, though, the fish leaped right into your cooler.

"English is an egalitarian language." Jacyn turned around and wrote *egalitarian* on the white board. "There's no central committee or board, like in France, that decides what's right and wrong. Sure, there are grammarians and linguists who have opinions." She wrote out *opinions*. "But the truth of the matter is that we all decide what's right and wrong in spoken speech every day by using the words we do in the way we do. That's what I was telling you in the first couple of lectures about language being an outgrowth of culture, and culture forming around language. Like hip-hop." She smiled and most of the kids of color laughed at the white woman trying to be down.

She had taught a similar class in the past, where she based most of the examples around Southern speech patterns and used Texan examples—such as Spanish words that had crept into everyday language. But at a predominantly black college, she'd had to rethink her entire message and lesson plan. Some speech patterns overlapped between what was often called "black speech" and Southern region speech, for obvious reasons, so she'd gone from there, from *y'all* and *ain't* to subject-verb agreement problems.

Another hand shot up. "Michael."

"So, you're sayin' that how people talk when it innit written down can't be wrong?" He sounded doubtful and slightly accusatory.

"Yeah, that's basically what I'm saying." She smiled when the classes' feathers ruffled and settled. "But don't quote me."

The rest of the class was an amiable back-and-forth with students giving examples of nonstandard speech and Jacyn explaining some of the ways that the usages could have arisen, but always bringing the discussion back to the point that usage is a marker for a group, a way for people to relate to one another, to mark who belongs inside a group and who doesn't. They seemed to accept that pretty readily. Most people do. Belonging isn't a made-up idea, it's an impulse, something innate about humans, maybe an outgrowth of pre human ancestry when being together meant survival, something primal.

By the time the class came to a close, only forty five minutes later, the entire room was gray in the fluorescent overhead lights, the window panes shaking and showing a low, threatening sky beyond the glass. The kids picked up their papers and backpacks and shuffled out in small groups and singles. Jacyn watched the clouds jumble up on top of one another as she collected her stuff and imagined a sudden squall over the Gulf, a green-gray with water spouts in the distance touching down. Thunder shook the room and she sighed as the windows repelled the first drops of rain. She slouched through the halls, dreading the run to the car. When she pushed the door to the parking lot open, she was immediately drenched by the rain whipping sideways against the building. It was so absurd she laughed and started for the car with her head down, hoping she didn't get hit.

She hadn't bothered to lock her car, so she flung the door open and hopped in lickety-split. Her Converse were soaked through and her socks soggy.

Hair stuck to the side of her neck and face. As she searched the front seat for something to wipe off her face—only a slightly greasy Krystal napkin— she wondered what kind of nonsense Kara had planned for tonight. The hard rain sometimes daunted Kara, who was used to the easy rain of the Pacific Northwest. But it was Thursday, so there was a good chance that nothing would stand between her and a night out. Glasses almost dry, she popped the keys into the ignition, immediately greeted by Avery murmuring to his murdered true love. She flipped the windshield wipers on and wrapped her arm around the passenger seat to pull out of her parking place. A weird sort of mood settled on her, melancholy with the clouds seeming to sit right on her shoulders near her neck. She decided she didn't like the music at all—something about it, eerie and wrong, and she punched the button on the stereo to put on the radio. NPR greeted her like and old friend.

The drive home was the usual Nashville bs fucktardery with people refusing to obey any of the traffic rules of North America. The infraction Jacyn loathed the most was when people used the middle turn lane as a regular traffic lane in order to pass all the standing traffic. No one ever seemed to get a ticket for this, so she wondered if maybe it wasn't illegal here. Unlikely, but possible. No turn signals, slamming brakes, running red lights, pedestrians darting into traffic—it was something like a game of Frogger if you were one of the cars, or Grand Theft Auto without the shooting and hooker-beating. The rain made the situation about thirty times worse since everyone refused to admit inclement weather was upon them and just kept up the road-Olympics as though no new variable had been introduced.

The street in front her house stretched out on both sides adorned with familiar vehicles, some belonging to her neighbors, some belonging to Kara's musicians and friends. Jacyn pulled up to the driveway and found that they had left her spot unmolested, and she smiled. The gravel popped under her tires as she angled the low-bodied vehicle up the steep driveway, feeling every bump, and bouncing and swaying in her seat. She sat for a minute in the bubble of the front seat, waiting to see if her mood would pass, if she would suddenly be steady and calm—like she was most of the time. But the rain and the setting sun conspired to make her feel like her internal landscape was just as gray as the external one. Water exploded on the windshield. The surface tension of the drops exploding into smaller and smaller drops, all running down the slick glass to pool and run together to the ground. She thought about all the victims in murder ballads who hadn't been fictional. Her thoughts spiraled to Jimmy Wayne sitting in the cab of his truck with the door

open, one leg hanging out of the side asking her
to explain cribbage to him and taking notes. She
hadn't ever asked him why he wanted to know. He'd
laughed when she told him she'd never lost a cribbage game in her life. The memory made her crum-
ble a bit inside. Jimmy Wayne taking off was
probably her luck rebounding on her hard, all those
games of cards and lucky job placements had to
even out. Jimmy Wayne had been the reckoning.

Her door flung open and Kara leaned in, her hair
matted around her face from the rain. "Hey, having
a nervous breakdown?" she asked with her soft,
raspy voice.

Jacyn just smiled up at her, a tight, fake sort of
half-smile. "Maybe." Maybe she was. Maybe she
had been. Moving to Tennessee seemed like an odd
thing to do after all in hindsight. Like her mama
said, hindsight was twenty-twenty.

"Come on." Kara reached in and snapped apart
the seat belt and tugged her out into the yard. "The
guys're here."

Jacyn couldn't help laughing. She let Kara push-
pull her toward the porch with an arm around her
waist. "The guys" meant any varied assortment of
musicians and engineers that collected in pockets
around East Nashville. Kara seemed to have a
knack for picking the best of them, the ones with
the most talent and biggest drive. She'd only put out
five albums on her tiny record label, but all of them

had been critical successes. Three of the acts were now on gigantic major labels, making big names for themselves.

The front door stood open, music and laughter breaking against the wall of depression the rain and her thoughts had formed. Jacyn untangled herself from Kara and beelined straight for the bathroom that adjoined her bedroom. Voices called out for her from the living room, Avery for sure, his voice crackling with abuse from smoke and whiskey, probably Teague and Tyler from Mississippi, who knows how many other people. She kicked her shoes off outside the bathroom, socks going with shoes and her feet really cold against the black-and-white tile of the bathroom floor. Even though it was just dusk, the sixty-watt bulb in the bathroom strained like it was full dark, giving the wide molding and bead-boarded room a homey feeling. Thunder vibrated through the room as she peeled her clothes off and flung them toward the wicker laundry hamper. She flipped the shower onto full heat, letting the enamel on the claw-foot tub heat as she wrapped a towel around herself to rummage in her room for clothes.

When she got in the shower, her clean clothes lying on the toilet seat in an unruly bundle, she could see straight through the transparent shower curtain, She wondered where Jimmy Wayne was right then, if he was alright—why she'd stopped taking his calls. Those kinds of random, self-destructive decisions were the worst kind, because she did things like that and then felt like she couldn't back down. It had been one of the many reasons her marriage broke down. Ultimatums come easy but admitting you're wrong doesn't. She stood in the shower until she felt like she might pass out from the heat.

Dressed in footless tights and a denim skirt and Jimmy Wayne's old Willie Nelson baseball-style shirt—she hadn't even noticed that she'd picked that up, though it didn't smell like him anymore— she padded into the living room. The noise had picked up some already, guitars thumping and pennies clanging in a jar, being used as percussion. Kara sat in her favorite yellow armchair, flipping through a stack of stained papers. Probably lyric sheets. Her head was bowed, a glass of whiskey in her hand. Jacyn felt the sort of happiness you could only feel when a longtime friend has found happiness. This wasn't the same lost girl she'd known in college, studying economics and falling in love with the wrong guy over and over. Kara had found a place for herself, even if it was a nonconformist place. Jacyn was starting to truly believe that "growing up" was overrated and only perpetuated by people who didn't have anything better to do with themselves.

Avery sat on the floor with his back against the foot of the couch, bobbing his head as Teague played a song about lightning bugs or that employed a lightning bug metaphor, Jacyn wasn't really listening. She tucked herself in the end of the couch against the arm, on the opposite end from Avery. He smiled at her genuinely, pleased to see her. Jacyn smiled back and laughed a little. His thick, curly dark hair fell in his face. She watched as he jittered around, long limbs moving with jerks and spasms. Avery was a big man who hadn't ever grown into it, held together like a scarecrow threaded through with wires. Jacyn watched as he turned back to Teague and Tyler goofing around and noticed Avery toying with the beaded necklace he always wore. She kept meaning to ask him about that, where he'd gotten it, because she liked the beads, little creamy carved hearts and crossed finger bones alternating. She never could remember to ask him, though. Something always came up, distracting her when she was just about to mention it.

Jacyn curled up with her feet tucked under her and watched Kara writing on Teague's lyric sheet. Tyler and Avery picked up a cord progression that one played and the other echoed in another key. When the melody finally kicked in, she realized they were playing some kind of improvisation of "Girl from the North Country" by Dylan. She thought that was appropriate, because in the nimbus of the hazy incandescent light mingled with the candles on the mantel, Avery, Teague, and Tyler looked like nothing more than a trio of motley balladeers from a fairyland masquerading as good Southern boys: Tyler with his thick gold hair that fell in a fan over his forehead and his blue eyes; Avery with his uncanny pallor contrasted against his dark hair and dark eyes; Teague with his reflective strawberry blond hair and knowing smirks. Large men, none shy of six one, in a small, disordered room, filling up the house from one small corner of it. Jacyn realized that maybe she was as close to happy as she could be expected to be.

The wind came with the rain, trying to pry the house off its foundations and away to another land far away. Jacyn wondered if there was a land under the rainbow, if that was the land of the Unseelie Court and the things that crawled into children's closets and sat on people's chests to eat their breaths as they slept. Tennessee was a lot colder than she'd figured on. Avery grabbed the afghan off the couch at one point and tossed it to her, handed her his glass of bourbon, and let her finish it off. She watched him—his easy smile and genuine good humor, but there was something under it, something broken maybe. Artists were like that, art often coming from some dark and dire place, maybe from under the rainbow. Jacyn thought about Jimmy Wayne, who was all sharp tobacco tang and the soft hum of a slight sunburn, light and green. He wasn't a

musician, though, not really. A sometimes singer
for his supper.

Barley's Taproom in Knoxville, Tennessee, was
one of those bars that college kids and hipsters
would call "authentic" and that Jimmy Wayne
would just much rather avoid at all costs. Unfortu-
nately, he didn't always get to pick and choose
where wackjobs wanted to meet him, and public
was better than private when it came to witches and
magic users of any flavor. He tipped his hat up and
watched the crew setting up the stage for the first
live act of the evening and hoped he could skeedad-
dle before they plugged their amps in.

The chick perched on the barstool next to him
didn't look any more like a witch than any of the
other kids in the place—low-slung jeans, long-
sleeved gray shirt under a short-sleeved black shirt
emblazoned with a heart with an arrow through it.
Her black hair fell long down her back and shielded
the sides of her face. She looked the same as everyone else, eyes sliding off her and on to the next person at the bar. That was the charm, the tell. Wasn't
nothing normal about her. Not her pale as a fish
belly skin nor her bright blue eyes, nor her black
as a void hair. Sounds pretty, Snow White and fairy
tale princesses. Jimmy Wayne knew better, knew
what those old stories hid.

This girl was a pure witch—the kind that spawned all those stories about put-upon little girls and evil stepmothers. Jimmy Wayne knew those stories were really about the struggle of one generation of pure witches scratchin' and bitin' like a cornered cat against the next. These folks eat their young or their young ate them, just the plain and simple of that matter. Power in the blood, and he really never wanted to delve too deeply into whether that was literal eating of one another or not. Looked a little like vampires, but unless he had to know, he'd rather not.

"You know who I am?" The girl drank an apple martini. Jimmy Wayne did his best not to snort at that.

"I know *what* you are." He sipped his Maker's and scanned the room. Her smile was like the sweet release of death after a long illness. His eyes skittered around her face and he didn't like her one bit.

"You think you do. It doesn't matter one way or another what you think about me and my kind." She twisted *my kind* in such a way that he wondered what her gig was. "I have particular opinions about propriety that . . . others of my kind do not."

A guy two tables down from the bar had a weird disquieting way about him, and Jimmy Wayne couldn't peg if it was a supernatural sort of twinge he was pinging or just a recognition of a crappy human being. "Look, whatever your personal damage is with your people, I ain't part of that." He looked up at those spooky eyes from under the brim of his hat. "I'm looking for something, and somebody said maybe you could help me there."

"Sadly, what you're looking for has transmuted, like winter into spring. I would have called you before now, but we have our own ways. I didn't want to get involved with my *sister* before I knew for sure." Her voice slithered over him like snake scales catching against his skin, pulling up his hairs and making his teeth itch. The word *sister* in particular slid under his fingernails like a needle.

He paused for a second, aware that his temper was overflowing in his spleen. Witches liked to use secrets against you, liked to turn your feelings into nooses and bring you to heel for their own uses. "What're you talking about?"

Tossing her hair over her shoulder, the witch sighed, "I was going to call you to me before this, to send you back to your lucky girl before this. Time is such a strange creature, jutting forward at its own pace. One never knows how fast or how slow."

Jimmy Wayne set his eyes on her and refused to let her compel him off. He could see straight through the skin of her cheek, could see the threads of veins and arteries, blue and red, pulsing and contracting like ink under wax. Something like a fainting spell passed over him, and he clutched the bar to hold himself up. Dislocation swamped him, the smell of seaweed and salt, the sound of music in the distance, the taste of oysters on his tongue. He heard his own voice, "I have to check out this one thing, baby, cursed bones maybe. It's a bad haunting, fierce. Come're." He could see himself talking to Jacyn, could see her standing at the sink in her mawmaw's kitchen with a dish towel in her hand wiping her hand. Her hair had been wet from a shower and he'd been wearing a Giley's T-shirt.

With a *pop* and a shock, he was staring into blue eyes and breathing secondhand smoke. He realized she'd just released him from some kind of spell. They sat there inches apart staring at each other for several long seconds. When his heart settled down to double speed, he realized his desperate need to track down the cursed bones and the source of the disquieting rumors of missing women had abated to a general curiosity over a mystery. The situation clicked into place, clear like thin air in the mountains—he'd been compelled on this hunt, magically forced to follow the compulsion to its end.

"Time got away from me," the witch said again.

"Why're you messin' with me?" He wasn't gonna bother telling her *not* to mess with him. Completely pointless with these kind of creatures.

She tilted her head to the side. "I'm not." Her expression was unreadable, but could've been confusion. "You are nothing to me. I want you to succeed in your quest."

He waited for her to go on, polishing off his drink.

When she didn't, he prompted with a sigh, "Have I been under some sort of compulsion?" He figured he'd at least get conformation if he could wrangle it outta her.

"Oh!" The word sprung out of her mouth with the exclamation point almost hovering in the air. "Yes. You have. Like in one of your stories. Droll. But that was not my work."

"What?" Jimmy Wayne was used to being jacked around by creatures of darkness, by neutral critters out for a lark and a laugh, by supposed good guys with hidden agendas. Some creatures taught lessons that one could apply to future encounters. These sorts of pure witches seemed to be inbred or something, a little simple or weird in the head that magic didn't account for. He'd never heard tell of one story involving a pure witch—a witch like this one sitting in front of him—that didn't involve death or torture, poison and madness. They lived according to rules beyond the understand of Jimmy Wayne Broadus.

"My *sister* hexed you. If it makes you feel better, I think she somehow miscalculated, because I doubt that it's you she cares about at all. Perhaps she's being subtle, punishing her through your absence." The witch looked at *him* like he was the simple one. "She was aiming for your female friend. The one with chance twisted around her."

His blood pressure jacked up hard and he had to swallow twice. "She meant to curse Jacyn?"

"Yes, of course." The witch blew smoke at him with one side of her mouth curled.

"Super." He fished a ten out of his pocket and slapped it on the counter. "You got somethin' for me or not. I'm just about done here."

When she smiled, Jimmy Wayne imagined flowers wilting and blowing away as dust on a breeze. She slipped a CD jewel case out of her back pocket and slid it across the bar and tapped the plastic a couple times with her red fingernail. Jimmy Wayne picked it up, staring her right in the eyes. He flipped it over. Avery Jenkins, *Murder Ballads for My True Love.*

"That is who you're looking for." She swung her hair back over her shoulder to obscure most of her face.

"He's the doer?" Jimmy Wayne looked at the guy on the cover, regular singer dude, floppy hair and depressed expression.

She nodded once, a curt bob of her head that shook her thick, glassy hair.

"Does time move for you in a steady pattern?" Her voice had picked up the serpent's rasp again. Jimmy Wayne assumed that meant no.

His hotel wasn't much of a walk. The air hung heavy with cigarette smoke from people hanging around the entrances to buildings puffing away, and pollen. Still fairly cool, only in the midsixties or so, but promising an early summer. He felt heavy, dragging, like he had ever since he left Mississippi.

Now, he could recognize part of that as a compulsion, the magic yanking him, tugging at him, and his natural inertia, his desire to get back to Jacyn and drag her to Texas. The two feelings strong and pulling in the opposite direction.

Witches behaved in ways that were unknowable to regular folks. Jimmy Wayne didn't know why a witch would want to separate him from Jacyn enough for a curse, or why another one would care enough to release him from the spell. He supposed that they had some kind of war between them. Witches were usually mostly concerned with one another and foiling one another's plans. Even with the magic lifted, he knew the heaviness he felt wasn't just the spell, it was heartsickness. Ever since Jacyn had stopped takin' his calls, stopped callin' him back, he'd felt nothing but tired and worn down. He'd known he was fucking up, knew it like he knew the cab of his truck and the smell of pine woods, but the road kept calling him, case after case, always just that one more. Jacyn had gotten more and more withdrawn, turtling up on her herself and then finally, just nothing.

Even knowing now what his problem was, that didn't change anything. She was out there thinking something else was more important, that he couldn't even be bothered for five months to take a couple days and see her. Jimmy Wayne tilted the CD case into the light of a streetlamp and squinted to read the production information. Amber, Jacyn's cousin, floated through his mind. All things considered, he thought she might help get Jacyn to at least have supper with him. The address for the production company was Nashville. Less than four hours away.

Jimmy Wayne crossed the parking lot of the motel as the wind picked up, whipping his hair into his face and stinging the backs of his exposed arms. He got the key in the lock and turned the knob just as a huge gust hit his back, rocking him on his feet and sending him stumbling into the room. The door banged against the far wall and papers flung themselves around the room. He had to near wrench his arm out of socket to get the dang door closed against the wind. Raking his hair off his face, he surveyed the damage. Papers everywhere. Suddenly, he felt old, tired, used up. His knee and his back ached and he was tired of the wind and rain. He just wanted a long day outside in the sun with a can of beer in his hand and Jacyn swimming close at hand.

He crossed the room and pulled his laptop out of its case to do some background searching on this Avery Jenkins character and Control Alt Delete, his record company. His mind kept circling around what the witch had said about Jacyn, though, that she'd been the focus of the other witch's attention. *The one with chance twisted around her.* Chance, luck, just like Pere Emmanuel and Tasha had said. He broke out in icy sweat. He felt something like terror, and he thought it was probably the closest he'd ever get to feeling fear for a child of his own.

Jimmy Wayne slept fitfully. His dreams slid around him with gunshots and the sound of running water. He woke again and again in a panic he couldn't explain. Giving up around dawn, he showered, shaved, and gathered up his stuff. The night clerk was still on duty when he turned his key in. She was a cute Indian girl who blinked at him with professional courtesy and not much else. He couldn't tell if that meant he looked every inch his years plus ten or if she just didn't have any time for white guys. Either way, no skin off his nose.

He ate his Egg McMuffin rumbling down I-40 listening to Avery Jenkins.

Cold, cold day when she broke my heart,
When her cell showed up his number.
Cold, cold ice when I pushed her in
And when I held her under.

Cold, cold nights, now I'm all alone,
Toss and turn in ice-cold slumber.
Cold, cold future without my love
Since she tore my heart asunder.

The melodies were traditional English folk ballads. The material was even pretty standard murder ballad material. But something about the songs, some crappy something burned low in Jimmy Wayne's belly. They felt real, authentic. They disturbed him on a level he could never explain, except to say he was weirded out. As the sun broke out, big and white, filling up the sky with UV, Jimmy Wayne was glad he wasn't trapped somewhere listening to this record in the dark where something could creep up on him. He saw twig fingers and yellow eyes staring out of the dark in his mind. Yup, weirded out.

After one listen, he popped that sucker out of the CD player and put on David Allan Coe. He spent the rest of the trip having a little Outlaw County sing-along all by his lonesome. Coe, Cash, Kristofferson, thinking about the sun in Jacyn's hair, the salt smell she had from the beach most days, how much he'd screwed this all up.

CHAPTER NINE

Jimmy Wayne really hated Nashville. Not for the usual reasons—the Bible industry, the plastic country music industry, big hair. Those things barely registered for him. He hated the town because it sat right between two big freako supernatural zones. Up in the hills, in East Tennessee and the rest of the Appalachians were the hidden critters, all the creepies and crawlies out of people's worst nightmares. Some people carried over the ocean with them, some were native. Not all of them were dangerous or malevolent. Some were even helpful. But just the idea of all that chittering and otherness creeped Jimmy Wayne way the hell out. On the other side of the state, lay Memphis and the whole Mississippi Magic Culture. Those people just got on his nerves. Always fighting among themselves and causing other people trouble. Jimmy Wayne just had no patience for that. For the most part, though, Nashville proper wasn't any worse than any other town its size. The location was just ill-advised.

He had friends in town, people he knew at least, but he decided just to go straight to the source when he got to town. He knew East Nashville pretty well and could picture the map of it in his mind as he coasted from I-40 to I-24, and then off the interstate at Shelby. The Jenkins guy's songs wouldn't leave him be. It was like tiny echoes of darkness kept reverberating through his bones.

Chapel Street was totally residential, which surprised Jimmy Wayne, since he had assumed the address of the record company would be at an office space. Instead, it turned out to be a sweet little wooden house with a wide front porch hung with fairy lights. The grass was just greening up and daffodils rioted along the driveway with yellow and orange fire. He parked right in front and made no other attempts at stealth, either, slamming his cab door and crunching the gravel of the drive under his boots as he walked up it, instead of the concrete steps to the sidewalk. A gold Volvo in the driveway had a Davidson County, Tennessee, plate, meaning whoever lived here had been in town at least long enough to change their license plates.

The sweet smell of pot lingered around the doorway. He knocked on the screen door and peered into the house through it. He noticed it wasn't locked. The inner door stood wide open and he had a good view down a straight, wood-floored hallway into the kitchen. The back door, which stood opposite the front, was also wide open.

A woman in a tank top and shorts banged open the door. She had a sleeve of magnolia tats on her left arm and some sort of Asian design on her left, a nose piercing, and black and white hair.

"I'm lookin' for Kara E . . ." He looked back at the jewel case. "Esayian?" Smiling with his eyes tilted down, he hoped he looked embarrassed and sweet. This women looked like she could be a bitch on wheels if she wanted to be.

"That's me!" She opened the door further and stepped back a little. "Come on in."

"That's a pretty name, never heard it before." Jimmy Wayne laid it on thick.

"It's Armenian." Reaching into her pocket to pull out a cigarette, the chick swept her eyes up and down Jimmy Wayne in a way he was both comfortable and familiar with. "I hope you're here to sing for me."

The laugh came all on its own accord, full and with real deep down pleasure. Women like this tended to be fun. Not his type, not ever really, and certainly not now with his heart busted up, but they made good friends, honest and real.

"Nah, I do got one, but nah." He presented the CD to her. "I was wondering what you could tell me about this guy."

Not bothering to take the case, Kara Esayian raised an eyebrow and lit her smoke. "You A&R?"

Jimmy Wayne ducked his head a bit and shook it. "Mainly, I'm unemployed and in the rodeo."

A couple of beats later, like she was waiting to decide if that was true or not, Miss Esayian smiled this real sweet, little girl smile and waved at him. "In that case, wanna beer?"

Jacyn loathed the grocery store. She always had, ever since she was a child. The frozen food section, in particular, she hated. Growing up in a semi-tropical environment where people routinely wore flip-flops and thin garments of cotton that barely covered them, the frigid air of the grocery store was a shock to the system. Her great-aunt had once told her when she was very young that going from one temperature extreme to another could cause a person to have a stroke or a heart attack. Even without being a superstitious person, this idea had lodged somewhere inside her, somewhere deep and hidden, like behind her gall bladder. The grocery store had been an ominous, brightly lit, place of random grief ever since.

People don't put stock in the right things, had always been Jacyn's opinion. Like the availability of the right brand of rice, for example. She was standing in the rice and bean aisle of the Kroger up the street from her house just then, looking over the assorted boxes of broccoli and cheese and chicken-flavored concoctions, but the one thing she wanted—Dixie Lily yellow rice—no, none of that. She had accepted that sort of lack when she went to college up North, but she fervently believed that in Tennessee she should be able to buy Dixie Lily rice. No dice. She gave up on the rice altogether and skulked over to the dairy case to grab some butter and cheese. The only staples they ever bought regularly anyway were cheese, bread, milk, and butter anyway. And beer.

Their neighborhood Kroger was a decidedly rundown affair with cracked linoleum, stained and scuffed with years of abuse, the sort of sour gray lighting that comes from fluorescents under a great deal of dust, and a clientele that looked like extras from some art movie about the degradation of the urban poor intermixed with hip, young urbanites in chunky glasses and $200 jeans. Jacyn knew she looked a lot more like the latter than the former and didn't think she liked that much. She hadn't spent much time around the kind of people who had fondue parties and talked about literary magazines since she'd left Austin—she was still technically on sabbatical, teaching at TSU on a semester contract to pay the bills—and she was vaguely homesick when she gave it any thought. She missed her family, but Amber was off in California solving the math riddles of the universe, and Jacyn just couldn't face her family with Jimmy Wayne pulling a bugout on her. They were just too over eager to look after her, too solicitous and wide eyed about it. Jacyn knew that her family had decided she was a lost cause, a divorce and rebound relationship gone wrong within a couple years. Soon they'd be trying to hook her up with older divorced men with kids and crazy-ass ex-wives who wanted to kill her. She'd seen it over and over again.

Stepping up to the self-scan aisle, Jacyn pulled out her keys to scan the Kroger discount card affixed to her keychain and set her plastic grocery basket on the shelf provided. The woman at the scanner ahead of her couldn't get the barcodes to scan, and the guy next to her couldn't negotiate the weighing of produce. This was sort of Jacyn's daily self-scan soap opera. She was always amazed at how flat-out impossible some people found the self-checkout. The poor employees who ended up "helping" the fools who couldn't figure out the touch screen with bright, color pictures and step-by-step examples always looked so haggard. Jacyn imagined it was the shit job people called "not-it" on at the beginning of shifts.

Grabbing her single bag, she once again regretted how she always forgot to pick up a canvas bag before leaving the house in the mornings. Yet another plastic bag to stick under the sink in the silly fabric tube bedecked with bright, dancing broccoli and bell peppers her mother had bought her at a crafts fair. What the so-called crafts people managed not only to come up with, make, but also convince others were total must-haves always flummoxed Jacyn. Why couldn't she just stick the plastic bags into another plastic bag and hang that up?

Stepping into the Kroger parking lot was a physical relief. She never noticed how tense she got in the grocery store until she was outside again. The wind had died down considering it was this far into March, and it was a good seventy degrees, sun shining in a thin, clear sky, the UV index had to be near on nine or so. Jacyn itched to get out onto the water and sit in the sun, get a sunburn and fall asleep by eight thirty at night, content on Bud fumes and a day well wasted. She rolled down both windows on the car and opened the sunroof for the three-block drive home. She went the long way round, down Gallatin Road and behind the drug store, past the Methodist school and up Chapel. More cars than usual spilled all down the street, but that could just as easily be the neighbors as Kara.

Jacyn left the windows down and the sunroof open, hoping the clear sky meant not having to dash out from the house at two in the morning to seal the vehicle up. There were a couple guys sitting on the swing on the porch. They called out, but she didn't recognize them.

"Hey." She waved. They waved back. Up close she still didn't know them. Young guys wearing ratty T-shirts and jeans, just more dudes like all the other ones she saw every day.

The front door was open, and Jacyn pulled open the screen door just as Teague and Tyler stepped in front of her, slapping each other on the back, two very tall guys, one with coppery red hair and the other with honey blond, both good-natured but as different as their accents were the same.

"Jay! Baby, where you been? We thought you deserted us!" Tyler grabbed the grocery bag as Teague slid his arm around her back.

"We're making a beer run." He pretended to look down her shirt. "Nope, no beer in there." He had this kind of artless charm that made anything he did forgivable. A charming rogue would probably have suited as a description a hundred years before. It helped that he was clearly in love with Kara, who was remaining willfully blind to it.

Jacyn followed behind Tyler, who constantly shook his head to the side to get his bangs out of his face, as he toted the groceries back to the kitchen to put them away. He was a Vanderbilt kid

who'd grown up in one of those crumbling Southern genteel families with long pedigrees, who were
now mainly academics, lawyers, and local politi-
cians. Jacyn watched him fussing with the groceries and wondered how long it was going to take
before he gave up on the whole big singing career,
went to law school, got married, and started his career aimed at the State Legislature of Mississippi.
Probably two years. Wild oats to sow and things
that never were to accumulate for later in life.

Teague stepped up behind her and slung his arm
back around her, balancing it on her shoulder so
that his fingers came perilously close to swiping at
one of her boobs. Since she never rose to his bait,
he never really tried to grope her. It was their dance.
The opening bars of "American Tune" by Paul
Simon struck up in the living room and almost the
entire house vibrated with several voices humming.

"Wanna come up with to the Three Crow tonight?" Teague swung his shoulders a bit, causing
Jacyn to have to sway with him.

"Hell no. The last time I did that, I couldn't remember half the night." Jacyn pulled away when
Tyler waved the tube the plastic bags went in.

"This damn thing's so jammed full I can't get another bag in here. Maybe you should recycle them
somehow. I've seen some people using them to dec-
orate trees."

Jacyn grabbed the bag and the bag the bags went in. She stuck the bag for bags back under the sink and tossed the new one in the trash. Tyler watched her as he swapped the habitual toothpick he chewed from one side of his mouth to the other.

"Bad day?" He was sensitive sometimes. Maybe a poet's soul, it was hard to tell under the Abercrombie and early twenties posturing.

"No, just moody. I hate the grocery."

"I told you I'd do that shit." Teague yanked his keys out of his pocket and hooked his thumb toward the front door. "Beer run."

Jacyn didn't wait around for that dog-and-pony act to kick back up, she just turned and headed toward her room, which was on the left from the kitchen. She plopped down on her back and thought about taking a mental-health evening—just lying in bed and watching television on her computer with headphones on, ignoring the rest of the house. There was a certain appeal there, wallowing in self-pity in one's underwear beneath a duvet really was one of the best modern conveniences.

Kicking off her shoes, Jacyn curled up on her bed strewn with laundry, fifteen pillows, and three duvets and rooted around until her hand hit the cool plastic and metal of her iPod. The earphones were still blessedly attached, and she pulled it out and popped it on. Since she was feeling pathetic, missing Jimmy Wayne and home, she cued up "Weather with You" by Crowded House and pulled the thinnest duvet over herself.

She must have fallen asleep somewhere in there between Crowded House and Jeff Buckley, because the bed dipped and for a static moment, she was elated. She expected a thick arm with a hundred little bracelets clicking together to wrap around her. Instead, she waited a tick longer than it should have taken and realized she could smell Kara's shampoo and cigarettes, that the weight behind her was far too small and the feet tucking in behind hers were attached to legs shorter than her own. She removed the earbuds from her ears.

"How you feelin'?" Kara whispered into her hair. They'd been friends for a decade. The first person Jacyn had called when things fell apart again. If Katrina hadn't hit right on the edge of her divorce, she would have been in Nashville months and months beforehand.

"Sad," Jacyn whispered back. No use lying about it or trying to cover it up.

Kara stroked her hair. "Why don't you get dressed and we'll go over to the Three Crow and Tyler will buy you drinks all night and act like a jerk when you give him advice?"

Jacyn smiled weakly at that. "I don't know if I could deal with him tonight. I feel old."

"Teague can buy you drinks, then. Hey, and maybe he can start a fight!" Kara's sarcastic humor made

Jacyn turn on her back laughing. Teague had a knack for attracting girls with boyfriends, often when the boyfriend was right there in the bar. The pretty didn't wipe off with a punch to the face.

"Who's playing?" Jacyn said it with as much innocence as she could muster, but they both knew it was a done deal now. Self-pity only went so far and the prospect of a good time with friends went much further.

"The kid I keep telling you about from Memphis. You don't like him. Doesn't matter." She gave Jacyn a squeeze and slide off the bed. "Wear something slutty."

They both laughed.

Wearing something not very slutty in the least, a below-the-knee kick-pleated black skirt and black-and-white Crowded House shirt she'd had since she was fifteen, Jacyn pulled her sandals on and hoped it hadn't cooled down too much. Avery and his ex-girlfriend Caroline were chitchatting with Tyler and Teague when she came out of the bathroom. That was a little weird, but most of the goings-on in Nashville were. Caroline was just too normal to sustain a relationship with someone who was about to break big. Avery's album had been reviewed on Pitchfork and might even make have a review in *Rolling Stone*. That changed people, changed relationships. In a close-knit scene, it could throw everyone off kilter, but so far all Jacyn had really noticed was Caroline getting more and more withdrawn and fragile until she and Avery flat-out broke up.

"Your hair's down," Tyler said with something odd in his voice.

"Don't feel like messing with it." Her hair had grown out to waist length by then, and it curled in little ringlets at the ends. It used to annoy her, but now she just really didn't care. The streaks that had been purple in Mississippi were now bleached out and colored over, dark to light blond in her sunbleached light brown hair. Tyler looked at her with his unreadable face.

"Are you gonna be a pain in my ass tonight?" She crossed her arms over her chest as he started shaking his head back and forth and waving his hands in the air.

"What? What? What do you take me for? I'm full of gentlemanly honor, lady! I am the soul of decorum."

Jacyn rolled her eyes and snorted, "Are you driving, old man?"

He raised his keys and wagged them. Turning on her heel, she headed for the car without asking where Kara was. No telling. Tyler always drove, because he was about seventy inside, drinking one or two beers at shows and complaining about the excesses of his elders, glowering and shaking his head at how the musicians wasted their talent on boozing and how playing to drunk audiences was a disgrace. Jacyn pictured him in her head as a little imp with a cane.

Avery and Caroline drove separately. Caroline at the wheel of her cute little Japanese car. Tyler, naturally, drove an old man's Toyota sedan—all electric with a moonroof and leather seats and wood detailing. Tyler chattered at her as they drove and Teague mumbled a running stream of commentary about how Tyler should shut up, which Jacyn didn't really hear. She watched the neighborhood roll by, old trees and cracked concrete, families with small children on lawns and guys with amps packing them into the backs of old vans.

When they got out of the car, Jacyn realized she had forgotten her sweater—something she always brought along in order to escape a few times during a show, to stand outside free of cigarette smoke and the suffocating Nashville bar scene. She turned to tell Tyler and as she opened her mouth, Kara stepped out of a cab and held it up to her.

"Y'all left me!" Kara tried to fake angry but ruined it by laughing.

"I thought you'd already left." Jacyn grabbed her sweater and wrapped a hand around Kara's arm. "The guys wouldn't ever leave you."

"But you would."

"Hell yeah!"

They showed their IDs to the guy at the door, who knew them both by face *and* name but was still such a dick that they had to show them every time to prove they were on the list. Tyler and Teague trailed somewhere behind, Avery and Caroline pretty much out of Jacyn's mind, as they pressed through the crowd.

The Three Crow was a small bar, like most of them in Nashville. Past the entrance a bar stretched across the back and right-hand walls, with tables all jumbled up on one another. The left side of the building was separated by a wall that started halfway through the room and contained the slightly elevated stage with the bathrooms in the back. Sometimes table were also set up in there, other times the tables were inexplicably cleared out on that side. The drinks were expensive for Nashville, and the crowd pretentious, just like in most of East Nashville.

Jacyn headed for the bar. The bartender was this girl she thought was named Kim but wasn't really sure. The ambient noise made it really impossible to have any sort of conversation in any way other than shouting straight into someone's ear. She waited patiently as maybe-Kim nodded and pointed at the bottle of Maker's Mark. Jacyn nodded with an ironic roll of her eyes. A girl with slanting bangs and a French-stripe top bumped into her and glared at her like Jacyn was at fault. Her immediate response was to flip the kid off. Instead she flipped her hair so it smacked the indy rock girl right in the face and laughed inside.

With her drink procured and the indication it should go on a tab made, she turned to scan the place. Lots of Vandy kids, indy scenesters, and to her right, Teague, who was being pawed by a cute girl in a jumpsuit dress and slingback heels. He was doing his best to fend her off without outright shoving her away, but it looked like it would get to that point pretty rapidly. Jacyn vacillated between feeling bad for Teague and being pissed off at him. He came from the same county as she did and they were close enough together in age that she really didn't know how she hadn't known him before Kara moved to Nashville. Good-looking didn't really cover the sort of aw-shucks bashfulness he could put on, with his fluttering, gold-red eyelashes, overly bright blue eyes, and his long, lanky frame and Jerry Lee Lewis hair. The guy was gorgeous and more important, he was smart. As a matter of fact, he was pretty much everything that women the world over complained daily wasn't real. Jacyn still wasn't sure if Kara was stringing him along or if she really believed he didn't care about her. Kara was a weird creature that way, all sass and a strong career woman, riot girl on the outside and a strange combination of self-doubt and self-reliance inside.

As much as they were alike, Jacyn and Kara had very different ways of dealing with relationships.

Neither of which appeared to be very swift. Kara was also divorced and had a string of epically disastrous relationships behind her.

Jacyn didn't see Tyler at all. He was probably camped out at the table next to the stage, glaring at all the other concert-goers, wishing he was sitting at home in his pajamas and slippers, sipping a brandy, and reading the paper.

A hand landed on her arm and Jacyn looked up to find Kara grinning at her with her with a pleased-as-peaches smile. "Hey!" she mouthed.

"Hey!" Jacyn mouthed back and her eyes flicked for just a split second over Kara's shoulder to catch startled hazel eyes staring back at her. His hair had grown out to about shoulder length and it was down. He ran a nervous hand through it, bracelets catching the overhead lights. Vertigo caught her and she had to reach out and hold on to Kara's collar to steady herself.

Jimmy Wayne's hand snatched out and grabbed her by the elbow. Stumbling against him, she smelled the peppery metal of gunpowder and under it, the warm smell of his skin. Her first instinct was to scream, her second was to scratch the side of his face as hard as she could. But his hand slid from her elbow to the small of her back and her hand followed his to twist her fingers against his calloused palm. Glaring up at him, she saw his fear there. Long lashes beating against his sunburned cheeks, full mouth parted in startlement or terror, he looked gobsmacked. Which pretty much meant he wasn't there to see her.

Jacyn turned to Kara who was watching with her mouth pressed together in a pucker and her eyes open wide like a plastic doll. In a flash, she crumpled and rolled her head and eyes. "Jay double-u equals Jimmy Wayne! Am stupid!"

A year ago, this would have been a strange coincidence, the kind that made her uneasy and confused. Now, Jacyn was sure this was related somehow to Jimmy Wayne's work, that he had stumbled on something here in her backyard and that Kara was involved. His visit had nothing to do with her. That much was plain. The fact that Kara somehow had fallen into some kind of supernatural who-did-ery wasn't in any way a surprise. She knew everyone and did a lot of stuff that was shady at best.

Jacyn dropped Jimmy Wayne's hand and stepped away from him. She snapped her fingers and pointed toward the door and didn't wait for him to follow her out. Threading her way through all the people out to just drink and screw and hear some music, she wondered when her time like that would come, when it would all be effortless goofing off without some dark thread sewing it all together.

The air outside was a blessing, car exhaust and all. She breathed in a few long breaths and did a

status check. She was shocked, no sadder or less
stable than earlier today. Maybe she could even get
some closure here.

Jimmy Wayne was wearing a teal and white and
red plaid shirt with white satin piping and snaps.
His jeans were old, holey ones she recognized immediately, the ones with an acid burn near the knee.
He jammed his hands in his front pockets and managed to look up at her through his eyelashes and
down at her from his height at the same time.

"Are you gonna say anything?" The flare of her
temper just erupted through all the faultlines he'd
created already.

"Where do you want me to start? I miss you?"
His voice broke, and she couldn't tell if he was being genuine or sarcastic.

"How about where the fuck you've been." Her
arms flew up in front of her chest to cross of their
own accord.

"On the road, you know where I've been." He
looked over his shoulder at a couple of drunk kids
stumbling out on to the sidewalk.

"You fucking know what I mean." The words
came out as a hiss. His shoulders fell and he pulled
a hand out of his pocket to wipe it across his face.

"Jacyn, baby . . ." he started, taking a step toward
her, but the whole scene was too much like an
episode of *Cops*. She expected some crazy methhead

to pop out of the bushes and set himself on fire and a patrol car to jump the curb any second.

"I waited . . ." And her voice gave out around the tears waiting for this second, when she admitted out loud that she really had believed in him, really had believed in what he promised and what she thought he was offering.

His mouth turned down and his eyes squeezed shut. "Will you just come with me some place more *private*?" The whisper crawled out of him, a hurt, broken thing.

She wanted so bad to just believe any line of bull-shit he spun, but that would make her a different kind of woman, the kind who turned a blind eye to affairs and told her friends the black eye wouldn't happen again. On the other hand, she knew he might have an almost decent explanation. She wanted there to be a decent explanation, but he would pay no matter what.

"You can come over, but I'm not . . ." She didn't get the *promise you anything* out before Tyler was standing behind Jimmy Wayne with Teague and about half a dozen other people behind him.

"Goin' home already?" Tyler had this way about him where Jacyn couldn't tell if he was clued into a situation or not. Could be that he just stumbled on this. Could be that Kara orchestrated it.

"That guy's too drunk to play, man, what is *with*

people?" Tyler rounded her and looked back over his shoulder. "Comin'?"

"I'm gonna ride with JW." Jacyn pointed at Jimmy Wayne and watched Tyler's upper-middle class eyes rake over him and dismiss him.

"'Kay," he said, walking to his car with a wave.

CHAPTER TEN

Jimmy Wayne really had always had shit luck. Couldn't catch a break with a mitt. The one thing he'd cried his sorry ass to sleep over, the one freakin' thing he couldn't get out of his mind, wanting it so bad he could smell it? It was sittin' right next to him in his truck and all he could do was fidget and try not to look too stupid.

She had her hair down. All washed out of that crazy color, gold and spun wheat catching the streetlights as they passed. What he had to say didn't make a whole lot of sense, not even to him, and she was a smart lady. Smart enough to know he was confused by it all. He was scared she was gonna misinterpet his confusion as being confused about her. He knew how to get back to Kara's place, which was good since Jacyn was crap for giving directions before you missed your turn.

When he parked, he rounded the front of the truck to open her door, but she met him half way with a shrug. "Don't worry about all that," she said in a tone he couldn't rightly interpret.

There was, unsurprisingly, some kind of party going on in full swing, even though the people who lived on the property had been gone. He looked over at Jacyn, but she didn't look worried about it. She didn't look a whole lot of anything, and that bothered him. Yeah, he was worried for his own ass, because, hell, he wanted her back, wanted all of this witchy garbage never to have happened at all. But more than that it broke his heart all over again to see her so blank. His girl was anything but calm and placid. She had an opinion on everything from toothpaste flavors (cinnamon was best) to text messaging (took too long to type, was boring).

His impulse was to nudge her with his elbow and make a face, but she marched up the steps to the house without looking at him. Following behind, he held the frame of the screen door to keep it from banging behind him. He waved at the guys smoking a joint in the living room who greeted him like a long lost relative.

Jacyn ducked into a room to the right at the end of the hallway between the front door and the kitchen and he followed her in. She was lying on her back on a white wrought-iron bed in the middle of a damned mess—clothes and books and papers and bedclothes all over the place. His heart beat in the back of his mouth.

"So, what's the deal. Make it interesting at least." Her bored tone broke him out of his fantasy world where he was gonna get to make this up to her the best way he had.

There was an old overstuffed armchair between a desk and chest of drawers and he plopped down on it, bracing his forearms on his thighs and hanging his head. "I was under some kind of compulsion."

"That's how I feel about smoking."

Uphill battle then. "A witch put a compulsion on me."

"Why and to do what?" She flopped her arm over her eyes.

Jimmy Wayne really wished that they could move on, because her ability to cut to the chase was one of the reasons he truly believed they would make one hell of a team.

"Why, exactly, I can't really say. The inner workings of the mind of the modern witch are sort of beyond my ken." The sarcasm bled in there even though he was doing his best to avoid it. He didn't want to discuss the fact that a witch had it out for *her* in particular, not so much him. He was just as upset as she was, and this was not anything near the ideal situation; he had envisioned sweeping her off her feet and taking her back home to the ranch when this whole gig was done. Now, he knew, no matter what he told her, she'd think he was only trying to get back into her good graces because he'd fucked up so bad by stumbling on her. She should know now that her damnable luck was probably the culprit here. Why, he had no idea and he didn't know how to broach the subject without scaring her half out of her mind.

"To do what, then?" She wasn't rising to the bait. He couldn't tell if that was because she was so depressed she didn't care what his damage was or if she was so angry she was waiting out his half-assed explanations in order to claw his eyes out at the end.

"To track down some cursed bones." He rubbed his eyes with the heel of his hand and sighed.

Jacyn rolled over on her side and looked at him. "Cursed how?" And he knew he shouldn't use her natural curiosity against her, but he was just a man. Just a very bad, weak man who was foolishly in love and heartsick. It was like pulling teeth for him to sit across the room and watch Jacyn tugging her hair out from under her and watching him with her little upturned nose and bright eyes.

"They're the bones of murder victims. The spirits aren't exactly excited about that and they're raisin' a ruckus. I need to get the bones back and offer them to the spirits to get them to move on." That was the condensed version anyway.

"Where are the bones?" She rolled over fully on her belly and propped her chin on one hand. It took everything in him not to grab her.

He closed his eyes and made a big show of looking around the room when he opened them back up. "I haven't got a damned clue."

"Then what the hell are you doing here?" She blinked at him, still without any real expression.

He pulled the CD out of his back pocket and tossed it on the bed. It landed with a thunk right in front of her. Pleasure over the perfect aim wasn't something that even a heartbroken man could suppress. She didn't even bother to pick the case up, just flicked her eyes from it back to him.

"Avery?"

"You know him?" Jimmy Wayne straightened his spine and ran a hand through his hair. This was her luck after all. It had to be. There was something about that witch. He was almost positive that whatever her deal was that it wasn't some kind of good-natured heads-up that caused her to help him or to tell him about the witch in Nashville. Something about Jacyn made her a pawn of some kind between them. He'd seen time and again how well that went for mortals who got caught up between two warring nonhumans. He wanted to keep her safe, to protect her, but he also knew holding back and lying to her would probably rebound on him like a slingshot to the face.

"He practically lives here. What does Avery have to do with this?" Even as she said it, though, Jimmy Wayne could tell she was clicking through something.

"The witch who pointed my feet toward the road gave me that. She had some ax to grind, I just don't know what yet." Like he'd said, he had no clue. He wondered if they made it through all of this alive if he'd ever really know what the hell this had been about.

"Well, I'm pretty sure I know where your bones are." She rolled back over and onto her feet. He was on his instantly.

"What? How?" How was obvious—she was uncanny, that was her way. Chance, luck, whatever it was. She knew things. He was just coming to realize that it was more than just being whip-smart and that he wasn't just judging her abilities through the haze of being head over heels. Whatever she could do was real.

"It's Avery's necklace. That part's obvious. The rest is the hard part." Her words trailed behind her as she left the room, left him standing still, feeling like his life had shifted a couple feet to the left.

In the way she did sometimes, as soon as Jimmy Wayne started explaining, Jacyn already knew where the whole story was heading. Probably that uncanny *whatever* that people called her luck, that something that made her able to read a game of

cards or know someone inside and out without any
effort on her part. There was no skill there, just this
innate niggle that unfailingly pointed her in the
right direction. And then left her on her ass around
the next bend. Lately, she was coming to be more
aware of her hunches. When she was growing up,
it'd only been normal. She'd been able to find
someone's keys or a lost pet or remember something no one else could. But she also always ended
up with no gas in her car or locked out of her house
or slipping on the sidewalk. For the most part, she'd
always thought it was her way of framing her life,
nothing *real*, nothing factual, just a worldview—
karma, balance. Now, though, she didn't know for
sure. Her life had taken a whole new path that was
full of the unexpected and the otherworldly. Everything had changed. She was starting to change, too.

Luckily for Jimmy Wayne, Leon was in the living
room with the rest of the pothead reprobates that
populated Kara's house morning, noon, and night.
Well, luckily if he wasn't too stoned and wanted to
talk endlessly about conspiracies concerning the
World Trade Center bombing or the invasion of
Iraq. If they were truly on a roll, Leon would be just
high enough and would have the exact information
they needed. Leon believed in magic. He believed
in witches and fairies and trolls and things that went
bump in the night.

"Hey, dude." He was ensconced on one of the

couches in Kara's living room with his fiddle in its case at his feet and a bottle of green tea in his other hand. Teague sat across from him in a high-backed wooden chair tuning his guitar. Out on the porch, Jacyn could hear a furious debate about makes of guitars going down. Leon shifted over on the couch to give Jacyn room to sit down.

"Hey, Leon," Jacyn started. "You ever notice anything *weird* about Avery?"

Teague looked up at that with a half-smile crumpling the corners of his mouth. Jimmy Wayne lounged with his shoulder against the molding of the double-arched doorway from the hall.

Leon took a sip of his tea and blinked his light eyelashes at her. He was wearing a knit cap over his shaved head, his bright red full beard shot through with white. "Weird *how*?" He blinked slowly at her.

"You know, like how you think I'm weird." That was how she'd first learned that Leon believed he was sensitive to "vibrations" and "feelings" and "auras" and the like.

Jimmy Wayne pushed away from the wall subtly and watched the conversation more closely. Leon glanced over at the movement. "You mean like how he's weird?"

Jacyn watched the light from the compact fluorescent bulbs reflect off the shine on Jimmy Wayne's hair, off the sliver around the pearl snaps on his shirt. She supposed that it would be normal if someone pinged her (of all people) as weird, then Jimmy Wayne probably screamed it in billboard-sized neon.

"Yeah, like that." She wasn't sure the analogy worked exactly, though. Leon's feelings about her seemed to have something to do with her luck—naturally—and Jimmy Wayne was just more of a regular guy who was caught up in a bunch of messes.

"Well." Leon started taking another long drink of his tea. "I'd say Avery made a deal with the devil."

That wasn't exactly what Jacyn was expecting. She didn't want to deal with any biblical implications about what had happened to her in the last year. The reality of creepy crawlies and the boogeyman was bad enough without bring anyone's immortal soul into the equation.

"Why you say that?" Jimmy Wayne asked in a casual, calm tone.

"It's all over ya, man. You got mojo bleeding off your skin like whiskey out of some drunk's pores after a bender!" Leon punctuated that with a few high trills of laughter.

"He meant why do you think Avery sold his soul to the devil?" Jacyn sighed and wiped at her eyes with her thumb.

"Oh. Yeah." Leon rolled his head on his shoulder and Teague thrummed a dramatic, Spanish-sounding intro riff. "You know, the old story. Some young guy wants fame and fortune but doesn't want to work for it. He gets nowhere, but then suddenly

out of the blue through a series of unlikely events
he has a bestselling album and indy cred at the same
time? Unlikely."

Jacyn thought over that reasoning. Minus the part
where they all lived in Nashville and that Kara was
majorly connected, she could understand looking
for zebras here instead of horses. But it *was* Nashville
and Avery did have talent.

"So, your opinion here is based on the fact that he
got his deal, or that you see something weird around
him?" Jacyn paused for a half beat. "In his aura or
whatever."

Leon winked at her. "He's got something seriously fucked up going on with his vibrations. He's
like the lying spikes on a lie detector readout."

"Huh," Teague said. "Maybe he got some bad pcp-
laced pot. Like some other people I know." Teague
had a way of delivering lines like that that made you
want to slap him and laugh at the same time.

"Hey, fuck you man! You'll see, he'll get dragged
back to hell by giant black dogs." Leon reached in
his pocket for his pot. "Wanna smoke a bowl?" He
offered the pipe to Jacyn.

"I'll pass." Jacyn stood up and walked over to
Jimmy Wayne, patting Teague on the head as she
went. She resisted pressing her palm into the swell
of Jimmy Wayne's chest muscles just barely.

She lifted her eyebrows at him and he followed
behind her into the unoccupied kitchen.

"So, what do you think?" She watched him as he watched her. He tilted his chin down to his chest and rubbed at the bristling stubble.

"I don't know, man." He shook his head. "If you were anyone else, I would say this wasn't even worth the gas. But I've seen old drunks and serious drug users who stumble into altered states and into bein' able to read magic like that before. Not surprised you know the guy, frankly. Leon's pretty much the sort of person I'd expect you to collect unintentionally." He smiled and Jacyn would have returned it, but she didn't really know what to make of what he'd said. She didn't want to know what he meant, more like it. This was all getting a little too close to home, because it was a little too much about her.

"So, deal with the devil?" Which is what she was actually asking him before he gave his impromptu speech on Leon.

"Nah, I've never once heard of the devil hisself comin' up outta hell to wheedle some sorry soul outta some fool sinner who prob'ly was gonna end up in hell anyway." Jacyn couldn't help laugh at that, and Jimmy Wayne smiled big and bright in return. "I figure this is the next step in the jig that my bitch witch has us dancing."

"Witch, seriously? I mean, what do you mean by witch? Old lady with fifteen cats and a wart on her nose?" Jacyn now firmly believed in voodoo, but that made sense in an off-kilter kind of way. It was more of a religion, just that the voudun gods were more interactive than most others, hanging around and waiting to possess people and act in the world. Esoteric magic really seemed like a whole other story. Gods probably didn't even apply in her worldview to Baron Samedi and the loa if she'd ever given it any thought, more like spirits.

"It's not really all that great an idea to stand around discussin' this stuff out in the open." He looked pointedly at the open windows and back door.

"Where are we supposed to go?" This felt like some kind of trickery to get her alone. But to be completely honest, she was just so glad to see him she barely cared about being manipulated.

"Hold up." He wandered over to the cabinets and flung them open and closed until he came across the spices. Picking through those, he scrutinized several cans and flung them back into the abyss of the dark cupboard.

With two cans firmly in hand he motioned toward the floor. "Sit down Indian style."

She rolled her eyes but did as told. He shook two streams of spices while walking in a clockwise fashion about her to create a circle that was big enough for him to sit in as well. When the circle was closed and Jacyn's nose was full of sage and red pepper, Jimmy Wayne sat down across from her and handed her a pinch of black powder.

"Toss a mite at the windows and a bit more at the door." His eyelashes fluttered against his cheek as he said it. She did as she was told again and watched as he mimicked her. With a loud series of bangs, the windows and doors to the yard and hallway all slammed shut.

"Well, that'll bring fifteen people running in here at once. Good call on flyin' under the radar." Jacyn glared at him as Jimmy Wayne started to laugh.

"You looked like you were about to piss your pants!" He slapped his leg and tossed his head back, cracking up. "Don't worry, darlin', nobody outside this room heard anything. It's part of the spell. It locks in sound."

"That would be useful in a house that's always full like this one."

He eyed her and she refused to blush because, yeah, that was exactly what she meant. Not that she'd been having any sex since she'd gotten here, no matter how insistent Kara had been about the benefits of rebound sex.

"Don't ask, don't tell," Jimmy Wayne murmured to himself.

"Ok, spit it out. What's up with the witch."

Jimmy Wayne's eyes wandered around the room, probably taking in all the ways of escape and possible dangers all at once.

"Witches don't work according to human rules for starters."

Jacyn interrupted. "Wait. Witches aren't humans who use magic and are female?"

He shook his head and rubbed at his eyes a bit. "There's a buncha different kinds of witches, and when someone talks about witches, who knows what they mean half the damned time?" Jacyn snorted at this. "But I'm talkin' 'bout what's called true witches. As far as I can tell, they're about as human as a porcupine."

"And about as prickly?" His jokes were telegraphed from about six states away.

"Hey!" Jimmy Wayne leaned forward and tugged on the hair that hung around the side of her face. "You gettin' tired of my dumb jokes already?"

Jacyn's stomach took a tilt-a-whirl ride and her heart went along for a laugh. She was three heartbeats away from jumping on top of him.

"Anyway, true witches, they're territorial, like weres and vampires and all the other big-time bullies." He tried to make eye contact, but Jacyn dripped her gaze to the backs of his scarred hands.

"Weres and vampires . . . forget it. We'll get into that later. Territorial? What does that have to do with anything?" She was five steps ahead, though, and sort of figured there was some kind of inexplicable manipulation going on involving two competing witches. Not so different than two women after the same man. "What are they territorial over? People? A certain place? The water supply?"

"Good question. It depends. They don't think like we do. They hate one another, play tricks on one another, steal from one another. Ain't nobody I know ever knew for sure what a true witch was after aside from screwin' over another witch." Jimmy Wayne broke off because the back door flew open and Tyler sauntered in.

"Uh-huh, and what's goin' on here, I ask you?" He wagged his finger at Jacyn.

Jimmy Wayne slid to his feet and shot a hand out to grab Jacyn's elbow and yank her along with him. At her puzzled face he whispered in her ear, "Spell only keeps out sound, don't lock the doors or nothin' like that." His lips brushed her ear and her nipples beaded up. Through her thin bra and shirt she figured he could feel them against his chest.

"Who's this outsider manhandlin' one of my wimmin-folk?" Tyler demanded with a fake swagger and thump of his chest.

"Don't beat me baby, you know I only love you!" Jacyn hollered in an over the top fake Southern accent.

Teague pushed open the door from the hallway right as she said that and snapped his fingers really loudly. "You been runnin' around on me with *two guys*? Aw, nah, that's not gonna stand!"

Kara peeked around his arm with a wave. "Everyone's goin' to Waffle House, wanna hit it?"

"Is Avery comin'?" Jacyn cocked her head and

thought about where the most likely places to find him would be. She also wondered if he had actually sold his soul, or the closest thing a person could, to this true witch, and how the hell she and Jimmy Wayne were gonna get it out of him. Getting a regular straight answer out of Avery was nearly impossible.

"Might do," Teague answered. Which of course meant . . .

"Hey, y'all, I think I'm gonna bail." Tyler said, and waved jauntily before bugging out directly through the back door.

Jimmy Wayne raised his eyebrows in query. "He's got some weird thing with Avery since he got his deal. Who knows."

"Boy crush," Kara said.

"You *hope*," Teague answered smacking her on the ass and grinning like a tweeked out methhead.

The planning stage for the trip to Waffle House took upward of an hour and a half, most of that time Jimmy Wayne sat on the couch and listened to Leon explain how come pixies really do steal socks and underwear.

"It's like this, man. Pixies, no one pays them any attention anymore, right?" He paused for Jimmy Wayne to agree or disagree to his own contentment.

"Right."

"See, back in the old days, people fed them all

the time, leavin' out bowls of milk and pieces of bread and talking to them as they went walking around in the woods." He paused to drink some of his seemingly endless supply of tea. "So who gives a shit about those little fuckers now? No one, exactly. Stealin' socks and underwear is their little revenge plot."

"What do they do with all of it?" This was by far not the stupidest theory Jimmy Wayne had heard about lost socks and underwear. That award probably went to the cousin of the chupacabra, the Sock-eater, that an old man in Amarillo had flogged until his dying day. Not eaten by a Sock-eater or anything else, bitten by a ten-foot rattler.

Leon shrugged. "Who knows the minds of woodland creatures, man?"

"Your little critters are more house spirits, though, wouldn'tcha say?" The stories of suchlike creatures went back to the dawn of people, so there was probably something to it at least.

Leon cocked his head at him. "I know you're holdin' out on me, but that's alright, man. We all got our secrets."

Jimmy Wayne thought Leon was the good-hearted sort of slacker-stoner, who couldn't ever be relied on to show up anywhere on time but who would always pull through in desperate times. He'd seen his fair share of those sorts of folks over the years, calm to the point of being sedated but big hearted, always giving away what they owned to the point of standing naked in a thunderstorm because someone else was going in want of a shirt.

"You know about Jacyn's luck then, right?" Leon glanced around the room to make sure they were really alone.

Jimmy Wayne did know about Jacyn's luck, or he had suspicions about it. He'd heard of people who seemed to have an uncanny way about them all his life. There were far and away tons of different sorts of uncanny—some people could taste the weather, hear someone else's feelings, pray and change the world. But the rumors of people who were half of one and half the opposite thing went back to when people first started learning to tell stories. Maybe Jacyn was really touched with some kind of Janus-tinged luck, half of it real good, half of it real bad. Like being part light and part dark, opposition set within one person. It was a workable theory, not one he particularly wanted to float by her, but workable in his head.

"I'll take your silence for agreement." Leon lit the bowl on his pipe and offered it over to Jimmy Wayne.

"Nah." Jimmy Wayne smiled and wagged his head slightly. "Too early for me still."

"We can't ever go anywhere without some kind of major production, dude. Where is everyone?" Leon pattered on around a large exhalation of smoke. "I mean, I just do not even get what takes so long to put your shoes on. I think they get sucked into some kind of time-dilation field whenever I'm hungry."

Jimmy Wayne figured it had more to do with the fact that so many people were at play; everyone had a list of things to do before leaving the house, and with seven different timelines, they all got added together instead of running parallel.

Jacyn wandered back into the room in flip-flops and the same cute skirt and old T-shirt she'd been wearing before. She'd pulled her hair back into pigtails high on her head that swung as she walked. Her smile peeped out like she didn't mean to show it. Goddamn, he missed her. He'd always hated witches, most kinds of them not just true witches, but if he'd blown *this* then he'd take up witch hunting as a full-time career.

"And like I told Teague the other day, man, you can't be too careful with women with black hair and real pale skin, because one out of ten of those bitches are witches. It's just better to pick up chicks with red hair or something instead of accidentally falling into that, you know what I'm saying?"

Jimmy Wayne saw Jacyn focus on Leon out of the corner of his eye as he did the same. "What'd you just say about witches, Leon?" Jacyn was pretty good at bluffing. She didn't sound anything other than curious.

"Oh, you know that girl that Teague was messing with last month? I was just saying that she had a weird way about her that I didn't like. I told him that he needed to look out for stuff like that around here. What with Nashville being a hub of weirdo activity and all the energy in the air. You know, feeding the things that go bump in the night."

Normally, Jimmy Wayne would have stuck around and had a long talk with Leon about his various theories, because he was near on to some actual reality here, but Jacyn wasn't having any of that.

"What did you think was strange about that girl." Jacyn paused and her eyebrows drew down. "I can't remember her name, neither."

"Oh, you know. Black black hair, not like a color but like the absence of anything. White skin like you could see her veins under it. Red mouth. Sounds like a witch to me, man. I'm not saying that girl was, but with the whole Avery thing, nobody can be too careful."

Bingo. Jimmy Wayne knew if they let this guy ramble long enough he'd get around to what they needed to know.

"I thought you thought Avery sold his soul to the devil. What's that got to do with a witch?" Jacyn sounded like she didn't buy a word of it, like she was teasing Leon. Leon just laughed high and bright, little bubbles of good humor breaking in the dim light of the room.

"I never said the actual devil came up in some kind of pneumatic tube from hell with a flaming pen and a singed parchment. Avery got taken in by a witch. I'm almost positive of it, man." He snapped his fingers for emphasis. Jimmy Wayne thought that Leon might be a useful ally if he could be steered away from his most wayward ideas and toward the more correct ones.

"Huh." Jacyn made the little sound in the back of her throat that could either be a neutral acknowledgment that she had heard what you said or an outright dismissal of everything you just said.

"A witch?" Jimmy Wayne leaned down to rest his arms on his thighs and looked up at Leon with his eyes half-closed, measuring. Natural suspicion came with the job, and Jimmy Wayne was ready to reassess Leon at any given second, ready to relabel him as more of a threat than a help.

"Yeah, no warts, though. Pretty thing. Not as pretty as the girls around here, though." He smiled up at Jacyn with a wink that looked more playful than interested. Jimmy Wayne shifted all the same and drew Leon's attention back at him. He wasn't the real protective type—the pissing upwind from a girl to mark his territory sorta guy—but he was a *guy* all the same. Leon just laughed good-naturedly with his chin tucked down to his chest. "Yeah, I feel ya, man. She doesn't want anyone but you anyway, I figure."

Jacyn butted in then making a loud, drawn out noise to cut through the bullshittery going down. Her eyes were rolling back in her head with annoyance when Jimmy Wayne met her eye and he couldn't help the bullfrog puff to his chest or the leering smile.

"What makes you think this chick's a witch?" Jacyn wasn't havin' the little boys' hour here, and Jimmy Wayne wouldn't want to cart her off back to Texas if she was the sort who would.

Leon wagged his head. He fixed his bright blue eyes on Jimmy Wayne's. They sat there for a second before Jimmy Wayne could tell if this was a standoff or a warning. "I just know."

A definite warning. Jacyn crossed the room all the way and reached out like she was gonna push Jimmy Wayne's hair out of his face, paused, and went to pull it back. But he caught her palm and brought it to his mouth for a kiss before she could get away. Sorta rolling her eyes, she broke into a sly smile, one corner up and one corner down. Leon chuckled and opened his bottle of tea again.

Mariah Partridge, the card read in a flourish-filled serif script. Under the name were printed a 615 phone number and a myspace address. Getting the card had been as simple as anything else in Nashville—someone had one in their wallet.

When everyone was finally assembled on the

porch to head out to Waffle House, Jacyn had leaned into Teague and asked "Hey, whatcha know about Avery's agent?" Teague scratched the red stubble under his chin theatrically and looked down from his ridiculous height with a squint. "Baby, you know if you want to hook up an act I've got a video camera and a Web site."

Coming from anyone else, it would have been the worst sort of sleazy-ass remark, the kind that gets a guy a red handprint on his face or bloodshot eyes from a glass of bourbon to the face. But from Teague it came out slicked with aw-shucks, just joshin' Mississippi pine and the first taste of beer after a long, humid day. Jacyn smiled despite herself, feeling Jimmy Wayne's eyes on the side of her face. She was almost embarrassed but figured it was pretty damned obvious that Teague was just a land shark always scenting for prey.

"The day I take up porn, I'll knock on your door." Jaycn smacked him on the face hard enough to sting but not to hurt really.

Teague smiled big enough to swallow the moon. "Man, you don't even know how many times I heard that song and dance." He pitched his voice up into a tinny falsetto. "Oh, you can pimp me out, Daddy!" He went back to his usual fluttering murmur. "Kids these days, no work ethic." He fished around in his back pocket and riffled through some cards as Kara came to peer over Jacyn's shoulder.

Jacyn was usually the one hurrying everyone up. The delay had caused Leon and several bandmates to settle on the porch swings, kicking softly at the painted cement, scuffing their Chucks softly with shushing sounds in counterpoint to an *a cappella,* harmonized version of "You Never Even Call Me by My Name."

Producing a card, Teague threw his head back and joined in the singing.

Leon's so-called witch was an all in one PR rep, agent, and booker. Or that's what her business card read. Jacyn had learned pretty fast after moving to Nashville that just because someone said they were an agent or an anything else didn't mean jack. Lots of eager, ignorant kids got pulled into that net like shiny, fat salmon. Big promises, lots of smoke blown up their asses, and nothing ever coming of it but heartbreak and more promises. It was a large part of why Kara had started Control Alt Delete Records, just to be able to really do something for at least a few of the acts that had the talent and drive to make a real go of it. Most didn't. Making a real go of it meant broken relationships, barely getting by, bouncing checks, and rotating which utilities were shut off, along with a hundred days or better on the road a year. Most folks just weren't cut out for that sort life. The reality of it was a lot more grime under your fingernails than getting your drinks for free.

When the guitars came out, it was clear that Waffle

House was off. Teague snatched Kara with an arm around her neck and sort of forced her into a stumbling two-step as Jacyn considered their options on this. Avery could show up in the flesh any second. She tried to frame in her mind how that conversation would go: *Hey, you sell your soul to the devil? Oh, and while you're up, get me a Coke.*

Jimmy Wayne pressed against her side and flicked the business card with his thumbnail. Sage and pepper from earlier overlaid his Dial soap and leather smell. "Check out this Web site?"

Flicking her eyes over the assembled idiots, Jacyn knew they might as well, nothin' doin' with those people for the rest of the night besides bourbon, beer, and bullshit. "Yeah, come on."

Her computer, naturally, was on her bed with all the other assorted odds and ends she never bothered to move. She didn't bother to make a show of everything and turn the light on, just kicked her shoes off and shuffled over to the bed. They both knew he'd offer to sleep on the couch and she'd turn him down, so better to just be real. She stepped out of her skirt and flopped down on the bed on her belly, tapped the button on the bottom of the laptop to wake it from hibernation as Jimmy Wayne settled next to her with all his clothes on, also on his belly.

"What's the address?" This felt like everything else in her life for the last year, real in an unfocused, gel-filtered way. *Of course* she was in Nashville

with Jimmy Wayne's bracelets clicking as he lifted
the business card of a possible witch to read it by
the ambient light thrown off by her laptop screen.
Of course she could hear three guitars, a fiddle, and
a mandolin on her porch accompanied by drunken,
jubilant voices. Life is what you make it, the old
saw went, and she hadn't ever really believed that.
Not with the unknowable right around every
bend—catastrophe, death, broken levies, and magical compulsions. She wasn't sure how she felt about
that explanation, or if she even bought it. Jimmy
Wayne was pretty out of her league, and she's
gotten so close to resigned that she'd been fooling
herself that she could have a life with him anyway.
She'd talked herself out of believing, of remembering, the way he would run a finger along her hairline with a startled, dazed expression and hum to
himself in the mornings. She'd convinced herself
that he hadn't ever really made biscuits and gravy
in nothing but nubby old jeans while changing song
lyrics to fit with her name.

The solid muscle of his arm pressed into her side.
He turned his head slightly, and she could almost
pretend he wasn't smelling her hair. She'd changed
her conditioner since she moved here. She wondered if he noticed.

"Myspace dot com slash triple moon agency."
His voice broke around the words, burred and half-
lit like the room.

Jacyn awkwardly typed in the address. The page popped up with a slick design, a crescent moon at the top with cascading stars dripping out of it down the left side of the page. "Subtle." Jacyn almost laughed.

"They have no reason to hide what they are. I don't even pretend to get the nonhuman types. Could be some kinda in-joke." He shifted his weight so he could lift his left hand to scroll down the page, his arm resting over hers. Comfortable, like they hadn't just spent months apart.

On the blog bit of the site, there was an announcement for a showcase the next night at the Mercy Lounge.

"This is elusive prey right here, son," Jacyn said mimicking Jimmy Wayne's accent.

"Hey now, we don't all got luck mojo bustin' out all over the damned place, doubting Thomasina." He made a quick biting motion, snapping his teeth together with dimples and mostly closed eyes.

"Sure, sure. I'm just better at this than you." Jacyn snapped the laptop closed and scooted around to rest her head at the other end of the bed. She settled against her white sheets with the bright yellow delft pattern printed on them. Jimmy Wayne moved to get up and Jacyn pinched his side with her toes. "Don't bother to go through the motions. I'm too worn out. Just lay down. You can't have the good pillows, though."

The bed dipped and redipped. Jacyn felt soft cotton against her bare arm. "Good pillows? Who can tell one from another?" Old joke, Jacyn and her fifteen pillows.

She floated toward sleep with the familiar smell of Jimmy Wayne's hair and the gunmetal tang that always settled over him when he was tired. When she was overcome with the paralyzed sensation right before total sleep, Jimmy Wayne resettled on his side and his arm came to rest over her ribcage, his entire body pressed against her side, his leg cocked up over her thighs. She immediately fell down an endless well of contentment.

CHAPTER ELEVEN

Nashville's an industry town. Actually, it's a three-industry town: higher education (Vanderbilt, TSU, Lipscomb, Belmont, Fisk), health care (HCA), and The Industry (Welcome to Music City, y'all!). Like most industry towns, everyone knows everyone else, or at least knows someone who knows someone. Kara knew most people and all the people who knew people.

After spending most of the day asleep and rising to find Jimmy Wayne reading the paper in a wife beater and jeans chitchatting with Teague, Jacyn had spent most of the downward slide into "time to go out" in the bathtub or watching Jimmy Wayne clean and tidy the house up while humming to himself. Too many people around to have any kind of meaningful conversation, whether about their relationship or about the witch situation. Jacyn was used to having a full house and living under the watchful eyes of a whole pack of meddling people. It felt right in the same way that fall turning to winter did, not really anything to remark on, natural, the order of the world. Teague appeared to like Jimmy Wayne, which was fine. Not like Jimmy Wayne would be sticking around, but it was nice that they could get on while he was in Nashville.

Jacyn thought about the natural order or things and how she felt like maybe there wasn't any such thing as she leaned against the side of Kara's purple Mazda 3. The guys (assorted, including Leon and Teague and the usual suspects) were all falling out of Leon's Volvo station wagon and Jacyn was grilling Jimmy Wayne about music. The cool was evaporating from the night, the breeze blowing warm with the green smell of the first real birth of full spring. Crickets sang love struck ballads to one another and drunk college students cavorted in unrestrained exuberance.

"I don't have any use for the White Stripes. Not even that Loretta Lynn album," Jimmy Wayne said as Jacyn pulled on Kara's cigarette. Somehow, Teague had coaxed Tyler out with him, and he stood a little to the side of the disheveled group of musicians arrayed around Leon, smart in a buttoned-down shirt with a tie, jeans, and Chucks. He looked like a disapproving younger brother, like usual.

The Mercy Lounge inhabited an old, converted warehouse. The parking lot sprawled where it should narrow and constricted where it should widen, like most of the paved surfaces in Nashville. The entrance was easy to miss, almost a throwback to when the best clubs were unmarked and discovered through word of mouth. At some silent signal, their entire party converged toward the little pulpit where the indy rock kid with black spiked hair, large gauge earrings, and star tattoos all over his arms checked the list for Kara's name. The downstairs of the club looked like the entrance foyer to a prewar NYC apartment building—octagonal white-tiled floor and old polished wooden staircase.

As the name check went down, it turned out (Who would have thought it?) they had enough people and plus ones on the list for everyone to get in free. The gatekeeper kid laughed and nearly applauded at the jiggery-pokery that must have come about to achieve that feat. Each hand was duly stamped and the madness decamped up the stairs to the venue with Teague and Tyler bickering about drinking too heavily at shows (Teague for, Tyler against) and Jimmy Wayne pressing his hand flat against the small of Jacyn's back. It was easy to lean into him, to let her hip bump his as they climbed the stairs, easy to turn and push a strand of his hair behind his ear where it had fallen out of the ponytail holder he had the thick honey mass constrained with. His hazel eyes fell on hers, the corners crinkling in a smile, the freckles high on his cheeks clear in the bright light on the stairs. The cord behind her belly button yanked, tethering her back to him, in all honesty just making itself known again since it had just lengthened and slackened while she gave up on him. His fingers on her back flexed and dug into her muscles more firmly. His smile melted into a parted mouth and fluttering lashes.

"Y'all're cute," Teague drawled from the landing at the top of the stairs. Jacyn and Jimmy Wayne were one step down, where the light faded from bright to gloaming. "Tyler, is this whiny emo bullshit night?" His attention turned to the sparkly, bright pop music flooding out of the speakers.

Jimmy Wayne stepped away from her slightly, and Jacyn grabbed him by a belt loop and laughed. He laughed along, burned embers and secrets right down to her fingertips, and brushed a hand through his hair, dislodging more of it from the hair tie. Kara was already in the middle of the crowd at the bar, chatting up some skanky looking dude in a Clash T-shirt, shorts, and flip-flops. Their party dispersed in clusters and pairs. Jacyn settled against Jimmy Wayne and his arm came around her.

The venue was a long room, seventy-five feet or so, with open rafters, a long bar on one side and blacked out windows on the other. The stage was small and raised on one end of the room, the bathrooms embedded in the wall opposite. The roof sat on pillars that ran the length of the room obscuring lines of sight throughout the place. That night, the place was fairly packed, all the tables running along either side of a wide center aisle created by the pillars were occupied by the usual Nashville sort—college students, industry dickheads, burnout cases, middle-class SUV drivers out for the evening.

Jimmy Wayne dropped his arm, grabbed her hand, and tugged her toward the bar. Leaning down he whispered in her ear, "A whiskey for the lady?" Jacyn laughed.

He shouldered his way between a girl in a bright orange University of Tennessee T-shirt and three pounds of makeup and a guy with a rattail and Lynyrd Skynyrd tour shirt from '74 and stepped back to let her have the spot, pressing against her back with his arm around her waist and hand pressed low on her stomach. His solid weight settled around her and she waved her hand above her head to get the attention of the bartender. Like the waitstaff at most hip bars, the service personnel exuded a sort of disdain for the clientele that extended just far enough from full-out hatred to keep the tips coming in.

They stood nestled together, Jimmy Wayne silently smiling as Jacyn turned her head as far to the

side as she could to whisper-shout to him about nothing in particular. The usual sort of bar babbling—
pointing out the other people in the crowd, making a
lot of eye contact, joshin' around. This felt comfortable, casual. They'd met in a bar. Re-met in a bar.
Something of an overdone cliché that wasn't really
even a cliché since no one *really* met in bars, right?
Jimmy Wayne's fingers dug harder into the softness
of her lower belly as they both tossed back their shots
of Jack, a little bit of mossy-flavored fire scorching
away a little of the propriety that everyone carries
around in the daylight. The night picked up the sort
of prickly focus that Jacyn associated with gambling
and the man whose forearm lay snug between her
breasts, fixing her in place in his storybook world
of magic, frantic sex, and intangible promises.

She knew, even as she sipped her Bud and listened to him sing along to Waylon being piped over
the PA between acts, that she should be pissed here.
Seriously pissed. Broken plates and busted egos
sort of pissed. But more than anything, she felt like
the last several months had been a enchanted sleep,
a long coma with her eyes open, where she was
stumbling through her days eating and speaking and
just getting by. Now she wanted to dance, to run out
into the street in bare feet in the rain. The taste of
wild onions and the smell of damp earth sat in the
back of her throat, memories of events that hadn't
happened yet.

As his body pivoted slightly, Jimmy Wayne pulled her along with him so that he rested his arm on the top of the bar. She leaned on his arm, held in an almost full circle in both his arms. They faced the stage as a scenester chick in high heels, tight dark jeans, and a teal off-the-shoulder blouse got up to tap on the mic and smile a coiling grin down at the audience. Jacyn felt a sudden tightening of her heart, like someone had reached into her chest and squeezed, hard, once. Her beer bottle hit the bar with a crack, reverberating up through her finger bones into her wrist, up to the elbow. The air stood still in her lungs, arrested, and Jimmy Wayne crumpled down around her gasping audibly, his teeth locking around a piece of her hair and tugging hard enough to hurt. The couple in front of them turned and watched without saying anything.

Tyler, however, appeared out of nowhere with a look composed half of disapproval and half of embarrassment. "Y'all ok?" He nervously pushed his mop of dark gold hair off his forehead with a sweep of the hand and a sharp flick of his head. He managed to steady Jimmy Wayne with a hand on his back and tugged Jacyn up with his hand under an elbow. Jimmy Wayne never let go of her completely, holding on to her left wrist with a hand fixed all the way around it.

Like a quick scene change, she was perfectly fine

again, standing up straight, looking between Tyler, who had his eyebrows both up and a wry quirk to one side of his mouth, and Jimmy Wayne, who had his free hand in his hair yanking at it as he glared at the stage. Flicking her gaze away from the way Jimmy Wayne's eyelashes caught the overhead lights, fragmenting them into copper and bronze, his freckles a grayscale of texture on his cheeks. Even as she caught sight of the odd tilt to the woman's head—the way her black hair seemed to move of its own accord, slithering slightly around her shoulder and back again, her motions disjointed, like a film clip with every tenth frame removed—all Jacyn could focus on was the superimposed image of Jimmy Wayne's jawline, the line of his straight nose sloping toward his ridiculous mouth.

His fingers constricted around her wrist and his broken nails pinched her skin as the woman onstage—had to be Mariah Partridge—disjointedly sashayed off the stage in a way that made Jacyn's skin feel tight. Jimmy Wayne ignored Tyler's good-natured inquiries, his joking "So, someone slip you a mickey of crank?", and his old man laugh accompanied with elbows flying and head wagging. Jacyn could see that his jaw was set, the muscle flexing as he gritted his teeth hard enough to be audible in a quieter setting. The band got rolling, a boy on bongos singing in an airy falsetto about wanting tea with lemon and a guy on a stand-up bass with floppy hair and a buttoned-down shirt.

Jacyn got on her toes and tugged Jimmy Wayne down so her lips blew his hair away from his ear. "What the fuck was that?"

He mouthed back, eyes wide open, angry— throwing down angry. "A warning."

That much was frickin' obvious. She meant more like why was she suddenly collateral damage here. Not that anyone around baby boy didn't end up collateral damage, which was his biggest malfunction anyway. Instead of feeling out of her element, Jacyn just felt angry. Why the hell did everything have to be so screwed up all the time? More than that, why didn't she just accept the chaos and ride it?

Tugging her arm out of Jimmy Wayne's grip, she started to thread her way through the crowd, pushing between two girls in halter tops and too much lip gloss before Jimmy Wayne could lunge after her. Negotiating rickety round tables and spindly chairs, coeds and soccer moms, Jacyn slipped from the bar to the shadowy, unlit area on the side of the stage, leading to the backstage area. Because it was a showcase, this whole zone was just as packed as the rest of the bar, and Jacyn was just another girl full of smiles and head bobs toward the guys fiddling with guitar cases and amps. She looked like someone's girlfriend, so no one questioned her.

The door backstage was wide open with people flowing both ways through it. A black door in a black-painted wall, opening to show an orange-tinted room with a bar running along the far side and couches and chairs scattered throughout. Guys ranging from mid-teens to late thirties flowed around and in and out of the room around the fixed center that was Mariah Partridge. As soon as she stepped across the threshold, Jacyn felt something like the air going heavy in the room. As both of her feet came to rest next to each other in the room, she could feel every inch of her skin pressing down into her flesh. Her bones hummed with a low vibration that tickled her head to toe from the inside. No one seemed to notice her, except the person she'd come looking for.

Mariah Partridge's hair flowed on unseen currents of air, fluttering and lifting around her face in alternating curls and straight tendrils, so black light didn't reflect off of it. Her skin against the black of her hair was pale, not porcelain pale, but waxy, like it could be scraped off with a fingernail. Her huge eyes were electric blue, startling, arresting maybe, but unnatural.

Jacyn knew she was rooted in place, fixed like the proverbial fly, without any higher thought.

You. I felt you. Something like a voice unfolded in her mind, not so much words as concepts fully born, beyond words, prior to words.

Leave Jimmy Wayne alone. That wasn't really the first thing Jacyn had intended to think at this creature, but she wasn't sure she was even in real control of her thoughts. All the same, that was the first thing that came to mind.

He is of no concern to me, woman. His affairs are his own. You I would cast away from me.

Jacyn saw Avery out of the corner of her eye and wondered why he had just passed by her without even bothering to say hey. She knew she should be scared, maybe panicked that this creature was interested in her, but she felt protective of her friends, of Jimmy Wayne, and she was more concerned about them than herself.

He does not see you. No woman is ever seen so close to me. There was no malevolence in the words, more like a kind of boredom. Like Jacyn wasn't even important enough to warrant complete focus.

You are as nothing before me. I will destroy you. The idea popped into Jacyn's mind. Jacyn felt calm, like she was maybe on the tip of shock. This thing hated her, that was clear. She felt like her luck was really screwing her here tonight. How did the witch know who she was or care one way or the other?

What I am is beyond your reckoning. Something close to thunder sounded inside Jaycn's head. She was dismissed with another crack and was left disoriented, standing on the outside of the backstage door, looking up at a nearly explosive Jimmy Wayne.

"Did you get hit on the head by the stupid stick?" he screamed over the music, loud enough to turn heads outside of the magical bubble the demonic PR agent had created. Jacyn opened her mouth to respond when Jimmy Wayne grabbed her arm and pretty much dragged her through the crowd. She pulled back, ready to argue, to stand her ground and assert her independence, but the look he turned on her was threaded with fear. That sort of vulnerability turned him vicious, and she didn't need him going to jail in Tennessee for domestic violence and assault when she created a scene and got him taken out by a pig pile of rowdy do-gooders. Plastering on a smile, she jogged to keep up and pretended everything was a-okay.

Down the stairs and out into the crowded Nashville night, she shoved him back with a hand flat on his chest and a twist of her body attempting to get away. He ran a hand through his hair, and pushing it off his face, turned his temper on the elastic in his hair—yanking it out and hurling it to the ground, grinding the toe of his boot on it like a cigarette butt.

Jacyn was running on adrenaline from her brush with the things that go bump in the night and her residual abandonment issues. Jimmy Wayne's misdirected anger wasn't tempering that any.

"What?" Jacyn exploded at him getting on her toes to scream in his face. "What is your problem?"

He stood completely still for what seemed like three minutes or better, though it was probably like a half a second. His right hand was twisted in his hair on the top of his head, his mouth hard, dimpled at the edges.

"I think we both know all too fucking well my problem is *you*." His words fell out soft, crinkled on the edges as his voice broke like his throat wanted to click shut. Jacyn could read lots of meanings in his statement. She had already decided to take the low road and choose the most insulting way to force a fight when he dropped his hand from his hair and tilted his chin up with his eyes closed.

She held her breath reflexively, because she realized that she knew this expression without ever having seen it before: He was hurting, on an edge she didn't even know he had. Pride got a lot of people by when they didn't have anything else. Pride's what held the pieces together when everything else exploded in your face. He wasn't going to say what he wanted to because he was holding himself together the only way he had.

Which made her both angry and depressed. She wasn't the sort of person who ignored someone else's pain because she had issues, too. He wasn't even trying to work her, which made it all the worse.

"Hey," she said, reaching out to take his hand hanging slack at his side. His palm was rough and calloused, warm, and he didn't respond at all as she held his hand tight. She tugged at it and he turned his face farther away. "I didn't mean to scare you." She knew he had panicked and was ashamed of it. For whatever reason, he was about as transparent to her as a white shirt at a wet T-shirt contest.

His face tilted down and one of his eyebrows went up, the pinching of his mouth grew worse, deeply indented on the sides. He was beautiful, yes, with his hazel eyes black in the darkness, his long eyelashes sweeping the freckles on his high cheekbones as he blinked, and his pissed-off mouth. But that somehow had faded to just be a truism. He was *Jimmy Wayne,* he was something beyond a concept of desire; he just was.

Goddamn it, she was insanely in love with him and that was all there was to it. She'd known it, but this was the test here. Full of her own problems, full of her own wants and needs and insecurities, all she wanted was for him to be happy. The impulse to put him first was so strong she knew she wasn't going to overcome it.

Holding on to his hand, she used it as leverage to press up against him on her toes and brush her mouth against the indention below his bottom lip. The wind picked up, the whirlwind of spring in Tennessee, and their hair flew around them, trapping their faces together inside a vortex of tiny stings from the whipping ends of gold and brown. His hand gripped hers, and came behind her to press against her back, wrenching her shoulder somewhat painfully. His tongue flickered against her top lip. His other hand cupped the back of her skull and tilted her head back so her spine bowed the wrong way. He leaned over her to twist his head and open his mouth wide against hers.

"Um."

The laughter was actually what registered first. The "um" only did a second later, when she realized there was a thigh between hers and her hand was in the front pocket of Jimmy Wayne's old jeans—well, some of her fingers were in the pocket and some were through the hole in the pocket . . .

"Now, really, kids." Tyler said in mock amusement.

It was Kara that Jacyn saw when she looked around Jimmy Wayne's shoulder. She rested her cheek against the solid muscle of his biceps and blushed. Kara was smiling, fighting laughter.

"I wouldn't have bothered you, but I didn't know if you had money for a cab." If it was anyone else, Jacyn wouldn't have believed a word of that. But as it was, Jacyn was notorious for leaving the house without her wallet or keys, so it was genuine.

"Y'all're leaving?" That was weird. What was

weirder was that their entire party faded toward the cars after she asked that and Kara stepped closer. Jimmy Wayne turned around, keeping an arm around her and held his hair back with his hand.

"Tyler and Avery got into it," Kara said rolling her eyes. Oh well, big shock. Tyler and Avery were always getting into it. Differences of opinion about rhyming schemes, song construction, extended metaphors, whiskey, lint in the dryer. Whatever there was to argue about. Tyler had been a wee bit jealous of Avery's record deal. Avery had been a wee bit insufferable toward Tyler about his record deal.

Jacyn thought about Mariah Partridge and Avery circling in her orbit. "Tyler might be right for once," Jacyn said. Jimmy Wayne pretended to look off in the distance, like an inscrutable cowboy type figure. Kara watched them both closely for a second.

"Okay, whatever's going on, y'all're gonna tell me after I ditch the three-penny circus." Kara inclined her head toward the cars.

"You get back to me when that happens." Jacyn smiled at her.

"So, cab fare?" Kara was persistently nagging when she got at it. The parking lot lights turned the platinum in her hair to yellow.

"We're good, sweetheart." Jimmy Wayne smiled down at her.

"I'm sure," Jacyn said with a dry deadpan. All three of them laughed, not really at the bad joke, but just as sort of recognition of camaraderie, of sharing adulthood in a world pretty devoid of grownups.

Teague and Leon started hollering at each other about flavors of Kool-Aid. Kara rolled her eyes and flapped her hand in good-bye at Jacyn.

"I see your peer group doesn't improve much no matter where you live." Jimmy Wayne smirked down at her and tugged her in closer with his hand at her waist.

"At least my peer group is human, puddin'head." She pulled out her cell phone and hit the speed dial for the Yellow Cab company. Cabs in Nashville were notoriously horrible. Not only did they not show up half the time, but even when they did, they overcharged, took the long way round, and pretty much grifted every extra cent they could out of unsuspecting or drunk fares. Which is why Jacyn had John at Yellow Cab in her phone.

"You take a lot of cabs?" The voice was amused but under it was a dissonant note, of caution maybe.

"You saw my peer group. I've been stranded a few times." The line engaged and as she told John where they were Jimmy Wayne muttered, "Too drunk to drive is what I reckon."

"Where are we going?" She looked up at him and the set of his eyes and his parted mouth answered that question pretty soundly. "The Holly Inn," she told John the cabbie.

Chivalry was always the sort of word that Jimmy Wayne thought people who didn't understand it very well threw around. Chivalry wasn't just opening doors and paying for supper and a movie. Chivalry was always something deeper, something inside, and a way of looking at the world, of thinking. Honor became outdated around the time folks started not automatically looking out for their neighbors like they would their own people. Honor and chivalry go together, like peaches and cobbler. Honor means that a man does the right thing not for any sort of reward. A man does what's right simply because it is. Right is the same as the blue in the sky—undebatable and unfaltering. Right comes before easy or simple.

Jacyn chatted with the cab driver. The guy was a long-haired yahoo smoking unfiltered cigarettes listening to 1970s guitar rock. The cab smelled like ten years' worth of Camel straights. John, though, didn't seem all that interested in Jacyn, didn't seem like he was just working an angle until the night she was drunk and alone to take advantage.

"Yeah, we ran into Karen the other day," Jacyn said, leaning forward on the seat and tapping John on the shoulder. He let out a loud groan and swore.

"That bitch. You know she got custody of the kids

even though she's got that biker sonuva bitch livin' with her up there in Inglewood?" He pulled a long draw on his smoke. Jimmy Wayne assumed that Karen was John's ex. How Jacyn knew her wasn't exactly crystal.

Jacyn pushed a piece of hair behind her ear and smiled back at him. "Karen's John's ex-wife. She lost her cab because she was dealin' crystal meth outta it." She smiled and he felt his honor putting up a struggle.

He told himself when he got his chance with his girl again, he wasn't gonna shoot it in the head before even looking it in the eye. She'd always given off this strange vibe like she believed he wasn't for real about her because of how they'd slept together before the first date. Weren't ever any dates, just sex and a domestic routine, bad things to kill and lots of need on both sides. Old-fashioned didn't suit her, but he'd had a long time to beat himself up and re-think every single bit of their freakin' strange relationship. He'd gotten it in his head that she thought he didn't respect her like he should, treated her like a passing thing, a girl in this particular port maybe. That was the last wrong-headed concept he wanted her deluding herself with. So, he swore when this day unwrapped itself like a lifetime's worth of Christmases, he wasn't gonna just toss her down on the nearest convenient surface and go at it, well, like they always did.

The sign for the Holly Inn reflected off the windows of the cab, the *L*s, one *Y*, and the second *N* were all burned out. Jimmy Wayne laughed, looked over at the pleased as peaches look on Jacyn's face and couldn't help running a finger along her hairline in the front. As good a man as he tried to be, in the end he really was just a good ol' boy, a bronc ridin', weak-willed man who was stupid in love. Love didn't make anything right, though, didn't take back all those months on the road compelled to leave his girl sitting at home thinking she'd done something wrong, fucked up, wasn't good enough.

The cab whipped up in front of the office of the sleazy-ass motel and Jimmy Wayne reached in his pocket for his wallet, but Jacyn whipped out a twenty from down the front of her shirt.

"You tell Kara she still owes me ten bucks from the other night when she puked," John rumbled as he made change. The radio crackled out Bad Company. Jacyn and John ran through some arcane tipping ritual and she slid out of the car with a shimmy and twist of her hips as John watched him in the rearview.

"That girl's special. I don't wanna hear nothin' bad later on, if you know what I mean." John lit another cigarette and looked as menacing as a jackass with a mullet listening to the same music he did in high school can pull off. Jimmy Wayne had seen worse.

"You don't gotta worry about me, son. I'm just as like to threaten you about not tryin' to roll her one night when she's had sixteen or so whiskey and sodas." He stared right back into the mirror. John jerked his head and popped the car into reverse. Jimmy Wayne stepped out of the car wondering if this was just a Nashville thing or if it was something Jacyn inspired in people. She did come off as a little too flaky to manage on her own if you didn't know her well. On the other hand, the South was the South, and a body was just as likely to end up parented by random strangers as having crimes committed on it by them.

The glass door of the motel swung open with a blast of stale, air-conditioned air. A grimy red runner stretched from the front door to the desk with a bald stripe down the center. The desk clerk was a rock chick with a shaggy haircut and a lip piercing. When he moved closer, he saw she also had star tattoos on the inside of her wrists.

"Yeah, I feel that," the girl said with a flat Midwestern accent. She handed over a big, brass key to Jacyn and gave Jimmy Wayne the once-over. He was used to roaming eyes, so he only took notice because she looked totally disinterested. No shy smiles, no ducked head, no fluttery eyelashes. Huh.

"Later, girl," Jacyn said and waved. Her hand slid into his as he gave the desk clerk one more glance over his shoulder.

"Yeah, she's gay." Jacyn laughed right in his face as they stepped back outside. "Shoulda seen your face." He smiled because she was, even though the joke was one him. "Vanity, thy name is Jimmy Wayne Broadus, for real!" She tugged him and he reached for her hair to pull it playfully.

"You seem to know pretty well the lay out of this place." He eyed her as she walked a straight line from the office to their room.

"Yeah, Leon owns this place." The key slid easily into the lock. The other side of the door was not exactly what Jimmy Wayne was expecting. No cigarette-burned carpet and tan polyester bed-spreads and cracked gold-flecked mirror and wheezing air-conditioning. The carpet was a deep green and the walls a warm beige. The bedspread looked like down, an Asian crane pattern in browns and greens. Bracketed into the wall was a shelf sporting high-end liquor. A huge television sat on a wall mount facing the television. Set in both walls were doors connecting the room to the ones on either side. "He keeps some of the rooms set up for himself and his friends to use when they want. Some kind of weird investment scheme."

"You've been holdin' out on me about some-thin'." He whistled. "Also, keepin' your money in your bra is sexy. Keep rollin' with that one."

Jacyn kicked her shoes off and pulled her hair back into a knot, twisting it and pulling the hair through the loop. "Leon's a weird bird. He owns a bunch of stuff, his own sorta financial diversification."

He made a motion with his hand to indicate that she should go on.

"Oh, I've never gotten a straight story about why he bought the hotel, but we have parties over here sometimes. Sometimes I stay here when there're too many people in the house. Kara stays over here sometimes, abandons the house to the riffraff."

Jimmy Wayne would just kick people out of his space with a couple warning shots and a big dog, but this wasn't his show.

"You didn't tell me the witch could do mind control at will," Jacyn said as she opened a bottle of Maker's Mark and poured a couple fingers into a glass. He watched her make him a drink, too, the dark gold of the whiskey throwing shadows against her face where the lamps against the far wall reflected through the glass.

"I didn't know she could." He sipped his drink and sat on the edge of the bed as she disappeared into the bathroom to run water in hers. Everyone'd heard stories about mesmerism and mind control when it came to true witches, but real facts were thin on the ground.

Her glass was empty when she came back out of the bathroom. Jimmy Wayne opened his mouth to ask her what'd happened when she was out of his

sight in the bar, but like he acknowledged to himself
earlier, he was just a weak-ass man. Jacyn stepped
up and knocked his knees closer together by brack-
eting them with her thighs. Leaning down, she
shoved his drink to his mouth. He could be a good
boy. The whiskey went down like a little piece of the
sun. The glass dropped to the carpet and his hand
ran up the back of her thigh under her skirt.

"Yeah," she said, turning her face down to him.

"Yeah, what?" he asked pulling her hair out of
the knot at the base of her head.

"Yeah to whatever. Whatever you need permission for later."

He knew he should pray then, pray for his soul,
because he thought if she asked him for it tonight,
he'd hand it over to her on a gold chain with a kiss
to seal the deal.

Whiskey tastes like the earth distilled, moss and
lichen and the dark, unknown things that live beneath the soul. The color of precious metals, bronze,
gold, copper, it links us to a past most of us choose
to pretend never was and the rest romanticizes. Jacyn could taste the history on her tongue, feel the
chain of lives stretching behind her—reprobates,
settlers, card sharps, people who took risks or who
crawled into a bottle to avoid them. She didn't know
which she was, wicked and wasted or terrified in the
face of change. Maybe she was neither, her choices

made for her by something beyond her, magic or
fate or the Illuminati.

The whiskey tang on the back of her tongue contrasted with the salt on Jimmy Wayne's cheek as she
touched the tip to his skin. Stubble lifted slightly, a
wiry nap that she ruffled as she settled on his lap.
She slid her legs so that her knees rested snug
against his hips. The denim of his jeans was soft
against the backs of her bare thighs, and when she
scooted higher, getting purchase with her toes
against the duvet, the fabric caught the legs of her
panties shoving them farther up her ass.

Withdrawing her tongue, she ran her lips over the
wet place she'd left, back and forth until the tickle
vibrated into her teeth and make her throat close
up, her head fall back. Stubble rubbed at her exposed
neck, too light to burn, but hard enough to bring
pink to her skin. When Jacyn moved to yank her
head away, Jimmy Wayne grabbed her hair and held
her in place in order to trail his open mouth over the
over-sensitive skin, the soft tongue flat between
his teeth caused a minor breakdown, causing Jacyn
to crumple around him. Her arms fell around his
shoulders, his muscles shifting as he moved to hold
her bowed back, giving him access to the underside
of her jaw and her neck.

Abandoning sitting on her knees, she rose up to
rest with her legs around his back. His groan when
they made contact chest to groin sank right into her

jugular, pulsing against Jacyn's eyelids and her fingertips. With one hand, he untangled her enough to pull her shirt over her head, the other hand went under her skirt to rub along the line of her panties in the crease at the top of her thigh and belly.

"Baby." His thumb slid along the damp line until his nail caught on hair tugging slightly. Jacyn didn't know if she'd be able to maintain even the infinitesimal amount of dignity she had if he started talking. Lips right under her ear, thumb just going for it, working between her legs, Jimmy Wayne spilled his tupelo honey voice right into her, down where she'd had a missing piece that changed shape with the words he spoke. "I was gonna try to wait." He shifted and his thumb hit a better position and her head fell so that her cheek rested against his shoulder.

Pepper and sweat and her own soap mingled. She kissed his neck right on the edge of his thin cotton plaid shirt. The fabric was shot through with reflective silver thread. The muscles worked in his arm and she could feel the tension all the way from his shoulder down his biceps to his hand. She knew the front of his jeans had to be soaked through and had to close her eyes when the edge came rushing up all of sudden like vertigo.

"Oh, Jesus Christ," Jimmy Wayne said it for her as she clenched her whole body around him and bit down hard on his shoulder. He fell back and brought her with him.

Rolling on his side to let her legs out from under him, he seemed to decide in mid-motion to keep going all the way so the he was pressing her down into a divot in the fluffy duvet. She hooked one heel over his thigh and let the other leg sprawl on the bed. Green eyes with sparks of gold around blown pupils stared down at her when Jacyn opened her eyes. She was relaxed, but nowhere near finished. Her want when it came to this man seemed to always increase instead of decrease. Tomorrow, she'd be sore and still not be able to keep her clothes on—she knew it like she knew the Gulf of Mexico had a diurnal tide.

He looked so young, no lines around his eyes when he wasn't smiling, caramel flecks over his nose and cheeks, the red in his beard unbroken by white. She felt like it wasn't enough to hold on and keep him here, like there was no way to ever have enough of him. As she tugged his undershirt out of the back of his jeans, his eyes fell closed and his lips brushed hers. Light contact in a back-and-forth motion like her mouth had done over his stubbly cheek. She could feel the indention on his bottom lip, the finer hairs under the full swell of it. Her tongue flickered out to catch his top lip, just barely inside, and he parted his mouth more and thrust his hips against her in a clockwise rotation.

Pulling back so she'd have to lean up, he kept the kiss open-mouthed and her tongue moved over his mouth randomly in tiny licks. His hips moved constantly against her and he dipped and retreated, teasing, his eyes closed, until she grabbed at his too-long hair and sucked his bottom lip into her mouth. Apparently that was enough for him, too. His hips lifted just enough to get his fly open and as she twisted her head to let his tongue in, he shoved her panties out of the way and thrust inside.

"Baby," she whispered into his hair as he pressed his face into the crook of her shoulder and neck. She pressed one heel into his lower back and held down his thigh with the other so that he could only move in small increments, never pulling out really, just rocking deep and deeper.

Stupidity comes in all kinds of flavors, and the worst consequences come from the things that feel the best, that seem the rightest. Jacyn held on as long as she could until the trepidation was stronger than the pleasure and pushed Jimmy Wayne away. He was six foot something of solid muscle and a thin coating if graspable padding and was pretty damned happy where he was, so shoving him off wasn't government work.

"Do you wanna be a daddy?" She pulled his hair hard enough to hurt and he lifted his head to look her in the eyes. His eyes skimmed her face, and his expression was probably best described as content.

"Are you offerin'?" He rotated his hips and Jacyn clenched around him pulling a croak from him.

"Get off, for real." She shoved and he rolled away

with his arm over his eyes. "Before I change my mind."

He groaned. "Woman, would you shut up before this gets six shades of fucked up?"

Jacyn rolled on her side, unsnapping her bra as she went. The bedside table was all rounded edges and brass knob pulls. She pulled open the top drawer to riffle through lube and rolling papers and handcuffs and things people really shouldn't just leave lying around. Jimmy Wayne pressed against her back and his hand fell between her legs over the fabric of her skirt.

"Gonna read the Bible for moral support?" His amused burr made the hair on her arms stand up.

Her fingers slipped across cool plastic packets and she pulled the roll of condoms out with a triumphant "Ha!" When she tried to roll over all the way, Jimmy Wayne held her in place by flipping the hem of her skirt up and pressing his fingers between her legs. She ripped one of the condom bubbles open with her teeth and flicked it at him. His laughter burst inside her belly when he withdrew to roll it on.

Mostly, he had two speeds during sex: slow and unrushed, languid like summer humidity and then there was this—pressing into her from behind fast and hard, his fingers working her like it was a contest. He bit her shoulder blade and whispered too low for her to hear. Clutching at her forearm, the twisting muscles straining under the skin, shifting in time with the strong, blunt fingers bringing her off, she came around him, and just held on to ride this out with him.

Soon, he tensed and collapsed his weight against her back so she had to cock her leg and roll mostly on her belly to keep from cracking her spine. He kept his hand between her legs, relaxed, familiar, and took his time pulling out of her. Somewhere in there, she sort of passed out.

Sleep fell off him like layers of water passing over his head and around his body. Fraction by fraction, Jimmy Wayne became aware of his environment. His leg twitched and arm jerked and he knew he was sleeping. An unfamiliar whir and click of an air-conditioning unit alerted him that he was probably in a motel room. The press of a smooth leg along his side signaled female companionship— Jacyn breathing in and out, her hand twisted in his hair at the base of his neck, finger pressed into the scar he'd gotten in Lubbock from the pastor with a sharp shovel. Even before he opened his eyes, he knew it was still full-on dark, the seemingly still hours of the early morning when very little good was to be found, the streets trickling with drunks and criminals and less human predators.

His skin felt a little too tight where Jacyn pressed into him, her naked skin sticking to his high on his thigh where his body hair faded to nothing, leaving him bare against her bare. Trying to match his breathing to hers, he kept his eyes mostly shut in the dim room and let his thoughts fly away from him in a wide arc like a line sweeping out over open water. Contentment settled into every pore—the good feeling of home that tasted like good sweet tea and the scent of fresh-cut grass on the back of his tongue—and something like fear pricked at the back of his neck. This was what he already thought he'd had before the witch two-stepped her way into their lives and exploded the whole scene like crickets abandoning one denuded field for another. He was terrified of losing it again. Jacyn was that thing no one had ever promised him that Jimmy Wayne had been working his ass off all his life to get. But she wasn't like a trophy belt. Nobody was just gonna stroll up and hand her over to him with a tip of his hat and a wink. The ride, the workin' for it, wasn't enough. Trust wasn't something a man could build when he said "couple weeks" and it turned into months. He couldn't swear up and down and twice on Sundays that all he ever wanted was to sit on the front porch of the ranch house sipping beer out of a can listenin' to Jacyn read the paper with commentary. He couldn't just ask for forever when he had barely managed a few months.

Not that Jimmy Wayne expected Jacyn to be a back at the ranch sorta girl. She wouldn't be left behind again and goddamn it he didn't know how he felt about that. Smarter than a three-piece suit on Easter, quicker than a two-dollar hooker, pretty like bluebells. He didn't know if he could drag her along after things that could do far worse than kill a person. He could risk bruises and stitches, but her soul was something he couldn't rightly be responsible for even if he wanted to be.

Fingers flexed against his scalp, stroking over the keloid hidden under his hair. Skin slid against skin and Jacyn's palm pressed over his belly button, soft fingertips brushing over the hair lower down. This was what he'd woken up for night after night aching in all the old ill-mended breaks in his bones. But he thought it might almost be worse if this was just a passing coupling for her, that she was building her life here in Nashville without him, that she had moved on and that falling into bed with him was just familiar in its own way.

"Tell me about your witches," Jacyn whispered into his arm before leveraging her leg up higher on his thigh, open against his thigh, and gripped his side to lay all over him with her face turned up near the underside of his jaw. His heartbeat jumped in his eyelids and tongue, and his hand came up to rub over his eyes without him consciously moving.

"I only know what most people know." If most people were those acquainted with magic, beasts, and demons.

"Do they steal people's souls?" That was just like her, direct and the punch not pulled, but the answer wasn't some simple yes or no scenario. Childhood fears couldn't be explained in black and white and red in adulthood.

"Depends what you mean by soul and stealin'." A bullshit answer for something of a bullshit question, but that was how Jimmy Wayne's life went. Jacyn whoofed out an annoyed breath. "Hey, don't get like that with me, Miss Priss. I don't make the rules, hell, I barely even know what they flippin' are half the time." His hand came down to hold hers on his stomach, so she wouldn't go questin' any further south while he was tryin' to get through this conversation without letting it slither into the underbrush of open-mouth kisses and stolen breath. "You know all the old kids' stories about witches?"

"Um, no, Cinderwho?" The pleased note in her voice cut the sarcasm. His smile came without his permission, pleased that she was pleased with herself.

"You ever wonder why all those stories were about some evil ol' woman, stepmother most likely, screwin' over some poor young thing who was all sweetness and light?" His voice bottomed out and crackled around the edges. Not enough sleep, too much stress, his shitty lifestyle exposing itself around Ks and Ss.

"Um. Well, not really. Seems sort of self-evident.

The story of youth being coveted by the older generation, the younger one lasting longer in the end to tell the story, history written by the winner. Could also be a parable about procreative destiny, the stepmother wanting to kick the offspring of a previous spouse out of her nest." The last sputtered out around a yawn.

"You think too much, innit good for your brain." Her laughter jiggled them both. "Somethin' like that. Most of them old stories are real. Well, some of it. Can't say how much as I'm hardly an expert. True witches hate one another. They're territorial like wolverines, pulling one another apart the same way, too. Don't much like any other women, human, spectral, whatever ya got. Don't like anyone with any sort of power that can oppose them, neither. They entrap people, trick them, screw them over."

"Huh. So the young ones move into territory occupied by older ones and get up in the old gal's faces and they duke it out until one of them wins? That's the natural order, so makes sense it'd be the unnatural order, too." Clearly, she was thinking about this on several levels, thoughts spinning around faster than his ever did. Jimmy Wayne didn't kid himself about this woman—he was good at what he did, but he wasn't a genius, just well trained. That suited him, worked for him. He wasn't a dull knife, just not Excalibur.

"Somethin' like that, yeah."

"That doesn't explain Avery, the soul-stealing, and the necklace, though." Jacyn sighed on his neck setting off a chain reaction down to his toes.

"Didn't have to, not really. Might not be related." He was about over this conversation in a general way.

"Hmmm." She wasn't sayin' anything else, lips pressed to the shallow dent in his chin, but she was definitely thinkin' it.

He grabbed her thigh and pulled her all the way on top of him, her hips sliding up so she straddled him perfectly, rubbing back and forth making him groan low, deep, rumbling up from somewhere near the bottom of his feet. Lips pressed to his ear and Jacyn's choked breath and broken gasps bled into him like mercury poisoning, his heart beating faster and faster, spreading her through him faster and faster as he slid two fingers up her spine to her hairline. Their hips worked in counterpoint, and his head went back with laughter as he flashed on the last time he'd been this worked up just rubbing on someone, tenth grade in the shade of his daddy's truck on an old beach towel, the taste of Boone's Farm too sweet in his mouth and a promise ring scratching him where Donna clutched at him too hard.

Jacyn broke all over him, her hair in his mouth and teeth tugging at his, breasts shaking with her too-swift heartbeat, her moans verging into whining. His hand on the back of her neck slid all the way into her hair and twisted her head so he could slide his tongue over her lips. The focus of near orgasm struck him with narrowed vision and nothing in his world but Jacyn. His mouth opened and pressed to hers, pulled back, tongue thick and barely working.

"Oh Jesus." Blaspheming was always natural for him, the Lord's name close at hand even when his own wasn't. His left hand slid up from Jacyn's hip and twisted next to the right in her hair, trying to hold her still, keep her face so close that she couldn't see in the darkness her hair created around their faces. "I love you. Oh, god, I love you, baby."

It was all over but the clean up after that. Jacyn collapsed on top of him and one of his hands slid down her back to rest on the swell of her hip.

"That didn't count. Said it during sex," she whispered right before he fell asleep, laughing to himself, exhausted.

Jacyn woke up a second time that night with sore hips lying on her side folded up around Jimmy Wayne who was snoring quietly, one arm draped over his eyes. A slim line of streetlight came through the slightly parted drapes. The strip of weak yellow illuminated a line down Jimmy Wayne's torso in a slash from his shoulder to his hip. Her fingers flashed over the patch, quick though not touching his skin.

A calloused hand caught hers and pinned it to his chest over his heart. "Go back to sleep." The timbre, a whole octave deeper than his usual speaking voice, probably presaged his voice in decades to come.

She went back to sleep.

Third time's a charm flitted through Jacyn's mind as she woke up again. That old saw cut at her a bit, though. Her thoughts jumbled together, and she wondered if there really was some kind of magic embedded in numbers. Three, seven, twelve, thirteen. Numbers floated through her mind like an old Disney cartoon.

"Got coffee." Jimmy Wayne rumbled from somewhere not the bed. Jacyn stretched out like a starfish across the scratchy sheets. She drew a pillow over her head and felt a sheet low on her back and down her legs.

"Arg," she replied, or something like it.

"Was thinkin' maybe we should talk to your buddy Avery about his take on all this." Paper crinkled and Jimmy Wayne said the second half around a mouthful of food. The greasy, pleasant smell of eggs and fried meat filtered under her pillow.

Sitting up, Jacyn didn't bother to cover herself or even run a hand through her hair. Jimmy Wayne sat in the armchair under the windows sipping a coffee from Hardee's in between mouthfuls of breakfast biscuit. "Where's mine?"

He wiped grease from his bottom lip with a paper napkin around a smile. "What you gonna trade me for it?"

Jacyn slid out of bed and snatched her egg, cheese, and sausage biscuit off the table before he could lunge at her.

CHAPTER TWELVE

Jimmy Wayne had cash, which was good, considering she didn't. The morning cabbies weren't her friends, and the guy who picked them up and carried them to Kara's house was a stranger to her, a middle-aged black guy in a Superman T-shirt who was so neutral about picking up a couple who clearly just spent the night having sordid sex in a motel room that his body language screamed "not asking!"

No one was stirring in the house when they got there. Jimmy Wayne swayed into the kitchen to make coffee and Jacyn grabbed fresh clothes and hopped in the shower. The tub in the main bathroom at first seemed to be period: claw-foot tub and tiled floor and walls. But the tub was fiberglass and the tile had replaced the original linoleum. Jacyn stepped under the filtered spray from the special chlorine-eliminating showerhead and tried not to think too hard.

Witches and weirdness she could deal with. Jimmy Wayne, maybe not so much. She wondered what she would feel if he wasn't the best looking guy she'd ever seen out of his clothes. All gold skin and mercurially hazel eyes, long lashes and wide, strong hands. His laughter made her want to toss her life away (again) and run off to herd alpacas or whatever he got up to under the seemingly unending Texas sky. Jacyn had always thought that people who tossed their entire life away for being crazy in love were idiots, or worse, delusional. Every time Jimmy Wayne hiked his jeans up by one belt loop or lifted an eyebrow in sarcasm at someone, she broke in a way she didn't even know she was cracked.

The bathroom door squeaked open and she didn't have to peek out from behind the curtain to confirm that the slightly limping gait belonged to the object of her thoughts. She rinsed the shampoo out of her hair smelling the bitter tang of coffee along with the medicinal Aveda scent of Kara's bath products.

"You're not makin' this nearly as hard as I figure you oughta," Jimmy Wayne said around loud sips of his coffee.

She knew that was true enough. But all the same, she firmly believed his explanation about the witch and the curse. Second-guessing that, she wondered if that made her a love-struck fool. Should she be tearing strips off him and demanding little blue boxes and flowers to make up for the months of self-recrimination and heartbreak?

"Maybe this's a sign. Time for me to give up this gig and settle down." His voice was too steady, practiced neutrality. Jacyn rubbed conditioner in her hair and swished hot water in her mouth to defeat the dry mouth she'd suddenly developed. "Love makes people stupid. It can also make them straighten up their act."

This was pretty much the conversation she'd been terrified of instigating herself. Her feelings felt like they rode on the outside of her skin, like a rash that everyone could see.

"Get to a place where you gotta believe in signs when you do this gig. Maybe the witch fiddlin' with us means we should do something else."

We. Huh. "Like what?" She could be cool about this. She used to be sorta cool, once upon a time.

"Ranch, what else?" He said it like she had a head wound.

"I spent half my adult life in college. Why'd I wanna throw that away to ranch?" She hollered as she squinted her eyes closed and rinsed the conditioner out of her hair.

The metal rings of the shower curtain scraped over the circular curtain rod suspended from the ceiling. Jimmy Wayne popped the button on his fly when she opened her eyes. His smirk let her in on the joke, but she knew it really wasn't one at all.

"I don't know, you tell me what you get outta the deal." His jeans dropped to the damp bathroom floor and he stepped into the tub reaching for her. Twisting an arm over her head, Jacyn adjusted the showerhead to spray him right in the face.

His laughter almost rattled the tiles on the wall, drowning sputters of good humor and pleasure. Thick fingers wrapped around her wrist and redirected the spray over both their heads. Lips moved over the side of her face. "Tell me you don't love me," he whispered.

That was something she definitely couldn't do and make it believable. His mouth moved from her cheek to her ear as she felt as close to passing out as she had since she'd been drunk in college. "I love you." His wet hair clung to her neck as his words vibrated the shell of her ear.

That should have been good enough, but people aren't made of should. People are made of stupid for the most part.

They fell back asleep to the wheeze of the central air struggling through the ancient ventilation system. Jacyn's wet hair was twisted back in a knot and her skin was still damp from the shower when she began to sweat from Jimmy Wayne's body heat. She sprawled on top of the covers, the books and Sharpies, the CD cases and notebooks, asleep almost as soon as Jimmy Wayne pulled her down on top if him.

She woke back up to the sounds of the morning rituals in Casa de Control Alt Delete. The smell of coffee filtered through the wall of the kitchen and someone was singing a Pixies song to himself . . . probably Teague, but the voice was too low to tell. Jacyn thought about not bothering to get up at all, but she knew that would only last until people got curious about her location and just banged on her door to to investigate. Jimmy Wayne released her when she tugged herself away from him, trying not to wake him, but she knew that was a futile battle. He was a light sleeper, naturally or from his training in the weird and wacky, she had no idea. Chicken and egg questions hadn't ever interested her anyway. Jimmy Wayne was a light sleeper, that was all that mattered, not so much how he got to be that way.

Rummaging around in the blended dirty and clean laundry pile, she extracted a kick-pleated denim skirt that came right below the knee, a couple of tank tops (one white, one black) and a black bra. The pile of detritus on the bed shifted and a package of Now and Laters slid to the floor as Jimmy Wayne sat up scratching his belly and shoving his damp hair off his face. Jacyn adjusted the wedgie her underwear gave her as she pulled her skirt up, and then adjusted her tank tops to be minimally unrevealing. The only light in the room came from the small space under her bedroom door and the ambient light from the *Smurfs* screensaver on her laptop's screen. Gray freckles against white skin, dark hair and unreadable eyes flashed at her as the screensaver faded from Gargamel to Smurfette.

Someone banged the metal on the metal in the kitchen and Jacyn swept her hair off her face and redid the bun in her hair. "There're some T-shirts in there you can probably wear."

This whole situation felt the same as ever with Jimmy Wayne—dislocated, strange, and eerily familiar and comfortable at the same time. She didn't feel like she had to explain herself to him, to make awkward conversation about the time that had passed with him god knows where and her alternating crying jags with shooting Tyler's pistol at cans to get out her aggression.

The radio blared in the kitchen, Sirius set to one of the talk stations. This morning's chat topic was about the dams on Lake Cumberland. Jacyn tuned it out and beelined to the dinette where Teague was reading *The Tennessean* and eating toast. Kara sat facing him reading horoscopes from the Internet.

"To get misguided tips about how to invest, check out Henry Blodget's *The Complete Bad Advice Column*. For crabby, mean-spirited counsel about how

to conduct your personal life, listen to Dr. Laura's
syndicated radio show. For silly chatter about trivial
subjects, read the 'most intelligent woman in the
world,' Marilyn vos Savant. But if, on the other
hand, you'd like brilliant guidance about where to
direct your substantial life energy next, tap into
your own intuition. The astrological omens suggest
that it's working better now than it ever has. It's far
more useful to you than any so-called expert's
blatherings." She paused and sipped her coffee
looking up at Jacyn with upturned lips. "Well, hello
there!"

Jacyn rolled her eyes and headed for the coffeepot. Her hippo mug was sitting next to the old,
beatup Mr. Coffee contraption, grounds all over the
counter and dried coffee sloshed in rivulets between
canisters and cups. Since someone else had made it,
Jacyn assumed the coffee was better than any she
could manage to make, so she didn't bother with
creamer or sugar.

"Hey, buddy," Teague drawled behind her.

"Back atcha, chief," Jimmy Wayne answered and
both men laughed in reflected deep rumbles. Kara
snorted in reply.

The floor beneath her feet was clean, free of dirt
or grit or unknown stickiness, which meant one of
Kara's artists had been over that morning to kiss ass
by cleaning. Jacyn hoped another would show up to
cook supper.

"What's your sign?" Kara asked Jimmy Wayne as Jacyn sat her mug in front of him and turned back to the coffeepot to get another cup for herself.

"Uuuuuh."

The paper rattled and Teague laughed to himself. "Just give it up, boy. Learn to give women what they want when they ask directly. All the rest of the time you can pretend to be stupid." That sounded exactly like Teague's life manifesto spelled out concise enough to be cross-stitched on a pillow.

"Libra," Jimmy Wayne said, around blowing on his coffee. He met Jacyn's eyes and she smiled at him. His returning smile felt like something private even in the middle of the kitchen with her yahoo friends sitting there.

"Okay," Kara started while combing her white-and-black-striped hair back from her face with one hand. " 'Ordinary life does not interest me,' wrote Anaïs Nin in one of her diaries. 'I seek only the high moments. I am searching for the marvelous.' Normally I might discourage you from pursuing that approach, Libra. You've got money to make and appointments to keep and groceries to buy, after all. And doing those tasks can make it hard to specialize in the marvelous. But for a limited time only, the planetary powers-that-be are granting you an exemption from the ordinary. More than that, actually: They're *insisting* on it. You need intimate contact with unreasonable beauty, sweet anomalies, beguiling ephemera, inexplicable joys, and small changes that inspire reverence."

Jimmy Wayne's lips compressed and pursed at the same time so that dimples popped out on both sides of his mouth. His eyebrows converged over the bridge of his nose, and his eyes flicked up to Jacyn's face. She figured the expression was consternation verging on anger. He lifted his eyebrows and flickered one in question.

"Mine was about expanding my horizons. I think that Website wants me to have sex with animals." Teague deadpanned.

Kara clicked the mouse on her laptop. "You're claiming you don't already?"

Jacyn laughed and Jimmy Wayne's annoyed face broke up a bit, like a cloud dissipating just enough for sun to shine through the gaps. She was about to make some kind of ill-timed and ill-considered comment about sheep and Mississippi when the outside door banged open. Leon strolled in with Tyler and several other rowdy guys in tow. Jacyn had hardly ever seen Leon in the daytime, and he looked out of place, younger than usual, a little impish with his shaved head and dull red beard and blue blue eyes.

"Gang's all here!" Leon chuckled and raised a hand in salute. Tyler busied himself by tutting over the mess on the counter, futzing under the sink for disinfectant and sponges, and setting to scrubbing.

A couple guys in slouching jeans with black

T-shirts and lots of silver and bead jewelry headed to the fridge and pulled out a couple of beers out of the crisper drawer. They had the good manners to at least offer one to everybody else. Everyone declined and the matching emo boys leaned next to each other against the counter across from the coffeepot and the diligently cleaning Tyler.

Teague folded his paper and took a bite of his jam-covered toast staring up at Jacyn. "You done forgot what today was, didn't ya?"

As a matter of fact, she had no idea what he was talking about. She raised a hand in the air and shrugged at the same time to indicate memory loss.

Leon ducked his head and scratched his forehead above his right eye. "Card day."

"Card *day!*" Tyler echoed with blistering enthusiasm that was really his version of sarcasm.

"Card day," Kara chorused with something like schadenfreude.

Jacyn realized there was no way she was going with Jimmy Wayne to look into this witch situation today. She was gonna be lucky not to be fall-down drunk by nightfall or breaking up a fight in short order. The sigh fluttered out completely involuntarily. Why they kept coming around for her to beat their pants, shoes, and even their hair off, she had no idea. Hazel eyes met hers over the rim of her favorite coffee mug, blue hippos drawing the green and gold out of his irises.

Leon cocked a finger at Jimmy Wayne and said, "Man, you a card player?"

Apparently, Leon wanted something here, which could be interesting. Jimmy Wayne wasn't much of a card player; that was a fact. Much more of a charmer, not so great in the skills department. Good with a bluff, bad with a long game. He seemed to agree, laughing and ducking his head down, his hair falling out of the loose ponytail around his face.

"No, man, I ain't never been good with cards." Unlucky at cards, lucky at love. Which begged the question of why they'd ended up together then. Maybe she was getting ahead of herself and the end of her story wasn't going to be so pleasant for her.

"Unlucky at cards, lucky at love. And all that other *bull*shit." Teague finished off his toast. Jacyn had that weird niggle in the back of her mind when Teague echoed her thoughts out loud, like something more than just normal coincidence was at play.

"Why you do bad at both?" Kara shot out.

"Beat me to my joke!" Jacyn and Kara met each other's eyes and laughed in matched staccato barks. Jacyn noticed that Kara was still in her pajamas (plaid cotton boxer shorts and tank top) and glasses. That pretty much meant Kara wasn't doing much that day.

Leon motioned to Jimmy Wayne. "If you aren't going to play cards with the kids, wanna get some coffee with me?" His tone was neutral, totally calm, but Jacyn knew without having to give it any notice that Leon was up to something. Jimmy Wayne could handle himself, though, and Leon probably just wanted to lay his theories about Masons on somebody new.

"Today's high is expected to be in the low eighties and tonight's low in the mid-seventies," the communications student manning the news desk at the public radio station droned out.

"Sure, coffee sounds good," Jimmy Wayne answered as he leaned back in his seat and smiled bright, throwing off dimples and white teeth.

CHAPTER THIRTEEN

Some folk ignore natural abilities they don't want to be bothered with. Some really can learn to believe some kind of uncanniness is nothing special, just a quirk or something other people don't talk about. Other folks, very few of them, put their abilities to use somehow.

"Huh," Jimmy Wayne said tipping his orange and white 'Horns cap up on his forehead a bit higher.

Second Avenue spread out on both sides of them, stretching down to Broadway and all the tourist spots which rambled along between the Gaylord Entertainment Center and the Cumberland River and back down toward the business district the other way. Jimmy Wayne looked over his shoulder and watched a cluster of fat tourists in too-tight shorts and T-shirts pushing into the Sun Records store. The iconic yellow and black shop looked out of place on the shaded street flanked by old brick buildings and sedate signage. Jimmy Wayne and Leon stood in front of a clapboard kiosk decorated with "spooky" lettering and stenciled tombstones.

"Yeah, it's a cliché, but sometimes they work." Leon shrugged and giggled briefly.

The kid in the ghost tour booth looked down at them with the indifferent, bored look a lot of those touched by the supernatural often affected after years spent scared out of their ever-living minds. "Whatta ya want?" His annoyed toned was clearly directed toward Leon.

The sun caught in Leon's dark red beard picking out the white strands, his hair flaming up into a copper and bronze prism. His companion had a lot more going on than most people chose to see. Jimmy Wayne was reserving judgment as to just what sort of something he was protecting with his conspiracy theories and wackadoodle ramblings. As he adjusted his cap again, the idea that the conspiracies weren't covering anything at all crept up on him like someone else's shadow. The crazy-talk about Masonic shenanigans and government terrorist coverups could very well be genuine.

Jimmy Wayne watched Leon's smile slide off his face right onto the shady pavement. "Whaddya know, kiddo? I wouldn't be here if I didn't strictly have to be."

The boy in the booth was tall, over six feet, smooth-faced and pale with hair that curled around his face and against his neck in that murky middle ground between light brown and dark blond. He looked like a college kid working a part-time job to pay the bills. Which didn't mean squat. Could be a supernatural entity wearing a human suit, could be touched with some kind of sight, could be clairvoyant or third-eyed or possessed.

Leon lit a cigarette, fumbling with his lighter; it took several tries to get the end going. He winked at Jimmy Wayne and ducked his head to indicate the kid in the booth with his chin. The kid shuffled around, back away from the open window and back again. "You didn't hear this from me." The voice twisted up with resignation and weariness, a lot of heavy stuff that a boy barely in his twenties shouldn't even have access to. Jimmy Wayne had been a boy like that once, what seemed like fifty years or better ago but was really closer to a decade.

"I never do," Leon replied with laughter ruffling the surface of his words.

"The spirits are unsettled." The hair on Jimmy Wayne's entire boy stood on end and his nipples hardened. The adrenaline brightened his vision and sharpened his hearing. The boy's voice crackled with dead leaves. Wind blew from inside the kiosk with the smell of mildew and moss, in the distance reedy voices called the names of long dead loved ones.

"You don't say." Leon drew on his smoke with his forehead scrunched up but the rest of his demeanor exactly the same as ever. "What sort of dead?"

The answer to that was obvious. There were only a few kinds of unquiet dead. Most of them fell into the murdered or summoned categories. Jimmy Wayne was willing to bet that Nashville's unquiet dead fell into both camps.

When he gritted his teeth together, a reflex from the stress of encountering the half-world, his teeth scraped dirt. He tasted decay, rot on his tongue. His eyes refused to focus on the boy in the booth right, the form moving slightly, like it was vibrating and a little bit blurry around the edges.

Leon calmly smoked staring into the booth and squinting.

"The dead do not serve the living willingly." The cool, weathered voice fluttered out of the rectangular window and wrapped around Jimmy Wayne with scrapes like broken fingernails over all his exposed skin. He reached up and scratched at his arms furiously, ready to get out of Dodge.

"Yeah, who wants to serve someone else anyway?" Leon flicked his cigarette in a wide arc into the alley behind the ghost tour booth. "Smell like witchery?"

The wooden flap that covered the kiosk window during off hours slapped shut with a loud bang and a mini-tornado of grave-scented air.

"Well, that answers that." Leon giggled and dug around in his pocket in order to withdraw a glass pipe with green peeking out of the bowl.

Jimmy Wayne cut his eyes over him, looked harder, thought about expectations and shaking them off a bit. He unfocused his eyes and watched Leon lighting his pipe and drawing on it. The shape remained the same, but the colors bled together and out of one another again. The smoke from the pipe curled around Leon's head in concentric circles and fell toward the ground instead of up to the sky. Jimmy Wayne blinked, and when he focused back on Leon, the world seemed to have reshuffled itself into a more natural pattern.

"You're a leprechaun." He rubbed his forehead and fussed with his cap until it felt more comfortable. Reaching into his back pocket, he pulled out a can of Copenhagen and stuck a plug between his cheek and gums.

Leon blew sweet smoke right into his face with a high-pitched giggle. "I thought you knew, dude."

His laughter was as bright and green as the marijuana he was smoking.

They walked back to the car in silence with Leon smiling, white even teeth flashing against the red of his beard. The chirp of the car alarm was loud in Jimmy Wayne's ears when Leon hit the button.

Since he was a teenager and he saw a were change outta nowhere for the first time—one minute he's talkin' to the town librarian, the next there's a puma sitting across from him on a wooden swivel chair yawning and blinking self-aware eyes at him—Jimmy Wayne had always been pretty cool with change, with weirdness.

"How come you didn't already know what was goin' on then?" That seemed a reasonable question. How in the ever-loving-hell had Leon not known what was going on from the get-go, and if had, why had he yanked him around like a fool?

They sat in the front seat of Leon's Catera with the air-conditioning cranked up and some bluegrass fiddling noodling out of the speakers. Leon took a few long seconds to blink at him and stare unnervingly into his eyes. The leather seats creaked under his weight as he shifted. "I don't get wrapped up in witches' bullshit, man. Those bitches don't live right."

Live right could mean a lot of things. Jimmy Wayne hadn't known any leprechauns previously.

A few gnomes and other sorts of fey creatures, but every variety had their own rules and behavior patterns. The old stories couldn't usually be counted on for much of anything, the big picture sometimes, sure, like different metals gave some nonhumans serious allergies, and you wouldn't see many vampires in the daytime. But Tennessee was a lot farther east than Jimmy Wayne's usual territory, full of creatures and beings he knew nothing about.

"Are you involved in this somehow?" Jimmy Wayne knew being direct could go either way with supernatural entities.

Leon lit a cigarette and turned the ignition over. "I am *now*." He pulled into traffic with a lazy tap on the gas and a twist of the radio knob.

They drove in silence, back over the arching suspension bridge across the Cumberland River and left down Second Street. Leon parked in a packed lot right off the intersection of three streets. Sweet smoke rushed out of the open door around Jimmy Wayne as he climbed out of the car into the humid afternoon heat. He felt mildly high from being trapped in the car with a heavy pot smoker, a little hungry maybe. The parking lot they were in looked like it serviced a bar later in the day. For now, a steady stream of people trampled back and forth between their cars and the coffee place across the street. Every sort of think-they're-cool idiot swaggered and sashayed across Eleventh Street. Tight jeans, hemp necklaces, sunglasses to protect damaged eyes from hangover-induced headaches, urban professionals in a sort of business casual that was too thought-out to be actually casual. Jimmy Wayne yawned and scratched his stomach under his borrowed, gray Batman T-shirt.

Leon glanced at him over the roof of the car and pushed his sunglasses up his nose. "Could you dig a Mexican popsicle?"

Jimmy Wayne could mainly dig going back to bed for a while. "Sure, man, they got pineapple?"

Leon's high-pitched laugher pulled a surprisingly easy smile out of Jimmy Wayne. He understood that this was part of a game. Leon was testing him somehow, feeling him out, deciding if Jimmy Wayne was an ally worth trusting. He'd done the same himself many times. He could play along for a little longer.

Bongo Java was the sort of trying-too-hard sort of place that Jimmy Wayne associated with middle America. Anything real had been disinfected away in a flurry of appearance over substance. The coffee had cute, rhyming, or punny names. The tables were rickety because they were cheap not because they'd been well-used. The onsite coffee roasting was in the open and affected. He missed cheap coffee from the Circle K. Burned coffee with irish cream creamer was better than three-buck, perfectly roasted brew surrounded by art school fuckwits and people checking their myspace on the free wireless.

"How can you stand this?"

Leon stood on the porch of the coffee shop with a smoke between his fingers, squinting through the plate glass windows toward a clutch of women in tight tracksuits and perfect makeup inside.

"I don't know, dude, people fascinate me." He blew on his coffee and smiled. "It's not like I don't know that coffee is a centrally controlled commodity that's used to oppress workers in the third world and as a shield for government importation of cocaine and heroin."

Jimmy Wayne blinked and narrowed his eyes. Now that he knew what Leon really was, how unreadable the guy was made a lot more sense. He still wasn't sure if the conspiracy theories were for real or not, though. Being the sort of person he was, Jimmy Wayne realized he probably wouldn't ever know.

"Bet Jacyn's taken the guys for all of her drinks for the next millennium or so by now." The giggle was expected. Jimmy Wayne realized he was getting used to this fey.

"Are you leading me on here?" The direct approach worked sometimes, more often for Jimmy Wayne than beating around the bush ever did.

Leon's eyes flicked over his face and landed somewhere over his right shoulder. "Not about Jacyn's kung-fu being mighty fu."

Jimmy Wayne just waited for a few seconds.

Leon's too-blue eyes swerved back to stare right through him. "This is my town. I love Nashville. I don't need anybody fucking with that. Especially people who are killing or binding people who are. I was waiting to see how this would play out. Now I know."

As far as answers went, it existed.

The thing about gambling was that if you knew what you were doing, it wasn't anything like gambling. Gambling implies some kind of risk, like the risk was the biggest part of it, that winning was unlikely. Jacyn's experience had always been something else entirely. Yes, she had her advantages maybe, but it wasn't really about that.

"It's not like a James Bond movie, you know." Jacyn tapped her cards together and pushed her hair out of her face. Tyler watched her with the huge grin that hid his actual feelings. His mask fell in place naturally, the aw shucks dripped off of him like condensation off of a cold beer on a hot day. Bluffing was his forte and probably had been since before puberty. Cockiness that covered insecurity was his liability. Cockiness made him play big when he should fold. Jacyn sipped her beer. Tyler's smile only brightened.

"Jacyn, Jacyn, I know this isn't a *Bond* movie. If it were, we'd be sportin' tuxes and you're be named something even *more* ludicrous."

The two boys in black, whose names Jacyn couldn't remember, both *J* names, looked poleaxed, like they didn't know if they were allowed to laugh or not.

"Just bet the cards, not what you're hoping to get from the dealer." Jacyn rolled her eyes and finished off her Miller Lite.

Teague slouched back in his chair and thumbed a card with his nail. "What's wild again?"

They were playing for chits for drinks because she wouldn't play them for money. Chits with red *X*s were for one drink, chits with purple were for five. She already knew she'd leave the table with enough free drinks to float her on a whiskey river all the way to the Atlantic Ocean.

Tyler's smile wasn't a tell. He wore that sardonic, bitter smile most of the time, but Jacyn already knew how the cards were going to fall in this round. Sometimes the cards sort of talked to her like that. She was holding a hand heavy in red hearts and diamonds, and she was pretty confident that Teague had a three of a kind by the tilt of his head. The new boys were wild cards, but something whispered to her that Tyler was the only one who could actually beat her today. His eyes flickered closed as he tossed two single-chit markers in the kitty with a flourish and a tap of his knuckle on the table.

"I see you and call, Lady."

Jacyn laid her cards out on the table in a neat fan and blew her hair out of her eyes at the same time. "Three queens." She heard something like leaves in the distance rustling against one another

The two black-clad J-boys had a pair between them. Tyler was one card short of a flush. Teague had a full house; he was the stealth opponent in this very relaxed tournament. The more he drank, the better Teague played. Jacyn was sure there was some kind of threshold there, beyond which Teague would start hemorrhaging drink slips like a frat boy dropping necklaces on Mardi Gras.

The air-conditioning clicked on, the register right under Jacyn's feet blowing frigid air on to her bare legs and feet. She wanted to put on pants, to get another drink maybe. She was only half in the room with the boys, her mind mainly focused on Jimmy Wayne and Leon. Coffee with Leon could mean anything. Usually it meant smoking bowls of pot in his car before having a Mexican popsicle at Bongo Java. Somehow, Jacyn doubted that Jimmy Wayne was hanging with Leon smoking up and eating sweets.

They played through five more hands with Tyler getting more and more visibly agitated, Teague becoming less focused, the two J-boys apparently getting bored, and Jacyn struggling to remain in the room. Her thoughts were on the necklace and Avery. She felt like Leon was excluding her for a reason, and that Jimmy Wayne was his knowing accomplice out of some misguided, outdated desire to protect her. She cycled around those thoughts as she idly dealt cards and won hand after hand.

Jacyn scooped the last remaining drink chits from the middle of the table into her massive pile. "What did we learn today, boys?" She didn't bother to actually gloat. It was pointless. Teague had about five pieces of paper in front of him, the other three musicians nothing at all but hard luck.

"I learned that either you've got some kind of mojo going on or the best fucking luck I've ever seen in my whole damned life." Tyler wasn't bothering with his sunshine pabulum, sweetness and light routine anymore. He sat back in his chair with his elbow over the back, long legs stretched out in front of him, one eyebrow sardonically up. For some reason, he was all over Jacyn's nerves.

"If you'd listened to me about betting big when you're looking at the cards in your hand instead of betting on what the next trade would get you, you'd have broke at least even." She'd meant for it to come out light and reasonable, but sometimes she had a hard time controlling her tone of voice, and sadly, this was one of those times.

Tyler shot up out of his chair. "On that note, I think I'll just be off." He swept out of the room in a jangle of car keys and a swing of his hair out of his eyes.

"Great," Teague moaned. He sighed and rubbed his eyelids with a finger and a thumb.

The two boys Jacyn was fixing to start calling Fall Out Boys, looked as blank as ever.

"Hey!" A familiar voice called from the back door. "I thought y'all were gonna call me before you started playin'!" Avery stared back and forth between the table, the little pieces of paper, and each face to the next with good humor. He had a twelve-pack of beer under one arm and his guitar under the other. Jacyn could see the bone necklace peeking out from under the holey collar of his Clash T-shirt.

"Oh well." He ambled toward the fridge and popped the door open. "We got the stuff for sandwiches?"

Downtown Nashville was dominated by the Bell-South skyscraper that stretched thirty-three stories into the sky, rising far and above any of the other mid-range office buildings. Both sides its apex were adored with tall spires, which inspired the common nickname for the building—the Batman building, due to its resemblance to the top of the iconic Batman cowl. Jimmy Wayne had no opinion on Nashville architecture or Leon's crazy thoughts on Freemasonry.

"What I don't cotton on to, Big A, is why you care one way or another about Masons or the Illuminati.

What's it matter to a supernatural creature?" Jimmy Wayne's belly roiled and rocked with foreboding. Witches freaked him out, and, worse yet, he was out of his element in Tennessee, far from backup and any familiar territorial markings.

Leon pulled on his cigarette and squinted at him from the driver's seat of the car. "Whaddya mean *super*natural, dude? I *am* nature! What's not natural about me? Before your kind started raping the land with pesticides and nuclear waste, my kind was skipping around in the woods hanging out, chilling, and eating mushrooms. Happy enough without you."

One of the reasons that Jimmy Wayne tended to avoid any real truck with fairies and other fey creatures was that they tended to think they owned the planet. Pollution and Paris Hilton were every human's responsibility equally. Jimmy Wayne hadn't had much to do with the Bhopal Disaster, and he wasn't about to take responsibility for AstroTurf or Velcro flies on pants, either.

"Hey now, don't get all riled up, I was just askin' why you give two shits about Freemasons."

Outside the car window, Jimmy Wayne watched as a scale reproduction of the Parthenon came into sight on the other side of a wide, green field of grass.

"The Parthenon? No shit."

Picnickers on blankets dotted the field, interspersed with Ultimate Frisbee players and unleashed dogs. The scene was dominated by college-aged couples and clusters of parents with small children.

Leon pulled into one of the many parking lots of the park. Jimmy Wayne had given up getting any kind of answer out of the guy. Most of the fey only lived by human rules if you didn't investigate to closely. They wore the clothes, maybe dated humans, slept with them, and had children with them, but all of that was a masquerade, an elaborate mime like the old Greek plays with masks and strict rules.

Throwing the car into park and snatching the keys out of the ignition, Leon squinted one eye closed and fastened the other on Jimmy Wayne's face. He pointed a long pale nicotine-stained finger at him about nose level. "It never occurred to you that there might be some truth to the numerology and symbology of Freemasonry? You of all people don't believe there's anything to the magic of numbers and signs? How about playing cards and dice?"

The hair on Jimmy Wayne's entire body stood on end and he stared Leon down. "You got somethin' on your mind you wanna share?"

Leon slammed his door open and clambered out of the car. "Nah, not really," he shot over his shoulder. Jimmy Wayne sat still for a few seconds and pondered whether he was ever going to get any sort of answers about Jacyn and her luck. Magicians and the fey weren't ever truly reliable, so he wasn't sure that even if he did get an answer it would be anything close to honest.

Swinging himself out of the car, he noticed that the fine hair on his neck and arms was still standing up. As he breathed in, there was a slight ozone tang to the air, a taste on the back on his tongue that had no name in his vocabulary—something like chili too hot to have a flavor aside from hot, damplike fog so thick it was like a cloud sitting on the ground, acidic like lemon juice in a fresh cut. The air pulsed with magic, no mistaking it. Some of the frolickers out on the green in front of the looming Parthenon even appeared to feel the arcing sparks of it.

Leon lit another cigarette and stepped up next to Jimmy Wayne. "Huh." The cherry on his smoke flared and smoke curled around his face in spiraling fingers. He stepped onto the grass of the field and headed in a zigzag toward the marble anachronism that flickered and stood against the sky like a photographic negative for several long seconds. Jimmy Wayne blinked and the building returned to normal.

Jimmy Wayne felt Jacyn behind him and spun around like a total fool only to find a girl on a blanket staring up at him like he'd lost his entire mind. When he turned back around, Leon was picking his way between blankets and students running on bandy legs. Leon moved in a scuttling motion with his shoulders hunched over and his body jangling in a way that betrayed his nature so that that Jimmy Wayne suspected it was purposeful. He was allowing his true self—his truer self anyway—to shine through the veneer of confusion he projected toward humans at other times.

The sun struggled to keep its head up, the day crashing off the sugar high of early evening into the sleep of true dusk. Purple crept overhead, shoving the blue away for another day, pollution streaking tendrils of pomegranate and saffron around the horizon like a frenzied embrace. The Parthenon sat on a knoll rising out of the far end of the large lawn before it. The columns rose high overhead in a colonnade on all four sides of the building, steps led from the grass up to the landing in front of the building. Jimmy Wayne climbed each stair with growing trepidation, watching as Leon nipped in between the massive wrought-iron doors at the top of the stairs. The ornate metal twisted in patterns Jimmy Wayne couldn't make out in the dim light. The spotlights on all four sides of the building were either not turned on yet or blacked out on purpose by the creature he was sent here to confront. He felt manipulated, his pride twisting up and in on itself, anger folded up around the impulse to protect Jacyn from something that might not even be a threat to her. Even the tiniest mote of a possibility that some supernatural force might harm his girl made Jimmy Wayne willing to toss himself on whatever sword was presented to him.

The iron of the doors was pocked under his palm, cracked and repainted countless times. The interior of the monument flickered with shifting blue and green light past the barely cracked inner doors. At the far end of an open space of around a hundred feet stood a forty-foot statue of a figure that was bound to be Athena. Jimmy Wayne took little notice of the statue. The gold gilding and fine details must be pretty for the tour groups and tourists, sure, but they held no appeal for him. His focus fell immediately on the shimmering nexus of shifting and shuddering light right in front of the statue.

Sliding into the room bit by bit, wary and acutely aware that he had no backup, no escape route or contingency plan, he prayed to Jesus and any saints who felt so inclined, that Leon wasn't on the side of the Devil here after all. Jimmy Wayne watched Leon stop right in front of the pile of shimmering lights weaving over and among themselves, the cigarette smoke adding texture as it passed through the kaleidoscope of what looked mostly like water seen from below—the rolling, shifting green-blue-green of the ocean from five feet under the waves. Leon stuck a hand on his hip and turned his head to look over his shoulder toward Jimmy Wayne as he motioned with his cigarette for him to hurry.

Drawing up on the wide expanse of floor before Leon, Jimmy Wayne was beginning to pick out shapes in the light show. Each ribbon twisting among the many, forming an ever-shifting hill that collapsed on itself into a large flat mass, and then rebuilt itself wraith by wraith, had the face of a person. Mouths wide open in eternal screaming maws, eyes blinking tears or squeezed shut in painful grimaces, each stretched out the normal human shape into something frightful and horrible.

Leon flicked his smoke with a snap of two fingers into the darker area of the room.

"What the hell is this?" Jimmy Wayne had seen some screwed up shit—weres who ate their young, shape-shifting critters that peeled their own skin off, genderless fey. Fear held him in place before this spectacle, though, because he knew instinctively that these were souls in thrall. He'd never seen hide nor hair of something like this, but some fairy tales were older than humanity, some whispered fears sit right in people's belly like a stone waiting to expose themselves. He glanced around the room, searching the shadows for the thing that had done this, fear so vital and real he could smell his own sweat and hear his own heartbeat in his ears.

"The souls of murderers." Leon raised an eyebrow at him, his face unreadable. The good-natured hippy had hid himself outside this room. Jimmy Wayne looked into the face of an unknowable creature who might be older than the English language, older than the sand on the beach of the Gulf of Mexico. "Do you pity them?"

Jimmy Wayne had survived for as long as he had because he wasn't rash. He didn't run willy-nilly into the mouth of the beast with guns blaring and revenge in his heart. He did what he did because there weren't anyone else to do it. Sometimes he dispatched creatures reluctantly, sometimes with righteous dispassion. Jimmy Wayne's game here was all about Jacyn. He'd come to Nashville compelled by some outside force playing games that humans couldn't ever hope to comprehend in earnest. He'd been manipulated and jacked around and gotten a second chance all the same. This witchy madness had nothing to do with him other than what did—Jacyn being at the end of his rainbow, waiting for now but that wouldn't always be the case. He had to turn this around to his advantage just enough to get out from under the notice of one witch or another.

"I have no feelin' one way or 'nother about someone who gets what they deserve." Drawing a hand through his hair, Jimmy Wayne averted his eyes. Weren't never no shame in knowing that the supernatural weren't your equal. He watched one ghost spiral along the floor, blue light white on the edges, as it crept back into the fray to disappear between two green shades. "Are they gettin' what they deserve?"

Leon made a clicking wheeze in the back of his throat. "Who cares? All I know is that this bitch isn't going to come to my town and set up a soul-battery to fuel whatever bullshit agenda she's got. Bad enough that cell of Illuminati moved to Murfreesboro."

Jimmy Wayne let the Illuminati thing go. No reason to poke the beast with a sharp stick. As long as they were getting out of there alive, that was all that mattered. Behind them, the iron doors moaned low and loud as someone opened them farther.

"Hello?" A high tenor called out. Jimmy Wayne recognized the voice. "Is this some kinda joke?" A reedy, nervous laugh brought the gooseflesh out on Jimmy Wayne's whole body.

Leon lit another cigarette. "Tyler, man, you have even less sense than I thought."

He sighed, expelling a thick bellowing of gray. Behind him a new wraith slid into the morass of bound souls, its eyes wide and staring with shock. Jimmy Wayne recognized Avery with the sort of cynical finality that made him feel ancient.

"The hell," Jimmy Wayne heard Tyler say from the doorway. He whipped his head around to watch from across the vast expanse of the arcade as Tyler touched the necklace now surrounding his neck. The shadow of the statute of Nike sitting in Athena's outstretched hand fell across on all three of them.

CHAPTER FOURTEEN

People use the word *luck* in a lot of different ways. Some use it interchangeably with kismet or destiny—a person's luck is like a guardian angel. Gamblers and risk-takers of every stripe tend to use luck in a personal way, almost always with a possessive adjective attached to it—someone's own luck, the luck of a companion or a rival to shake a head at in wonder. Most often when people talked about luck, what they meant was some sort of amorphous net that covered the world, an attribute to be ascribed when something marvelous or surprising happened, a near death escape or lottery win. Jacyn had always thought of luck in that way, a way to frame the world for people who didn't want to ascribe good fortune to God or fate. Luck was a random thread people sewed into their lives to make the chaos understandable.

Some days, though, Jacyn had to admit that she'd generally left the table richer than poorer, that she often got the good piece of pie or the super discount coupon at the boutique. Sometimes, rarely, but it happened, her run of good luck seemed to affect those around her.

The kitchen rumbled and clattered around her with pleased men in good humor for no other reason than they were young, a little silly, and slightly tipsy. She rinsed a glass in the sink and wondered what Jimmy Wayne and Leon had gotten up to. Not a whole lot of good, probably. The glass between her finger and thumb was slick, the smell of the caramel-scented dish soap strong, the whooping of the boys hard to resist. Her phone vibrated in her hip pocket. Wiping her hands on the front of her shirt, she fished the rectangle of black plastic and metal out and flipped it open.

"H—" she began, but the noises emanating out of the receiver were clearly not chitchat. Loud bangs and the sound of wood scraping against something—probably concrete—was overlaid by several voices. The loudest was Tyler's.

"Hey now, let's not be too hasty!" His nervous laughter had Jacyn turning around and snapping her fingers at Teague and Avery, who were saluting each other with their beer bottles over and over, glass clanking against glass and their resonant voices raised in mirth.

Teague's eyes were mostly hidden under his bangs, but his mouth closed around a small smile. Avery rolled his eyes and tossed his shaggy brown hair from his face. He leaned with an arm over the back of his chair. The two emo boys sat silently picking at their shirt hems and looking washed-out, like water-colored people in a room full of Fauvism.

A low hissing spun around Tyler's voice on the other end and his laughter stumbled out into heavy breathing and background sound.

"Do you have a dream?" A female voice fluttered down the line, something horribly familiar about the tone, but with the vowels stretched out wrong, the consonants jumbled up together like felt letters fallen off a kindergarten board. Jacyn's pulse beat in the back of her mouth; her blood pressure bottomed out and she swayed.

The smell of hops and cedar soap and the feel of a large hand wrapped all the way around her forearm, a palm against her back, freeze-framed through her mind, one piece snapping into place fast before it faded and her mind moved on to the next sensation. Soft cotton, a rumbling voice, a higher-pitched voice in the distance, fingers on her face. A sudden shock of cold against her lower back brought the world into sharp focus. Teague smiled down at her and moved back slightly from where he was propping her up to show her the condensation-covered beer can.

"Wakes ya up, huh?" His smile was wilted around the edges, a facsimile of the real thing. His worry sat between them in the slim space between his large body and Jacyn's more average one.

"Tyler . . ." she started, but she didn't want to explain the witch and Leon and the merry-go-round of hobgoblins and snake-women and child-eating that was her current life.

"Misdialed your number." Avery's cracked-gravel voice answered. The motion of his hand drawing through his hair caught her eyes. "Is in dire peril, yadda." He lifted one eyebrow and managed to look ancient in his Ramones T-shirt and Chucks. The necklace ringing his neck peeked out of his collar, reminding Jacyn of a noose or a garrote.

The overhead compact fluorescents in the kitchen cast everyone as a grayer version of themselves, like the preview of their shades in the underworld.

"You knew?" Jacyn croaked out weakly at Avery.

His face moved through several emotions, denial, annoyance, aggravation, guilt. His arms came up to begin his normal cycle of frantic gesturing. "I mean . . ." His head bobbed. "There's knowing and there's *knowing*, you know?"

The easiest answer to that would be no! But it would be something of a lie. We all live our lives ignoring the little niggles that make us suspect the bubble we've made for ease of use in this world was constructed on quicksand and swamp. Ignoring is simple. Ignoring the indications that your lover is cheating allows you a stable relationship. Ignoring the desperation of others around us allows for a streamlined society. Ignoring death allows life to be livable.

"You think Tyler . . ." Jacyn didn't have any doubt that he had gone off in a fit of pique and enrolled himself in the Big Soul Scam of the century. The road to hell had to be at least lined with the souls of ambitious young men with more pride than sense.

Teague pulled her against his side subtly and tilted his body so that he interposed himself between Jacyn and Avery. "Soooo." He flipped his hair out of his eyes. "Couldn't resist the easy way out, huh? I gotta admit, the easy way is like one of those Bible illustrations with wide lanes and flowers all along the sides. Pretty as a black-haired girl in a red dress."

Jacyn lifted an eyebrow. Her mind clicked, wondering if Teague had turned down the same deal Avery had accepted, if he was some kind of supernatural creature (which would explain his looks), how everyone always seemed to know more than her, and if Kara knew about all these shenanigans.

"It wasn't like that!" Avery shouted, becoming

more animated, beginning to pace back and forth in front of the dinette where the two boys in black looked on with bored expressions. "You don't understand! Everything comes easily for you!"

Jacyn shoved Teague away softly with her elbow and stepped away from him. Teague, left to his own devices, moved to the middle of the room with his back to Jacyn and front toward Avery, sticking his hands in his front pockets.

"Ambition and jealousy are the ruin of man," Teague sighed and shook his head. Avery stopped pacing and turned in a tight circle on the ball of his foot.

"What?" He looked much the same as he did when Jacyn and he discussed politics or philosophy, interested and focused, not unhinged or deranged.

"Well, it's like this, you know: There's always an easier way, magic or intrigue or nepotism. The rewards are more important than the journey. Man, haven't you ever listened to the Buddha? You gotta let all that bullshit go and learn to live without desire." Teague's voice filled the room from the ground up, like a flood working in under the doors and through the cracks in the foundations of the house. His voice pressed the air out of the room and made oxygen precious.

"What?" Avery said again in a confused, faint voice. "What?"

His necklace began to glow, pearlescent energy

pulsing in small coronas around each of the matryoshka-shaped beads. The lips of the small shock waves began as a bright white and became bluer and bluer, with Avery's face lighting up from beneath, giving his flummoxed expression a wry cast. His eye sockets fell into total shadow, black voids where his brown eyes had been seconds before. The shadow from his nose angled straight up in a line over his forehead bisecting his face. As Jacyn watched, the shadow widened and Avery's mouth faded to black, like his eyes.

He didn't scream or speak as the glow from his necklace became an imploding nova and he blipped out of the kitchen head first. One shoe clattered to the ground as air flooded into the space his body had been occupying microseconds previously.

"Um," Jacyn said.

"Man, I'm tripping balls," one of the kids in black muttered to the other.

"Totes, dude," the other replied.

Jacyn stood in the kitchen contemplating her options. She didn't really see all that many. Teague and the two card-playing, black-clad boys sat out on the porch leaving her and Kara alone in the kitchen. Jacyn's first call had been to Kara.

"I'd assume you were insane, but that just gets me to having to deal with you being crazy." Kara sipped a Pabst and blew her hair out of her face. "Something about this feels . . ." She trailed off. Jacyn watched her for a few seconds as Kara looked out the window in the door to the back porch.

"True?" Jacyn could substitute a bunch of other words—nuts, disturbing, depressing—but that moment didn't feel like the time. Jimmy Wayne was on his way back to the house with Leon and Tyler in tow, and that felt ominous, like the rise in barometric pressure before a storm.

"Avery's music changed almost overnight." She sighed. "That's not an exaggeration. Maybe it was a week? I don't know. A very short time. But it's art, you know?"

Jacyn didn't say anything. She got it. Art was art. Sometimes people stumbled onto genius. Jacyn had the suspicion that art and inspiration were words that filled in the blanks on a lot of supernaturally influenced scenarios. Music was an old theme in fairy stories, witches and elves were always attracted to musicians and poets and artists. Jacyn knew an old explanation of that was that nonhuman creatures couldn't create, only consume. She somehow felt that was a human self-inflation. Being the only creatures with the ability to create art would put something of a pretty spin on being moral—bright, bright stars that burn out too swiftly but are all the more beautiful for art. Something hollow rang there, like the rationalization was too close to the surface. The lie was too evident. Easy answers often came with false dichotomies. The equally likely alternative, that humans were the prey of supernatural creatures and were fragile and in constant peril, wasn't as romantic but seemed more in line with the rest of reality.

Life was precarious at the best of times when all humans had to survive was disease and war and technology. The supernatural world seemed unfair on some level, like loading the deck. How were people supposed to get by when they could be ensnared in a witch's trap when they didn't even know witches existed? Had humanity wished away belief in the things that preyed on them, leaving them completely exposed to the predators, not even knowing something circled in the dark, at a disadvantage that no other animal endured?

The back door banged open and Teague stood framed, backlit by the yellow porch light, his face unreadable and shadowed. "Y'all ready for this?"

Clearly whatever he had to say was pretty horrible. Teague rarely went serious, using humor to diffuse and charm. Kara tensed and the cigarette in her hand shook like she feared the worst. Jacyn wasn't sure what *the worst* even meant anymore. She tried to picture Jimmy Wayne hale and hearty and in one piece, but instead kept dredging up a horrible image of him with a black eye and long line of blood down his cheek.

"The cops just found Caroline's body." Teague

brushed a hand through his hair leaving it standing on end like a cockatiel's feathers.

"What do you mean found her body?" Kara never sounded anything but grounded during a crisis, always the adult in the room no matter what the situation. Jacyn barely knew Caroline; her first thoughts were for her parents. Dead, so young. Just like so many others, which is what made the situation tragic—because it was just so commonplace.

"Well . . ." he sighed. "They found her buried in about a foot of dirt out behind the Kroger."

Jacyn's stomach dropped to the floor.

"Just like his songs . . ." Kara voiced Jacyn's thought.

"Pretty much." The screen door banged closed behind Teague as he faded back out onto the porch.

Kara stubbed out her cigarette and blew the last drag of smoke away from Jacyn. "My feelings are at best conflicted."

"Yeah, there's not really a correct response to finding out your friend's been ensnared by something evil and done something evil in turn." Jacyn used to have the sort of life where watching *Cops* was about as close as she came to crime. Now she was hardly even rattled by cold-blooded murder. She felt compassion and regret for Caroline, even felt sadness that Avery's ambition had been so intense that he would be willing to trade his life—or his soul—for fame. But she wasn't surprised. Becoming cynical felt oddly natural, like this was just the next normal stage of life.

Her phone rang, vibing first and making her just about jump out of her skin. She pulled it out of her pocket and flipped it open. "Are you alright?"

"If all right means alive and in one piece, yeah." Jimmy Wayne sounded tired, worn out. "If it means happy, then fuck no, I'm not."

When Jimmy Wayne was pretty young, eleven or so, he trained for most of the year for a calf-roping contest that seemed to be his entire world. He practiced between chores and after school, every waking moment he could get away. He roped the couch and the dining-room chairs, the dogs who snapped and nipped his hair in response, and once, memorably, his mama. Three days before the competition, he took a bit of buckshot in the thigh when he was out duck hunting with his daddy. It was only much later that he realized that "duck hunting" was really just practice for his real life's work, many rodeos later, and many pieces of metal in his flesh later.

"It's not fair!" Jimmy Wayne said, laid up in bed with seventeen stitches and some seriously bruised pride. Even as the words spilled off his tongue, tripping on a whine, he knew that was the worst possible thing to say. He knew there weren't no such thing as fair, knew that only babies screamed and blubbered about fair.

His daddy sat there on the edge of his bed, tattered Wranglers stretched across his thighs, faded plaid shirt over a stained white T-shirt, and pulled his hat off. Gazing out Jimmy Wayne's bedroom window, he wiped an old kerchief over his dark hair and sighed. "You're damned right it ain't fair, JW."

At the time, Jimmy Wayne thought his daddy was old as Methuselah, ancient like bleached steer skulls and the Mariah, but when he remembered that day later, he always laughed to think how young his daddy had been then. Less than thirty-five, barely a gray hair on a head that eventually became full-on steel gray later in life.

His daddy looked away from the window and dead into Jimmy Wayne's eyes. "Is it fair when no rain comes and a family loses their livelihood or when a snake takes a child or when the Lord doesn't listen to your prayers?" Jimmy Wayne didn't know if his daddy really wanted an answer. He thought hard, scrunching his face up and really *thinking* on it. His daddy's hand came down on his arm, thick, scarred fingers and banged-up gold wedding band. Jimmy Wayne was comforted by being so close to his daddy, his family, like the in-out of his own breath in his lungs. "Life ain't fair, but sometimes a man can try to make it more so."

Standing in the bullshit mock-Parthenon on a spring evening in Nashville, Jimmy Wayne thought again about fair and how mostly fair ain't got much to do with any human's life.

Tyler held up his hands palms outward in the universal expression of denial, shaking his long mop of hair and making scared kitten noises. "Hey now, no one said anything about immortal souls and murder and stuff like that."

Leon let out his uncanny, high-pitched giggle and lit a smoke. "Didn't anyone ever teach you to be afraid of running into traffic or to look out for snakes in tall grass? Some things go without saying after you've already been warned over and over."

"This isn't fair. Don't you gotta actually *sell* your soul to sell your soul, if you know what I mean?" Tyler looked from the writhing wraiths behind Leon to Jimmy Wayne and Leon. Jimmy Wayne really hated it when people got all flippant when they clearly needed some serious saving from something highly retarded they'd walked into on their own. The air tasted like eternity, full of dark promise and some taint without a name. He felt old and tired. Tired of little boys who should know better and how there never were no victimless crimes when it came to the supernatural.

"What did you think were gonna trade for instant fame and endless ass?" Jimmy Wayne almost snatched the smoke out of Leon's hand and started puffing. There always was a lot of stupid to go 'round in the world, but rich kids with a sense of entitlement really set him on a low boil. Why was he the one who had to put his ass on the line for some kid whose worst experience had been having to shop at the outlet mall instead of at the boutique shops? How do you explain the endless unknowable to someone whose concepts of the arcane were shaped by The Count from *Sesame Street* and Anne Rice novels? This was the whirlwind that the world was creating by taking all of the wonder out of the world. When science explained away ghosts and revenants and a school kid could recite the periodic table like his peer a hundred years before could have recited the Bible, then there were gonna be a lot of casualties at the hands of the paranormal. Tyler and his ilk were nothing but good eating for the evil things in the world. Right that second, Jimmy Wayne felt like throwing them into the shadows with a steak wrapped about their necks for the risk that had come to Jacyn. He knew that was irrational, but irrationality was a huge part of being human. Goddamn it.

Tyler looked defiant, bitchy, and confused in equal measure. Jimmy Wayne had little pity to spare, but this kid wasn't really doing his all to solicit it.

"Hey, man, as far as I'm concerned, you can lay in the infernal bed you made, but mainly I want your sugar mama outta Nashvegas. So pony it up, where's the cunt who promised you a major label deal?" Leon had his own style, and Jimmy Wayne could appreciate that. If he got results, that would be that.

"She said she had some business in Knoxville and to come over here . . ." He shook his arm out to look at his watch face, which was illuminated with a press of a button on the side. "About now."

And wasn't that ominous? Leon ducked down into a crouch with one hand balanced on the marble floor. Jimmy Wayne craned his neck back to look up at the ceiling. The wraiths wove in and out of one another, not seeming to be aware of any looming conflagration. In and out, in and out, blue over green over blue, elongated faces set in gaping maws of silent screams. They gave off a light like ripples reflected on glass through water, ominous and oppressive. Jimmy Wayne didn't want their light to touch him.

The beads on Tyler's necklace began to glow, one bead at a time, starting with the oval resting in the indenture at the hollow of his throat and working counterclockwise. As each bead brightened, one of the ghosts in the pile flew across the room in a wide arch, the spirit twisting and bobbing and flipping over like a seal in a pool. They circled Tyler five times each widdershins and disappeared with a shower of green or blue glitter into a bead. *Zip*, *zip*, *zip*, staring eyes and wide open mouths zoomed across the hundred-foot-long hall in wide arcs to disappear at they smashed into the stunned-looking kid in Converse and a thrift store blazer. Jimmy Wayne looked on with growing fear. This was uncontrolled, unknown. Since Jacyn was the pivot for this in so many ways, he was damned sure somehow this was going to backfire on her again.

When the last wraith wrapped around Tyler's throat and vanished into its bead, Leon let out a long whistle. "Guess we just gotta lop your head off and smash the necklace then!" he said with enthusiasm.

"What?" Tyler's high-pitched panic rattled Jimmy Wayne's fillings. He wiped a hand over his head and let out a long sigh. The kid's hand shook hard enough to be visible from yards away.

"He's just yankin' your chain." Jimmy Wayne glanced over at Leon and lifted an eyebrow. Leon returned the gesture with a smirk. "I think."

"What?" Tyler screamed.

The marble and metal were still eerie, lit by the security lights set in the floor, now that the otherworldly glow of the spirits were gone. The bad mojo still vibrated through the space. Jimmy Wayne thought it would be a very long time before the Parthenon was cleansed of what had transpired there that night and probably many nights previously. His thoughts tripped over the witch and what her new plan was. He had no doubt that this wasn't the end of her games.

Mainly, he was exhausted.

The headlights of Leon's car strobed in the front bay window elongating and bending the shadows of the people slung in chairs and couches in Kara's living room. Unsurprisingly, the first person through the door was Leon, who smiled like the imp he was and shook his head in a way that probably indicated something profound or nonsensical or both, and bypassed the room altogether for the kitchen. Tyler followed a few ticks behind with a new accessory, his skin pale like a corpse except for streaky pink high on his cheeks. Jimmy Wayne slammed the door behind him, feet scuffing on the old, worn boards of the floor, his flip-flops smacking against his feet. He had his hat in his hand, as he came into the room brushing his hair back off his forehead. Tyler followed Leon, his head down and shoulders hunched in on himself. Jimmy Wayne twisted his head to the side to crack his neck and stared Jacyn down without blinking.

"Your boy's got some bad times comin' ahead if we don't figure out how to get that necklace off him." He knocked his hat against his leg for emphasis, dust exploded out of the brim.

Teague sat still with his hand propped on his chin and Kara looked to Jacyn. Suddenly, Jacyn felt old and terribly young at the same time. She should be chilling in the backyard eating corn on the cob and shooting the shit with the neighbors, her biggest worries a mortgage or a car payment, not supernatural forces from out of kids' books. She should have a parent to hold her hand, to look after her, to advise her, someone who could make this all go away or instantly better with a cookie and a glass of milk. Instead, she got up out of the old, battered wing-back chair Kara refused to send gently into that good night and stepped up to Jimmy Wayne. He raised an eyebrow and half-smiled, displaying a dimple in his right cheek, his hazel eyes darkening to brown in the dim light of the house. Her hand slid to his lower back, the deep furrow of his backbone between the muscles on either side almost made her sigh.

"Ok, who needs a beer?" She tugged on Jimmy Wayne's shirt and hauled him along with her. She realized that without a parent at hand, she was turning to Jimmy Wayne automatically for comfort, to ease her with a hug or a hand in her hair.

The kitchen was deserted. The porch light was on behind the house and the *zip-zip* of the bug zapper sounded over the ambient hum of the refrigerator. Jimmy Wayne's arm came around her side and he let out a long, low *hmm*ing sigh. She felt the same inside, comfortable to have him press against her after the stress of the night—of the last year. In a world with no answers, where witches could trick impressionable young men into murdering for personal gain, you had to cling to what little hope you could scratch together.

"It's too bad your luck don't extend to people around you, kiddo." Jimmy Wayne brushed Jacyn's hair out of her face as she turned to look at him.

Her "luck" had always been more of a superstition to her until she'd met Jimmy Wayne. It was a simple shorthand to explain the weird confluences of events that happened to her for good or ill—four hands of blackjack in a row or her ex leaving her for a younger model, meeting up with Jimmy Wayne after a one-night stand or him being cursed into abandoning her. She'd never really meant anything by it, but lately so much had been strange in more than a simply passing way. But her glimpses of luck, her feeling that it wasn't such a passing thing, had been growing and growing since she'd know Jimmy Wayne.

"Do you think maybe I can?" She stepped away from him, his salt and soap smell fading, leaving her sort of deprived.

She'd known since he'd shown up in Mississippi, pretty much immediately on meeting him for the second time, that Jimmy Wayne used his pretty, thousand-yard stare to cover how quick-witted he really was. This wasn't a fool or just a farmhand, all molasses slow thought and hobbling preconceived notions about the world. This man was a lightening strike, a blade in the dark, a flash flood.

"That maybe that's why some certain witchy someone might not want you in play in this deal?" She could tell that Jimmy Wayne was seven steps ahead. More than that, she could feel something in the air, like a spark, like ozone heavy in the back of her throat—similar to the way she felt playing cards on a good roll, at a craps table with the dice tumbling her way, or the few times she'd bet at the track, with her horses placing, showing, and winning. The world clicked into place with something near an audible snap that was more metaphor than descriptive. Like opening your eyes after they've been shut and realizing *I can see*. Or taking earplugs out of your ears, that first onslaught of untempered sound.

The kitchen seemed brighter, white bright, and everything out of her direct line of sight faded to a black corona of nothing, holding her bright world together like surface tension on a bubble. The *something more* she felt increased and she let it bank and amplify until she was thinking six moves ahead—outside, Tyler on the step, necklace in her hand, floating up and away far away into the sky up, up, up, and south the air currents calling.

She didn't remember walking outside or how the necklace ended up fisted in her hand. The calculating look on Leon's face as he stared at Tyler's prone body lying half on the porch and half hanging off, limp and fragile-looking, moored her back in her body. Jimmy Wayne's hand around her wrist hurt, bruising—she could feel the capillaries bursting and knew the imprint of his hand would be there for weeks maybe. His eyes were what held her down, though, pinned her right in place with direct reproach.

"What . . ." *What happened? What did I do? Is Tyler alright?* Leon pushed Tyler's hair off his forehead with the hand holding his cigarette and sort of grunted.

"He'll be fine. Just in shock from having the magic ripped out of him." He looked up at Jacyn with his usual half-deranged smile. "Man, you had one hell of a masking spell on you, Jay, because I didn't even sense you!" Leaping to his feet he threw his arms over his head and let out a whoop. "I mean, you gotta get up pretty early in the day to pull one over on me, but you managed it." He paused and pointed his cigarette at her as he blew smoke out of his mouth. "But it wasn't you, was it? Nah. You didn't know, right? But you know those old stories, wicked stepmoms and princesses, you know?"

"No," Jacyn said faintly. She wasn't negating what he was saying or disavowing knowledge, either. She didn't really know what the hell to say. One minute she was standing in the kitchen thinking about her luck and the next she was standing outside with some kind of evil whatever in her hand. She looked down and realized it wasn't in her hand anymore. Leon and Jimmy Wayne both followed her line of sight to find the necklace was now a triple-stranded bracelet around her wrist. "No," Jacyn repeated, her luck turning now, like it always did. Something good traded for something horrible.

"With great power comes great responsibility and

all that garbage." Jimmy Wayne slid his hand up her arm gently until it rested on her elbow. The look on his face didn't tell her much, his work face, stern and thoughtful.

"*Spiderman*? Really? Your girlfriend's a changeling and you're quoting Spiderman? Weak." Leon lit another cigarette.

Jacyn touched the beads against her wrist, held them up to the light. Iridescent gold and purple over red glass. She knew her luck had definitely turned in some direction, but she didn't know which way yet.

EPILOGUE

Iced tea on a hot day has a special taste, flowery and complex, like actual plants, sunshine and photo-synthesis and dirt. Jacyn liked her tea barely sweet, just sweet enough to take the bitterness out of the drink, but not sweet enough for it to be properly sweet. Jimmy Wayne always put two packets of Splenda in his tea before drinking it. He stood in the kitchen of the house his granddaddy built, looking out the window over the kitchen sink with its red-and-white-checked curtains, drinking his super sweet tea out of a thin, clear glass with yellow, half-rubbed-off polka dots on it and watched Jacyn in the yard talking to the UPS guy. The deliveryman wiped the back of his hand against his forehead as Jacyn signed for her package; his hair was plastered to his head from the heat. Jacyn had her hair up on top of her head in some complex arrangement that allowed enough strands to escape that she had curls tucked along her hairline in the front and back. She was dressed for work, in a light blue cotton sundress that wouldn't have looked out of place fifty years before. Her work wasn't animal husbandry or tending their garden patch—but she pitched in when they needed her help.

The screen door banged open and Jacyn slammed the inner door with her foot as she crossed the room to the drawer with the knives and scissors in it. Jimmy Wayne followed and stood behind her, close enough to peer down at the return address. The brown parcel paper was stained, the return address smudged into illegibility.

"Who's that from?" He rattled the ice in his glass and tipped it up to get a piece to nip off and chew. Jacyn cut the packing tape on one end of the parcel and struggled a bit when he wrapped an arm around her waist to pull her back against his front.

"Ew, seriously, you're covered in grime." She struggled harder, and Jimmy Wayne pressed his condensation-covered glass against her cheek, causing her to whip her head back to press into him, her hair gliding and catching on the stubble under his chin and the package clattering to the floor as she tried to get away when he moved the glass down to her neck. "Stop stop!" she hollered as he started to laugh. The glass flew across the room with a thunk, ice flying every which way, but the heirloom remaining intact. He got both arms around her. Sweat from all over him soaked straight through her dress, the fabric on her back melding into the cotton of his filthy T-shirt.

"You're already dirty now, might as well enjoy it." His mouth slid over the salt on her neck, his tongue flickered out to taste the clean water from the side of his tea glass. She went limp in his arms and her right hand came back to run a couple fingers along his hairline. His foot knocked against the package as he started to shuffle them down the hallway to the bathroom. He glanced down to see Leon's crazy-ass scrawl on a note peeking out of the edge of the half-torn wrapping.

Leon sending another book.

The beads around Jacyn's wrist tugged at the hair on his arm when she wrapped her fingers around his wrist.

His heart lurched and he squashed her tighter to him, always standing on the edge of the abyss waiting for the second she was gonna get snatched away from him. Her hair smelled like violets and sunshine and she was a solid weight against him, but he knew she was made of spun glass and night air.

Jimmy Wayne was a simple man with simple expectations, but Jacyn Boaz was his happily-ever-after that might never come. He held on to her as tightly as he could, hoping to hold her in his little bit of perfection, right here in Texas, right here against his beating heart.

He let her go, pushing her back toward the kitchen. She cocked her head to the side and watched him, waiting. Usually, she let him explain himself before flying off the handle when he did something unexpected. That was one of the many reasons he was scared to lose her. That kind of reasonableness didn't come ringing every Tuesday and twice on Sunday.

Running a hand through his hair, he lifted his head back toward the kitchen. "Parcel's from Leon. Just thought." He paused to pull his shirt over his head. "You oughtta get on that lickety-split in case it's got something livin' in it. Or, you know . . ." He trailed off as she wiped her hand down the front of her spoiled dress.

"If, you know, it's got a magic charm in it?" Her smile came with a slow sweep of her eyelashes against her cheeks. He wasn't giving up getting the bracelet off or figuring out exactly what kind of magic had affected her. She watched him as he turned away and flicked the light switch in the bathroom on. "This might not be curable, JW. You know that, right?"

He grunted and closed the bathroom door behind him.

Jacyn rolled her eyes at the closed bathroom door and walked the fifteen feet back into the kitchen.

Jimmy Wayne's mama was in San Antonio for some Red Hat convention—or so she claimed. Jacyn was dubious there, so Jacyn thought about cooking dinner and worrying about Leon's package afterward. She pulled the left over pot roast out of the fridge and set the platter covered in Press'n Seal on the old linoleum countertop. The old pipes in the house grunted and strained as Jimmy Wayne took his shower. Jacyn laughed to herself as he shouted out an expletive when she turned the cold water to wash her hands. She let the water run for a few seconds longer than necessary for him ruining her clothes for nothing. The tile floor was cool under her feet. The heat was getting worse as August came on, the livestock panting, cows sleeping during the day around their watering holes and birds keeping to the shade.

The allure of the package overcame her as she stood contemplating whether to make the roast into some kind of salad or fake Mexican something. She pulled a battered pair of black-handled metal scissors out of the same drawer that Jimmy Wayne's mama kept her recipes on scraps of paper. The package was crumpled and beaten like everything that Leon sent. She imagined him storing the parcels and envelopes in the glove compartment of his car for days at a time until he finally hauled his ass to the post office to mail them.

Inside the parcel was an old, leather-bound journal

held together by rubber bands. The cover had once been ox-blood or burgundy, but was now a flaking brown and pink color. On top of the journal was a piece of paper folded several times indiscriminately with her name written on it in Leon's scribble-scrabble: *Jacyn Elsbeth Boaz.*

Leon always wrote out her full name like that. She had grown used to it over the last few months, knowing that he was a creature of old ways underneath the veneer of a flighty pothead. Names had meaning and power. Leon was the most paranoid person she'd ever met, so she assumed that he wove some kind of concealment spell into the letters of her name when he wrote it. A sort of magical For Your Eyes Only stamp.

The letter read:

This is such a pain in my ass. I know people are afraid of change, but this would all move much faster if people learned to use the Internet, you know what I mean? I know you do. The enclosed journal used to belong to one of the Scots fey that lived in your area. Or so I was led to believe. You can't trust a tinker. Remember that. You think you've gone in to buy some charcoal and a lump of clay and come out with six pots with holes in them and a broken pencil. That was a true story, by the way.

*My new working theory is that you probably
have a fairy godmother. Probably. You could
still have a fairy in the woodpile, though. I will
admit defeat on the full changeling status
thing. How was I supposed to know that you
look just like every other female member of
your family? I was working blind. Fairies steal
babies. This is a known fact. Haven't you ever
seen a super ugly kid and thought to yourself—
that kid's head looks like a potato! What human has a potato for a head? None. But fairies
sometimes do. Scoff all you want. Wait until
you run into Mr. Potato Head and let's see
who's laughing.*

*The journal has all kinds of stuff in it. I flipped
through. Your answer is bound to be in there. If
not, well, it should lead you to all kinds of
trouble. Good thing you have Heehaw there to
look out for you. Swing by Nashvegas soon. We
miss you.*

The letter was unsigned, but that was typical of
Leon. Jacyn had known from day one that she
wasn't really a changeling. Not that she doubted in
the least that some fey probably stole children and
replaced them with mutants or animated clay figures or puppets or whatever suited them that day.

But she was too much like Amber and her mawmaw and her mother to not be blood relation.

The beads of her bracelet were cool against her skin. She touched a place on the cover of the journal that looked scorched and felt the uneven texture of blistered dye. The shower cut off down the hall and Jacyn wondered how she was going to break it to Jimmy Wayne that she wasn't a fairy princess after all.

Her laughter pulled a "What turned over your laugh box?" from the open kitchen door. Jimmy Wayne stood there in a towel flicking water out of his hair with an answering smile on his face, without even having to know what the joke was.

TOR
ROMANCE

Believe that love is magic

P lease join us at the website below
for more information about this
author and other great romance
selections, and to sign up for our
monthly newsletter!

www.tor-forge.com